"You're staring," Angela said, a slight smirk pulling across her face.

Ellington smiled. "I was. I couldn't help myself."

She closed the folder in her hand. She sat forward in her seat, resting her elbows atop the table as she folded her hands together in front of her face. "I'm sorry," she said softly.

"For what?"

"For running away last night."

"Is that what you were doing? Running away?"

"Not really, but I was avoiding you and what I knew would happen between us."

"And what was going to happen between us?"

Angela smiled, noting the smug expression across his handsome face. She chuckled softly. "I imagine," she answered, "that you were going to show off your best boxer shorts and those scrawny legs of yours. I didn't want you to embarrass yourself."

Ellington laughed heartily. "There is nothing scrawny about my legs!" he said as he moved around the table to stand beside her.

Angela sat back in the upholstered chair and lifted her eyes to his. They stared at each other for a moment and then Ellington leaned down to press his mouth to hers.

Dear Reader,

I so love what I do! And sometimes I do it well and other times, maybe not so much. But I always bring the necessary energy to tell the best story that I possibly can. I loved writing Ellington and Angela's story and tossing in the mystery surrounding his brother, Parker, was some very sweet icing on top of some really good cake!

Fleshing out Ellington Black came with challenges. As the story came together, I got to know him as you will get to know him. He surprised me more than once and I still find him to be a fascinating specimen of maleness. He meets his match in love interest, Angela Stanfield. His protective nature kicks into overload, but Angela is a woman so secure in her stiletto heels that she has no need to be protected! I absolutely adore these two and their adventure is one for the record books!

Thank you so much for your support. I am always humbled by all the love you keep showing me, my characters and our stories. I know that none of this would be possible without you.

Until next time, please take care and may God's blessings be with you always.

With much love,

Deborah Fletcher Mello

www.deborahmello.blogspot.com

IN THE ARMS OF
THE LAW

——

Deborah Fletcher Mello

HARLEQUIN
ROMANTIC
SUSPENSE

HARLEQUIN®
ROMANTIC SUSPENSE™

Recycling programs
for this product may
not exist in your area.

ISBN-13: 978-1-335-73815-8

In the Arms of the Law

Harlequin Enterprises ULC
22 Adelaide St. West, 41st Floor
Toronto, Ontario M5H 4E3, Canada
www.Harlequin.com

Printed in U.S.A.

A true Renaissance woman, **Deborah Fletcher Mello** finds joy in crafting unique story lines and memorable characters. She's received accolades from several publications, including *Publishers Weekly*, *Library Journal* and *RT Book Reviews*. Born and raised in Connecticut, Deborah now considers home to be wherever the moment moves her.

Books by Deborah Fletcher Mello

Harlequin Romantic Suspense

To Serve and Seduce

Seduced by the Badge
Tempted by the Badge
Reunited by the Badge
Stalked by Secrets
In the Arms of the Law

The Coltons of Colorado

Colton's Secret Sabotage

The Coltons of Grave Gulch

Rescued by the Colton Cowboy

Colton 911: Grand Rapids

Colton 911: Agent By Her Side

Visit the Author Profile page at
Harlequin.com for more titles.

To the Princess and the Paw,
You two bring your MeeMi much joy.
I love you immensely!
Now, stop running in the house!

Chapter 1

Defense attorney Ellington Black surveyed the crime scene as he and his brother, Chicago Police Captain Parker Black, waited for their father to arrive on-site. What had once been a beautiful room was now spattered with blood. The sheer white curtains that framed the double windows were no longer pristine, and blood puddled on an expensive oriental rug. A silk duvet had been tossed in a corner and knickknacks that had decorated the dresser were strewn haphazardly around. Most disconcerting was the body, which lay beneath a plastic tarp on the floor. The body of district attorney Jonathan Wyler. Ellington knew Jonathan well. The two had gone up against each other in the courtroom many times and had socialized in the same circles a time or two. Now he was going cold under a sheet of blue plastic.

Ellington was there in an official capacity at his brother Parker's request. His brother the police captain with the formidable reputation in the Chicago community had needed him. What would typically be a straightforward murder investigation was anything but, considering the prime suspect was Parker. Their father, Jerome Black, was the superintendent of police for Chicago. Whispers of a possible conflict of interest were already sweeping through the investigators on-site.

Many of the detectives in the room believed Parker had fired the shots that killed Jonathan. A domestic dispute gone awry. Ellington knew there could be no way his brother was involved. How Parker found himself in this position was mind-boggling, and Ellington had more questions for his brother than Parker probably had answers.

Forensic specialists and techs from the local crime lab were crawling through the home. The county coroner had come to claim the body. The tall, bearded man with a lazy eye pulled back the tarp, exposing the body as his camera captured every shot that had riddled the victim's chest. Someone had emptied the clip from Parker's department-issued Glock. Seventeen shots total had been aimed straight at Jonathan's chest. Ellington lifted a silk handkerchief from the breast pocket of his suit jacket and pressed it to his mouth and nose. He fought the rise of bile that bubbled in his midsection, threatening to swell to the back of his throat and spew what had been a pretty decent breakfast of waffles and bacon.

Parker sat on the edge of the king-size bed, his head hanging in his hands. His gray sweats and white T-shirt were stained with Jonathan's blood. Parker's face was blotched from crying, and he looked as if he'd been dragged behind a bus. He was broken and his pain was like a neon sign painted across his forehead.

Per police policy, to preserve the integrity of any statement Parker might make, a uniformed patrol officer had been assigned to help monitor his well-being. The officer's name was Michael Danube and the young man had only been with the department a few short months. He stood guard over Parker, not allowing him to move freely through the space but staying beside him if he did.

Ellington sighed as he drafted a text to his siblings and pushed the send button. There were seven Black siblings in total. He and Parker had two sisters, Vaughan and Simone, and three brothers, Armstrong, Davis and Mingus, and there was nothing they would not do for each other. Parker would need their support, now more than he had ever needed it before. Because Jonathan Wyler had been the love of Parker's life.

Jerome Black suddenly stood in the doorway, his eyes skating around the room. A senior detective from Parker's precinct whispered into his ear. Ellington watched his father's expression fall as his gaze landed on his eldest son. He clenched his teeth tightly together and his jaw tightened. He was visibly distressed, and Ellington braced himself for whatever might come. Jerome hurried to Ellington's side.

"I'm told he called you first?" their father asked curtly.

Ellington shook his head. "No, sir. He called 911 and reported finding the body first. Then he called me."

"What was he doing here?" Jerome questioned, his voice a loud whisper.

Ellington swallowed hard. "It's my understanding he spent the night."

Jerome paused, seeming to take that in. He scowled and his voice dropped an octave. "How long has he… this…" He took a deep breath. "How long has this been going on?"

"For a while now, Dad," Ellington said. "Almost two

years, I think. He didn't want you to know but he probably spent more time here than at his own town house. He and Jonathan considered this place their home."

"Two years?" Jerome shot a look at Parker, who still sat with his head hanging, looking like he'd lost his soul.

Jerome turned back to Ellington. "Did they get into an argument? Was Parker defending himself?"

Ellington shook his head. "Parker says he was in the shower and didn't hear the gun being fired, but when he came out of the bathroom, he found the victim shot dead on the floor. He's adamant that he didn't pull the trigger and he doesn't know who did."

Jerome swiped a large hand across his face. "Unbelievable!" he said, spitting a string of expletives past his full lips. His cell phone rang. He stole a quick glance at the caller ID, then cussed one more time. "This is your mother. I have to take this," he said as he turned abruptly and hurried out of the room.

Ellington closed his eyes and took a deep breath. Drama continued to haunt the family, despite them doing their best to keep it at bay. In the past six months they'd had to face their parents being blackmailed and discovered that their mother had an illegitimate child and their father was the half brother of one of Chicago's most notorious criminals. Ellington's very pregnant sister had taken a bullet in a drive-by shooting and survived, and a family vendetta had almost taken out his baby brother. Now another family secret had been exposed and he was going to have to defend his brother against a murder charge. Ellington couldn't help but wonder if the Black family curse was ever going to end.

When he opened his eyes, Parker was staring and their gazes met. Ellington knew that despite being lost in grief, Parker wanted to find the killer who'd taken Jonathan from him, more than he wanted anything else. Clearing his own name didn't matter to Parker as long as Jonathan got the justice he deserved. From all the whispering going on in the room, Ellington sensed that wasn't going to be as easy as either of them would have liked.

He moved to his brother's side. "You going to be okay?" he asked.

"No," Parker said.

Ellington nodded. "I get it. What can I do to help you right now?"

"I need to change. And I need to get out of this room." He tossed a glance to the body on the floor and his eyes misted. He looked back toward Ellington. "What did Dad say?" he questioned.

"Not much. But I'm sure it's coming. You need to ready yourself for the hurricane that is our father."

"This was not how I wanted him to find out I'm gay," Parker muttered.

Ellington shrugged his broad shoulders in sympathy but said nothing.

Jerome reentered the room, joining the two of them. Seemingly oblivious to his son's pain, he did what he did best and snapped orders. Being a father suddenly came second to being the superintendent of police. The moment was awkward, and Ellington could nearly feel his brother's discomfort.

"Any police-involved shooting follows strict protocols. The investigators need your clothes. Then you need to give an official statement down at the station. Right now, you're not under arrest, but that could change. I've already notified the district attorney's office. The deputy district attorney and a special investigator are already en route and should be here any minute now. Their investigation will be independent from the department's.

In fact, there will be overlapping investigations and you need to prepare yourself to face a barrage of questions coming at you from different directions."

Jerome tossed a look over his shoulder, turning his back to Officer Danube. His voice low, he continued, "You don't talk to anyone or make any statements without Ellington. You have officially invoked your right against self-incrimination. Is that clear?"

Ellington and Parker both nodded. They knew the drill. Parker's refusal to provide a voluntary statement to detectives meant his statement couldn't be used against him in court. However, he would be compelled to make a statement that could only be used for the internal administrative investigation. He would be asked to file a police report and to put his statements in writing in the presence of his attorney.

"I didn't do this," Parker responded. "I didn't kill Jon. I loved him."

Father and son stared at each other, and Ellington looked from one to the other. It looked like the large vein that pulsed in their father's neck might burst. Parker bristled, fighting back tears. Ellington could feel a kettle of emotion simmering and he knew it was only a matter of time before it blew. He took a step between them and gestured toward the bathroom with his head.

"Change. I'll drive you to the station," he said.

Jerome stared at Ellington as he gestured to the officer who stood off to the side, the man's hands folded politely in front of him. "Officer Danube will have to do it. You can follow him there. Danube doesn't leave Parker's side until I say so, is that understood? The first thing they'll question is what we did and didn't allow him to do."

Ellington nodded. "Yes, sir."

Without saying another word to either of them Jerome

made his exit, stopping to give a long list of directives to the homicide detail detectives and field supervisors. A second uniformed officer followed Parker into the bathroom and Ellington knew the man would stay by his brother's side until he collected the clothing that would be used as evidence against Parker if this went to trial. They were ensuring a clean chain of custody.

Ellington waited until the officer exited the room, carrying a plastic bag that contained the garments Parker had just discarded. Minutes later Parker stepped out wearing denim jeans and a plaid button-up shirt. With one last look at the investigator gathering samples, he practically ran from the bedroom, Danube on his heels.

The brothers found their father standing in the living room. He held a silver-framed photo in his hand. Parker brushed past him, heading straight for the front door. Ellington paused, glancing over Jerome's shoulder. The eight-by-ten photograph had been taken on Parker's last vacation: he and Jonathan posed side by side, cheek to cheek in Aruba.

Ellington tapped his father's shoulder as the patriarch rested the photograph back where he'd found it. The two exchanged a look but said nothing to each other. Outside, Parker leaned against a patrol car. Officer Danube slid into the driver's seat. Ellington moved to the driver's side of his luxury Mercedes. As he disengaged the door lock and pulled open the door, Ellington heard Jerome call Parker's name. He turned.

"Yes, sir?" Parker answered.

"It's going to be okay, son," Jerome said. "Trust and believe, we're going to get you through this."

Turning back to his own car Ellington slid into the driver's seat and started the engine. He appreciated his father's efforts to show Parker some compassion. He only wished he was as confident about things being okay.

Special Agent Angela Stanfield wearing heels was proving to be a problem for everyone except Angela. Before she'd even made it to the front door, two officers had commented on the four-inch Jimmy Choo stilettos she sported, as if investigating a murder in a high-end home necessitated flat-footed brogans to be successful. Her frustration with men questioning her abilities was palpable as she arrived at the South Clark Street home. So much so she almost missed the three men standing together at the end of the driveway. Almost.

There was no missing the family resemblance. Clearly, they were related. Each stood well over six feet, the younger two with lukewarm complexions that were a rich tawny with just the barest hint of the older man's mahogany hue. They had the same chiseled features—sculpted cheekbones and strong jawlines, solid builds and broad chests and shoulders. Two wore suits, while the third was dressed more casually. Her mother would have called them pretty and they were. But one, his expression less strained, caught her attention and held it. Concern blanketed his face, not the anger and sadness that painted the countenance of the other two. There was an air of determination in his eyes that seemed to indicate he was the rock others leaned on. He was handsome but she didn't get the sense that he knew it. He had a magnificent presence and she imagined that in a crowd he stood out easily.

She watched them enter their respective cars, one riding in a police patrol vehicle with a uniformed officer. She was curious to know how they were related to her case and stared until they pulled out of the driveway and rounded the corner at the end of the block. She turned her attention back to the property the men had just vacated.

The pristine South Loop gem was tucked away in secluded Dearborn Park. A gorgeous tree-lined courtyard led to the front door that had been painted a vibrant shade of fire-engine red. As Angela stepped over the threshold, she became acutely aware of the tension through the space, the investigative team all seeming to walk on eggshells. A detective from the local precinct rushed forward to greet her, his hand extended to shake hers.

"Special Agent Stanfield, it's a pleasure. I'm Detective Mike Caswell."

"Detective Caswell, thanks for the warm welcome."

"Under the circumstances, we appreciate an unbiased eye on this case."

"What do we have?" Angela questioned.

"The primary suspect is one of our own. My captain, Parker Black. His father, Jerome Black, is also the superintendent. You just missed them both, as a matter of fact. The victim was a lawyer with the district attorney's office. Apparently, he and Captain Black had a relationship."

Angela didn't miss the snark wrapped around the man's tone. Nor did she miss the snide comments and hushed chortles from the other officers in the room. She could only imagine the boys' club jokes and flagrant bigotry she'd been blessed to miss. That narrow-minded ignorance only served to further fuel her disdain for some of the men she often found herself working with.

A moment of recognition washed over her, but she didn't bother to mention that she and Parker had met briefly once at a conference for law enforcement officials. She pushed both hands into the pockets of her trench coat. "I need your people to clear the area for me. I need fifteen minutes."

Caswell frowned. "We're still collecting evidence…" he started.

"And that's fine. You'll be able to go right back to it. I just need to assess the space without the noise and commotion. I promise, I won't take long," she said, giving him a bright smile. "And I'm sure your boys will appreciate a break. No doubt it's been a long morning for them."

Caswell nodded. "Yeah, we could use a few minutes."

"And any samples your people have taken need to go to the state crime lab," she stated.

"But we have a good facility…"

"Under the jurisdiction of your superintendent. Which someone could claim is compromised if you proceed to trial against his son. There's no point in taking that risk if we can get clean test results from the start. But we can talk more when I'm finished here," she said, effectively dismissing him.

Caswell nodded. His eyes narrowed and Angela felt it was on the tip of his tongue to challenge her, but he didn't, instead turning an about-face to scurry toward the other side of the room.

Minutes later, Angela stood in the quiet of the space. Someone's taste was minimalistic and decidedly masculine. The colors were muted but warm. Hardwoods were prominent and the space felt extremely comfortable. The decor was simple, and pictures of family and friends decorated the shelves and tabletops. There were multiple photos of the two men, and she saw they had traveled often. They had been a pretty couple, smiling and happy. Much love had filled their home.

In the kitchen, a pot of coffee had brewed on schedule, two empty cups resting beside it. Someone had left a container of eggs and pack of bacon on the counter. She opened the refrigerator door. Foodstuffs were stacked neatly on the shelves and from the contents she fathomed one or both had loved to cook. There was a whole chicken marinating in a stoneware bowl that fit into a five-quart Crock-Pot, which rested on the stove top. It was clear that someone had already planned dinner.

She moved from the kitchen to a spare room that had become a home office. Two identical desks faced each other, matching executive chairs on either side. Law briefs rested on top of one desk, and criminal files on the other. The file folders were all neatly labeled, by someone meticulous, thorough and maybe even a tad anal. Angela flipped through the pile in the center of the desk. She opened the desk drawer, noting the folders lined neatly inside. The space revealed both men occasionally worked from home and seemingly worked well together.

She moved into the master bedroom, pausing at the door to take in the whole room. The body hadn't been removed and rigor mortis was beginning to set in. The shots had been fired at close range. The first two or three had knocked him to the floor. The rest had been fired as someone stood above him, intent on finishing what had been started. The shooting felt very personal, a crime of passion for some perceived offense. Or overkill to just make it look that way.

A box of condoms rested on one nightstand and there was an empty bottle of wine with one empty glass on a wicker tray. One of them had drank the night before, she thought, the other hadn't. A Breitling Navitimer wrist-watch, a contact lens case and a Stephen King novel rested on the other nightstand. A pair of men's briefs lay on the floor at the foot of the bed and a black silk worsted wool suit hung on the back of the closet door. A dresser drawer was open and a silk necktie hung haphazardly from inside. Multiple cologne bottles and a boar bristle brush had also been knocked to the floor. They had been dressing, getting ready to start their day, when things went left for them.

Angela stepped past the body and eased into the bathroom. Water dripped from the shower faucet. The last person inside had dropped the bar of soap and it was now a softened mess resting over the drain. White towels had been kicked into a corner and an electric razor had fallen into the sink.

Back in the bedroom she took one last look around. There was an oversize fireplace with a heavy mantel that held more pictures as well as a gold trophy. She moved closer to read the inscription engraved in the nameplate. A personal dedication from Jonathan to Parker and signed with a heart spoke volumes about their relationship. They had been head over heels in love. *So why,* Angela wondered, *did Parker Black shoot his lover? And if he didn't do it, who did?*

She was making her exit just as Detective Caswell was reentering the home.

"You're leaving?" he asked.

Angela nodded. "For now. I'll be at the police station if you need me. Meanwhile get me a list of all the forensics and make sure you date and time stamp everything you transfer to the lab. We wouldn't want this case derailed because someone made a rookie mistake."

Ellington stood with his back pressed tight to the concrete wall. His hands were pushed deep into his pants pockets. He had stepped out of the interrogation room to field a call, Parker assuring him that all would be well until he returned. Now he just needed a minute to think it all through. His brother had consented to a sobriety test and a gunpowder residue swab. Neither had any doubts about him passing both, which would force the police department's hand. They would have to consider another suspect or dig in their heels to prove Parker was guilty and somehow gaming the system. Both had known too many men railroaded by cops determined to override fact with fiction of their own making, an arrest and conviction being more important than the truth.

Ellington saw her well before she saw him, roused to attention by the woman standing at the front desk. She was long and lean with legs that seemed miles high. She wore a form-fitting, gray, plaid pencil skirt with a matching blazer and white dress shirt. Her stiletto heels were a vibrant shade of burgundy red, and she was stunning! Box braids had been twisted into a high bun atop her head and her ebony skin tone was complemented by glossy red lips. She'd captured the attention of everyone in the room, people pausing to stare as she commanded the space. The woman had a regal presence, and as he watched her, Ellington wanted to know more.

Ellington stood taller, and as he pulled his suit jacket closed, brushing a spot of lint from the lapel, she spied him out of the corner of her eye. There was a hint of recognition, and her gaze was curious as she looked him up and down and then up a second time. Then just like that, she turned in the opposite direction, following an officer who'd come to escort her to the other side of the building. She blessed him with one last glance over her shoulder and then she was gone.

He moved to the front desk and the female officer who was monitoring walk-ins and phones. Officer Maxine Jenkins had been employed with the Chicago Police Department for as long as Ellington could remember. She'd watched him and his siblings grow up and there was no denying her loyalty to his father and his brothers. She was a buxom woman, the top buttons of her uniform pulled taut against her full chest. Her closely cropped hairdo was winter white, the gray strands having taken a firm hold of her head for the past ten years. Her smile pulled from ear to ear as he stood before her.

"No, I can't go out with you, Attorney Black," she said teasingly. "I'm old enough to be your mother. Maybe even your grandmother!"

Ellington laughed. "You keep breaking my heart, Officer Jenkins."

"I know. I hate turning down all you good-looking men, but someone's got to do it."

"Well, since you won't have anything to do with me, maybe you can tell me the name of that beautiful woman who was just here?"

She grunted, "Humph! You're just like all the others! Can't trust you as far as I can throw you. It didn't take you any time at all to move on and start chasing after someone else. And all this time I thought you loved me!" She shook her head.

Ellington shrugged. "I was simply curious. She looked familiar. You know you'll always have my heart!"

Officer Jenkins laughed. "You lie so sweetly! You know full well that woman wasn't familiar!"

Ellington laughed with her as he leaned across the desk. "So, are you going to help a brother out?"

The woman rolled her eyes skyward. She leaned toward him, her voice dropping. "She's with the mayor's office. She's here to see your father. Her name's Angela Stanfield."

"The mayor's office?"

Officer Jenkins nodded. "A special investigator assigned to your brother's case."

Ellington's eyes danced from side to side, suddenly sensing this woman's presence was not at all good for any of them. He tapped the older woman's hands.

"Thank you," he said softly.

"Anytime, baby," she answered as she winked an eye at him.

Ellington moved back to where he'd been standing, resuming his lean against the wall. Minutes passed, people coming and going as he waited. When his phone rang, it surprised him as he grabbed it from the breast pocket of his suit jacket. His father's photograph appeared on the cell phone screen. He took a deep breath before answering it.

"Where are you?" Jerome questioned, not bothering to say hello.

"Still here at the station. Waiting to take Parker home."

"Home?"

"Probably to my house. Or yours."

"I need you to join me for lunch with the mayor."

"What's going on?"

His father's voice dropped slightly. "We'll talk later," he said. "I'll text you the address and meet you there."

"Yes, sir."

As Ellington disconnected the call, the phone rang a second time. This time it was his mother on the line, her face smiling up at him from the screen in the palm of his hand.

"Hi, Mom!"

"Hey, son! Where's your brother?"

"He's here."

"Is he okay?"

"He's been better."

"He needs to come here when you're done. Your father said they're not going to hold him, so I want him to come home. He shouldn't be alone."

"I agree. I'll talk to him and see what he says."

"Tell him I'm not asking. I'll see you both soon."

Ellington chuckled softly. "Yes, ma'am. I'll let him know."

The door to the room suddenly flew open, a technician hurrying out of the space. When Ellington entered, Parker sat at the table, staring off into space.

"Everything okay?" Ellington asked.

"Why do people keep asking me that?"

Ellington shrugged. "Probably because we don't know what else to say."

"Well, nothing's okay. And I don't know if anything will ever be okay again."

Ellington stared. He understood his brother's loss was monumental and he would have done anything to help him get through it. He just didn't have a clue what that should be.

"We're done here. They've opted not to hold you pending the results of those tests. But you've been officially relieved of duty until further notice. Your weapon is currently being held as evidence and you'll need to hand in your badge."

"Dad pulling strings again?"

"Professional courtesy. Too many questions that don't make this a cut-and-dried case."

"I need to figure out who did this."

"We will. Until then you need to take some time to grieve."

"I need to call Jon's mother. She doesn't know…"

Ellington shook his head. "The family's been notified."

Parker stood up abruptly. "I should go see her."

"I don't know if that's a good idea."

"I didn't kill him!" he shouted, his voice rising an octave.

"And it's still not a good idea, under the circumstances. Let Mom reach out on your behalf."

"He wanted to be cremated," Parker said, his voice dropping back to normal. "And there needs to be a memorial service. We have friends that need to be called and…"

"Let Mom help," Ellington said, interrupting his thoughts. "She's waiting for you. I told her I'd drop you off at the house."

"I need to go back to Jon's…"

"It's a crime scene, Parker. You can't."

Parker seemed to deflate before his brother's eyes, his energy waning and every ounce of fortitude gushing from him like air from a popped balloon. He was a broken man, barely holding himself together, and it hurt Ellington to his core to see him that way.

Ellington reached out to hug him as Parker fought back a low sob trapped in the back of his throat. Ellington sensed he wanted to wail but was conscious of where he was and who might be listening. Instead, the two just held tight to each other, minutes passing before either considered letting go.

"Mom will send out a search party if I don't get you home soon," Ellington finally said. "It'll be okay once you get to the house and Mom can love on you some."

Parker nodded. "Do you really believe that?"

Ellington smiled. "No, but it sounded good," he said as he led the way and his brother followed.

Chapter 2

Mayor Clarence Perry was sharing a story about his tenure as a state prosecutor and the many cases he'd notched on his belt. Ellington listened with half an ear, trying not to let his disinterest show on his face. The man was chatty, and no one was there for it. He still had no idea why it had been necessary for him to join the conversation. Even the superintendent, brow furrowed with frustration, was finding it difficult to hide his annoyance.

Mayor Perry stopped midsentence, jumping to his feet abruptly. "Here she is," he exclaimed, not hiding the excitement in his voice.

Ellington and his father both looked up at the same time. Jerome reacted before he did, standing to greet the young woman headed toward them. Ellington met Angela Stanfield's intense stare with one of his own, his surprise registering on his face. For the briefest moment, his breath caught deep in his chest. She was even more stunning up close! Her complexion was dark marble, melanin-rich and glassy as ice. Her full lips bore the faintest hint of a pout, the rich red lipstick complementing her skin tone. And her eyes! Her eyes were large pools of black water and he suddenly wanted to lose himself in the depths of them. He stood as his father made the formal introductions.

"It's good to see you again, Ms. Stanfield. Allow me to introduce you to my attorney. This is my second eldest son, Ellington Black. Ellington, this is Angela Stanfield," the patriarch said. "Angela is the special investigator who's been assigned to your brother's case."

Despite the stoic expression on her face, Angela was surprised to discover that lunch with her new employer also included the family of the man she'd been asked to investigate. The looks both were giving her hinted at them being as surprised as she was. Angela held out her hand, her eyes locked tightly to Ellington's. As her fingers slid across his palm, a current of electricity shot through her feminine spirit. It rushed like a storm wind up her spine and back down again, and her knees quivered just enough to make her rock slightly on her high heels. Ellington Black was one of the prettiest men she had ever had the pleasure of meeting. Eyeing him from the distance didn't begin to do him justice. He was gorgeous! He was tall, standing a few inches over six feet. His cheekbones were chiseled, and his eyes were a pale shade of hazel green. His complexion was lighter than his father's but there was no denying the familial resemblance. Both men wore pristinely tailored wool suits, with bright white dress shirts and complementing neckties. Dress shoes were polished to a spit shine, and each boasted a hairline that was meticulously edged. The two men were good-looking, but the son took her breath away. "Mr. Black, it's a pleasure to meet you," she said.

"The pleasure is mine, Ms. Stanfield."

The mayor chimed in. "Ms. Stanfield works for my office. She was hired for situations just like your brother's. She helps me keep my city officials honest."

"I try to find the truth in implausible situations," Angela said.

"Exactly!" the mayor said, sounding too eager for Ellington's comfort. "Let's all take a seat."

As they settled around the table the waiter came to introduce himself. "How is everyone this afternoon? My name's Bernard and I'll be your server today!"

"Bernard, I need a drink. Whiskey, straight, please," the mayor said. He tossed a glance at Ellington and his father. "You gentlemen should join me!" he added, seeming to ignore Angela's presence.

Angela interjected, her eyes rolling skyward. "Water with lemon, please."

"I'll have the same," Ellington said.

Jerome shook his head. "Coffee for me, please."

The mayor shrugged. He was a small man with beady eyes, a narrow nose and chin, and a bad comb-over. He also liked to hear himself talk and he talked incessantly. As they waited for their drinks the three listened to him chatter about the economy, his favorite hockey team and social media's influence on state politics.

"I really should get right to the point of this meeting," he suddenly said, tossing back his second shot of whiskey.

"Please, do," Jerome responded.

"You and I have been friends for years. You've done a brilliant job turning the police department around. Community trust is at an all-time high. I can't tell you how much I appreciate the job you've done. But unfortunately, I think you should step down now."

"You think I should quit?"

"No, not quit. Take an early retirement. I'll make sure there are no issues with your pension. Your contract leaves you with a very nice retirement bonus. We'll even throw you a going-away party. You retire and it'll make it easy for all of us."

"No disrespect, Mayor Perry, but how does my father retiring make it easy?" Ellington questioned. He shifted forward in his seat.

"Ellington, your father and both your brothers were already being scrutinized by Internal Affairs. We've had multiple complaints that they don't always follow the rules, but I was willing to overlook that because you could always trust that they would get the job done. However, this situation with Parker is proving problematic. I can't turn my head and hope it blows over, and I can't let your father or your brother Armstrong run slipshod over everyone trying to solve the case. Armstrong is a great detective and he's already making demands of the officers assigned to this case! This is an election year and I have to consider how the optics may look to my constituents, especially if Parker is found innocent. While this case is pending, I need your father to step down and Armstrong needs to take some vacation time." He gestured toward the waiter, shaking his empty glass for another drink. "Obviously, you'll be defending your brother, but the rest of you need to stay as far from this case as possible. For the optics and all!"

"And if I refuse to step down?" Jerome questioned.

"Jerome, I appointed you to the position because I believed in you. I still do. But if I must remove you, it'll be a blemish on my record as I start out on the campaign trail, and that can't happen."

Ellington repeated the question. "And if he doesn't step down?"

"I'll let Internal Affairs sort it out. But you'll be out here on your own, Jerome, and any questions they have about your actions…well…it won't be my problem. Unfortunately, this thing with your son has made you a liability."

Ellington and his father exchanged a look. Angela sat back in her seat, her arms folded over her chest as she watched them, her eyes shifting back and forth as if she had front-row seats to a tennis match. The mayor's smug expression was disconcerting at best, and she couldn't help but wonder what she'd gotten herself into. Her eyes shifted to Ellington's face, and when he sensed her staring, he met her gaze, his expression blank. She sensed that he wasn't happy and neither he nor his father was going to take the mayor's request lightly.

The mayor continued. "Meanwhile, Ms. Stanfield will officially be taking over this murder investigation. She and anyone working the case will report directly to me. I don't want you or anyone related to you, who's employed by the city of Chicago, anywhere near this. And that's an order. There will be a press conference later this evening. It's important for the community to know that we're going to be fully transparent, most especially since this involves one of our officers. Agent Stanfield, you should plan to be there. And have a statement ready. Something short and sweet. If need be, the city's communication office can write something down for you." He downed another drink.

Silence fell over the table. Ellington knew his father would never step down. He also knew that depending on the time of day, the case and the mood of Internal Affairs, any investigation into his father's decisions or his brothers' actions might prove to be problematic. All three had been known to skirt the lines between right and wrong to catch the bad guys. Dismissive of public scrutiny, they did what they needed to do and damned the consequences if it meant getting the job done. The many commendations and accolades each had received proved their choices hadn't been so wrong. He also knew that whatever his father chose to do, Armstrong and Parker would follow his lead and he would support all three.

When his father stood, Ellington wasn't surprised. Jerome Black didn't take orders well from anyone.

Jerome threw his napkin to the table, then turned to Angela and apologized, politely excusing himself. "If I or anyone on my staff can assist you, Ms. Stanfield, please don't hesitate to ask," he said. "Because we will get to the truth." He tossed the mayor a narrowed glare as he headed for the door but said nothing to the man.

Mayor Perry called after him, jumping up to follow. "Jerome, don't be like that. Let's talk! Jerome!"

An awkward silence descended over the table. Ellington sat back in his seat, falling into thought. Angela broke through the layer of quiet, startling him from his thoughts. "You have another brother with the police department?" she asked.

Ellington nodded. "My brother Armstrong is a detective. So is his wife, Danielle."

"Ellington, Armstrong, Parker… Someone was a jazz enthusiast." Angela smiled.

"The only thing our parents love more than each other and their children, is their music. My siblings and I were weaned on jazz."

"How many of you are there?"

"Seven. Parker, who you've met, and Armstrong. Then there's my brother Mingus, who is a private investigator, and my brother Davis, who is a city alderman. We also have two sisters, Simone and Vaughan."

"Are they in law enforcement, too?"

"Simone is an attorney and partner in my law firm and Vaughan is a political lobbyist. Until recently she was working on Davis's political campaign."

"Are you all close?"

"Are you asking because you want to know more about me or because you're gathering information to help you build a case against my brother?" A wry smirk pulled at his lips.

Angela smiled. "I was curious. And it's not my job to build a case against your brother. I just want to find the truth."

"Well, the truth is Parker didn't kill Jonathan. Those two were in love."

"I know," Angela said matter-of-factly.

He stared, her comment surprising him. "So, you don't think he's a killer?"

"I didn't say that at all. I agreed with you that from what little I do know so far, they were very much in love with each other. So I'll ask again. Are you and your siblings close?"

Ellington nodded. "Very close. And I know it probably sounds a little cliché, but we're all best friends."

"Actually, it sounds extremely sweet. I have one brother and we're not close at all. There's a twenty-year age difference between us. Stephen is more like a second father."

They were suddenly interrupted by their waiter. "Mayor Perry apologized, but he had to leave. He paid for your lunch before he left, though. Would you like to hear our specials?" Bernard asked.

Ellington gave her a look, his brow raised.

"I'm hungry," Angela said. "So I would love to hear the specials."

"The lady has spoken, Bernard. What's on the menu today?"

Bernard eagerly read off the list of chef's specials. At the top of that list was a lunch portion of surf and turf, and they both perked up as the young man described it.

"It's our classic pan-seared rib eye steak, cooked to your satisfaction and served with our creamy garlic shrimp and crispy asparagus."

"I'll have that," Angela said. "And I'd like my steak rare."

"And for you, sir?"

"I'll have the same," Ellington answered as he returned the menus back to him. "Thank you."

"Your meals will be right up," Bernard said as he refilled their water glasses before heading back toward the kitchen.

"So, if you don't mind me asking, what's your background?" Ellington questioned. He reached for his glass and took a sip of his water.

"I graduated from Chicago State University with a degree in criminal justice. Then I went to the police training institute at the University of Illinois at Urbana-Champaign. I got my initial investigative experience with the Champaign Police Department. I discovered I was good at it and my career evolved from there. As a backup, I also pursued a law degree and worked for the Illinois state attorney general's office. The 'special investigator' title," she said, using air quotes to highlight the term, "is just a pretty way to say I'm a high-priced detective who's really good at what I do. My last special investigator gig was with the New York City Police Department. When I heard Chicago was looking for someone, it was the perfect opportunity for me to come back to Illinois and be closer to home."

"Do you still have family in Champaign?"

"All of them are still there. My parents are still in the family home and my brother lives near them with his wife and kids."

"You're an auntie!"

She smiled. "I am. Two nieces and one nephew."

"My youngest sister is pregnant with her first child. A boy. He'll be the first grandchild and nephew."

"Uncle Ellington!"

"I can't wait," Ellington said, his grin wide and full. "My brothers and I are already battling to see who'll be his favorite!"

Angela laughed. "Toys, candy and cool trips are the trick! Never visit empty-handed."

He shook his head. "This kid is going to be so spoiled!"

"It's what I love most about being an aunt. All I'm required to do is spoil them!"

The conversation was easy. They continued to chat as they enjoyed the meal. He asked questions and she answered them readily. He discovered her penchant for graphic novels, her dislike of Christmas movies and her necessity to shake pepper on everything she ate, even dessert. They chatted about everything except work and the case. Much like any elephant in a room, they pretended it wasn't there at all. Two hours later Ellington had ignored the fifth call from his father, and he knew the good time he was having had to come to an end.

Angela stole a glance to her own cell phone. "I need to head back to the station. But I really enjoyed talking to you. It was nice to take a break."

"I had a good time as well. I appreciate you giving me

an opportunity to not be so serious for a moment." His phone chimed again.

Angela stood, adjusting her skirt as she did. "You should probably answer that. I don't get the impression your father will take being ignored lightly."

Ellington nodded. "You have a good afternoon." As she started to walk away, he suddenly called after her. As she turned back toward him, his expression was eager and hopeful.

"Yes?"

"Would you have dinner with me tomorrow night?"

Angela smiled. "Wouldn't that be a conflict of interest for both of us, Attorney Black?"

Ellington grinned. "I won't tell if you don't."

Without an ounce of hesitation, she answered, "Yes, I'd love to." Then, like that, she was gone.

Ellington liked her. She was smart and funny, and he appreciated that she was straightforward in how she approached things. She didn't dance around issues and had no problems saying whatever was on her mind. He rose from his seat, leaving a sizable tip on the table for Bernard. Once he was settled back in his car, he dialed his father. The patriarch answered on the second ring.

"Have you spoken to your brother since you took him to the house?" Jerome asked.

"No, sir."

"Your mother's not answering, and I wanted to make sure he was okay."

"You can call him, Dad. I'm sure he'd appreciate it."

There was a moment of hesitation and Ellington sensed his father was conflicted. He clearly didn't have the words to verbalize what he was feeling, and Ellington knew he didn't want to say the wrong thing. He continued. "You're going to have to sit down and talk with him at some point."

"Right now, son, I'm struggling with the fact that your brother didn't think he could talk to *me*. But that's not your concern." Jerome changed the subject. "Ms. Stanfield has requested an interview with Parker. You'll need to make him available so he can give a statement."

"I'll talk to him and then I'll call her to arrange something," Ellington said. He found himself wondering why she hadn't just asked him directly. And when had she had the opportunity to make the request of his father? As he maneuvered his car through downtown and back toward his office, he had questions for Angela Stanfield that he knew he might never get answers for. He only hoped he'd be given ample opportunity to ask them.

Ellington Black was clearly a distraction, Angela thought as she sat in the parking lot of the West Harrison Street Police Station. She had broken one of her cardinal rules, their business lunch about everything but business. He was the attorney for the primary suspect in her investigation, which made any encounter between them problematic. Making herself susceptible to censure went against everything she had ever strived to achieve. But there was something appealing about the man. Something warm and welcoming about his spirit. He made her laugh and he had been easy to talk to. She liked that he didn't take himself too seriously and he was humble. He had a kind heart and kindness went far with her.

She had already done her research on the Black family, wanting to understand the dynamics of all the players. Theirs was considered the First Family of Chicago law enforcement. All of them in the public spotlight, doing their civic duty to make the city a safer place. The parents had paved the way, their mother a federal court judge who was highly respected. His father's ascension through the ranks to the position of superintendent, where he oversaw Chicago's entire police department, had been duly impressive. There had been the expected accusations of nepotism when his sons had joined the police force, but Angela sensed Parker Black and his brother Armstrong had both worked hard to accomplish all that they had. She didn't fault them for the door that had been opened by their father because she knew each had needed to prove himself in the field to earn the respect of those officers who supported them. Most spoke highly of the two brothers, and the few who didn't had either bumped heads with one or the other, or resented the success that had not been theirs.

Armstrong had married months earlier in a lavish ceremony, pictures of him and his bride making the *Chicago Tribune*'s celebrations page. There had been multiple articles about all their successes and accolades, including Ellington's most efficacious legal wins. They were also no strangers to drama: the sister being shot in a drive-by, and the popular alderman's issues with a stalker. Little had been written about Parker Black's personal life and even less about Ellington's. Angela blew a soft sigh past her glossed lips.

Exiting the vehicle, she put on her game face and sauntered slowly through the front door of the building. Inside, there was a flurry of activity, the noise level reminding her of those days when she'd walked a beat, making arrests. There was something cathartic about the synergy in a bustling police station. As she moved through the narrow halls to the office that had been re-

served especially for her, she drew much attention from
the officers in the Bureau of Detectives, and there was
no missing the whispers that followed her.

She closed the office door and took a seat. Someone
had gone to great lengths to make her comfortable. New
office supplies, a phone directory and a small bowl of
assorted candies sat atop the desk. The candy made her
smile. There was also an envelope with her name on it
that sat propped against a cup holding pens and pencils.
The bold print looked like someone had written it quickly.
She reached for a metal letter opener and slid it easily
beneath the flap. The sheet of paper inside had been torn
from a legal-sized notepad, the block print done in permanent marker.

Angela read the note once and then again. After the
third time she dropped it into the side pocket of her
leather attaché. She sat back in her chair, folding her
hands together in her lap. It was five words, and on the
surface, there was nothing significant about it. *TALK TO
RAY-ANNE HARLOW.*

Who is Ray-Anne Harlow? Clearly, Angela thought,
someone had information they wanted her to know. But
that someone wasn't willing to come forward in person
to give it to her. She had to question the legitimacy of
the information. If this were a diversion and the anon-
ymous writer of the note was wrong, sending her on a
blind search, it could send Parker Black to prison and
implode her own career at the same time. But considering what little she did know to be fact, she couldn't afford to leave any stone unturned. And curiosity pulled
at her. She now wanted to not only know who Ray-Anne
Harlow was and maybe learn what this woman might

know about the prosecutor's murder; but even more, she wanted to know who had left her the note and what they had to gain from all of this.

Chapter 3

An unsettling pall had descended over the Black home, keeping at bay the ripple of laughter and energy that usually swept through the historic Gold Coast residence. It was almost eerie, Ellington thought as he moved from the front door to the family room at the back of the house. His sisters were both there, the youngest bemoaning the state of her ankles.

"I can barely wear shoes I'm so swollen," Simone was saying, her palms resting atop her very pregnant belly.

"It'll pass," Vaughan muttered, clearly not interested in the conversation. She looked up anxiously as Ellington entered the room. "Saved by the bell!" she exclaimed.

Simone rolled her eyes skyward.

"Where's everyone?" Ellington questioned, dropping onto the sofa beside his little sister. He pulled her legs into his lap and began to gently massage her swollen feet.

"You're my favorite big brother," Simone purred as

she settled back against the sofa's arm. "At least some-one in this family loves me." She shot Vaughan a look.

"And you're still whining!" Vaughan quipped. She turned to Ellington. "Mom and Dad are in his office pre-tending not to argue. Parker's resting upstairs."

"Paul called in a prescription for him to help with his anxiety," Simone said, referring to her husband, Dr. Paul Reilly, the medical professional in the family. "Parker was in a bad way."

"Do you know what happened?" Vaughan questioned.

"I just know it doesn't look good for Parker. I know he didn't do it, but everything seems to be stacking up against him right now."

"It doesn't make any sense," Vaughan said. "Parker adored Jonathan. They were happy. He would never hurt him."

"We know that. Hopefully, Jonathan's family knows that, too. But we may have to prove it, and that may not be easy."

"It's already made the news," Vaughan said. "They're saying a person of interest was being questioned."

"Did they mention Parker's name?" Ellington ques-tioned.

His sister shook her head. "No, but they made it sound like an arrest was imminent."

"How's Dad handling it?" Ellington gestured toward the office door with a nod of his head.

"He hasn't said much." Simone's voice dropped an octave. "But he and Mom have been at it for a good while now."

Ellington sighed. "I should probably go talk to them."

Simone lifted her legs and swung her feet back to the floor. "You should go do that. This is hard enough without them being at each other's throat. I'll be glad when things get back to normal with them."

"If things ever get back to normal," Vaughan interjected.

"Do you have to be such a pessimist?" Simone snapped, her gaze narrowing.

"I'm being pragmatic. With everything they've had to deal with, it's a wonder they're still together."

"It's not that bad," Ellington said.

"Thank you," Simone quipped. "She always has them divorced, about to be divorced or thinking about divorce. I keep telling her marriage requires a devotion and commitment to the *effort* that needs to go into the relationship as much as the relationship itself."

Vaughan scoffed. "Says the pregnant broad who only made it down the aisle when she got knocked up."

"But I made it down the aisle," Simone said as she waved her ring finger in the air. "I have a man who was extremely excited about marrying me. You're still playing house with Victor vibrator. I wouldn't judge if I were you."

"And on that note," Ellington chuckled, rising from his seat. "I think I'll go check on our senior citizens. You two carry on."

"I'm not paying Simone an ounce of attention," Vaughan proclaimed.

"You started it," Simone responded.

As Ellington moved down the hall to his father's study, his two sisters were still bickering. Standing before the closed door, he knocked reluctantly. He could hear his parents on the other side, their conversation sounding a tad more contentious than the one he'd just left. He hated that the seriousness of the situation had them all on edge, ready to snap at the slightest infraction. Usually, the sly

comments between them were more humorous than hurt-
ful. The digs were genuinely good-natured and not spite-
ful. The stress they'd all been under suddenly had them
throwing daggers at each other.

Judith Harmon Black threw open the office door. His
mother couldn't hide her frustration, her porcelain complexion a brilliant shade of rage red. His father stood
behind her, his own warm skin tone equally heated. She
feigned surprise at seeing him. "Ellington! We weren't
expecting you. Isn't this a pleasant surprise!"

Ellington shook his head. "That works on Davis, Mom,"
he said as he leaned to kiss her cheek. "You okay?"

She took a deep breath and held it for a moment. "I'm
sure I will be," she said, her voice dropping to a loud
whisper. She stepped aside, gesturing for him to enter
the room.

He extended his arm to shake his father's hand. "I
didn't mean to interrupt but I wanted to check on Parker.
Maybe see what I can do to help."

Jerome turned an about-face, moving to the chair behind the desk he'd been leaning against. "The way things
are looking, your brother is going to need all the help he
can get."

"My son did not murder his best friend," Judith snapped.
"And the two of you need to make this go away."

Ellington gave his mother a look. He had always
thought her to be the most beautiful woman he'd ever
known. As a little boy, she'd been a goddess of monumental proportions and there had been nothing she couldn't
do. Eyeing her, he realized Judith Harmon Black had
aged some in the past few months. She looked exhausted,
the impact of everyone else's problems showing on her
face. Her silver gray tresses had been pulled back into
a ponytail and she wore the barest hint of makeup. Her

eyes were crystal and they shimmered with determination. His mother was his heart, and a source of strength for all of them. But for the first time ever, she looked fragile, and he understood that she couldn't fix what was broken and she was having a difficult time coming to terms with that. He reached out to hug her, and when he did, he felt her hang on to him, her body deflating ever so slightly against his.

Ellington wanted to tell his mother that everything was going to be okay, but he knew he couldn't say the words and sound convincing. He wasn't certain of anything, least of all being able to get Parker out of this mess. He blew a soft sigh as his mother pulled herself from him, swiping at her eyes with the back of her hand.

Jerome interrupted the moment. "Did you speak with Ms. Stanfield?"

"Not since lunch, but she did leave me a message about deposing Parker." Ellington shifted the conversation. "How did you and the mayor leave things?"

Jerome waved a dismissive hand. "That fool is going to make me do something he'll soon regret. I'm not stepping down. If he wants me gone, he's going to have to put me out. But you don't need to worry about that. I want you fully focused on proving your brother's innocence."

A knock pulled at their attention, and the three of them turned toward the door as it slowly opened. Mingus Black peeked his head around the corner. "Is this a good time?"

Judith waved her third oldest child inside. She wrapped him tightly in a warm hug. "It's always a good time to see my children," she muttered as she tapped him gently against his broad chest.

The two brothers shook hands and Mingus gave his father a nod of his head. He pushed both of his hands deep into the pockets of his leather trench coat. "Tell me what you need," he said, his eyes shifting to stare at Ellington.

"I want everything you can find on Jonathan. Everything. And don't let Parker know."

"Done."

"I'm interested in past relationships, business associates, friends, family—particularly anyone he may have pissed off or who had a grudge against him. Also, what cases he was working on for the last year. Dig under every rock. If he had secrets, I want to know what they were."

Mingus nodded. A private investigator by profession, he was known to dig up dirt others had difficulty finding. He was a former police lieutenant who didn't always play by the rules, and he had a notorious reputation for breaking many of them. Mingus was just as dedicated to the municipality as the rest of his family, but he worked alone, sometimes with the dregs of society, beneath the cover of darkness, getting his hands dirty. Many times, he did what others weren't willing to do, and he did it exceptionally well.

"I also need you to dig into Parker," Ellington continued. "If there's anything they can use against him, we should know that before they do."

"I hate this," Judith muttered. "Parker doesn't deserve to have this happen to him."

"Is there something else we don't know that you might want to tell us?" Jerome quipped, a wealth of attitude in his tone. "Something else you've been hiding?"

The two brothers exchanged a look, both feeling the energy shift as Judith bristled. She didn't bother to respond to the question. Instead, she moved to the door, pulling it open as she tossed the patriarch one final look over her shoulder. "You might want to sit down and have a conversation with your son instead of bullying the rest of us for your mistakes," she snapped. "Instead of being mad at me because I did know, ask yourself why Parker didn't want you to know about his sexuality. Question how you managed to fail your eldest son so that he was afraid to be open with you. That's what you should be asking."

The door slamming vibrated long after Judith was gone, the three men standing in the silence of it. No one was quite sure what to say, not wanting to stir up the dust that had been thick and stifling and was only just beginning to settle around them.

"Well," Jerome finally murmured as he moved back to his seat. "Do you two think I failed Parker, too?"

Ellington shot Mingus a look, suddenly feeling cornered. "Dad, you need to talk to him. You really do. Only he can explain himself and why he made the decisions he made."

Jerome sighed. "I treated all of you the same. I never favored one over the other. I tried to ensure you each had individual, quality time so that you never felt left out. I did the best I knew how."

Ellington nodded. "You did. You were always there, preparing us to be the *men* you expected us to be, and disappointing you wasn't an option." He shot Mingus another look, and his brother nodded.

Jerome sat back in his seat, still staring at the two of them. Ellington didn't need him to say anything to know that his father had gotten the message. They were a family of high achievers, and failure had never been an option for any of them. Jerome had spent all their lives telling them what *real* men did and didn't do. How *real* men took care of their wives and children. That *real* men were strong and independent. A *real* man wasn't weak, never cried and had tough skin. And though he had never explicitly said so out loud, men loving men failed his *real* men test. His belief system had been nurtured by a church and community too ready to criticize and criminalize things they chose not to understand. He had never been made to question his own intrinsic bias, and so he'd turned a blind eye, choosing instead to ignore what didn't impact him personally.

Parker's fear of failing their father had kept him closeted all his life. He'd been too afraid to risk the possibility of being rejected by the man they each idolized. All the family except the patriarch had known he was gay but had banded together to keep his secret, their own uncertainty about Jerome's reaction helping to fuel their decisions. They wouldn't have to face what they never talked about. They trusted their father's love but, being acutely aware of his shortcomings, had kept a wall of reservation high and wide around them in order to keep the peace in their tight-knit family.

Ellington imagined that with so many family secrets suddenly being exposed, Parker's sexuality was just the tip of what else might come. He had to question if the Blacks could stand up against the scrutiny and come out unscathed on the other side.

His father interrupted his thoughts. "I love you, boys. All of you. You are my sons and all I have ever expected is that you would be decent, honorable men who are productive members of society. That you would make your mother and me proud. And just like your mother, I have only wanted you to be happy with whatever choices you made for yourselves. I never thought I needed to say that, because I always thought it was what I was showing you."

"You should say that to Parker, Pop," Mingus said firmly. "He needs to hear you say it."

Jerome nodded. "I'll make sure each of you knows that. Until then, though, I need you two to figure this thing out and get Parker out of this mess." He moved from the desk to the door, turning to give them both one last look. Contrition painted his expression. He took a deep breath, the air pushing out his chest and pulling his shoulders back. He seemed to stand taller and then he opened the door and exited the room.

In that moment, Ellington was reminded that the father they idolized, who'd been a god in their young eyes, was still just a man, beautifully flawed and finding his way with each new day. He blew a soft sigh as he turned toward his brother.

"This one's bad. I'm not even sure where to begin building Parker's defense. We barely have a five-minute window where someone entered the home, shot and killed Jonathan and made his escape. All while Parker was in the shower. I can't come up with one scenario that sounds plausible. That's why I need you to dig deep. Find me something I can use."

Mingus nodded. "I'm already on it. As soon as I get something, you'll be the first to know. Are they still processing the crime scene?"

Ellington nodded. "I'll send you everything I get in discovery."

"What do you know about the special investigator the mayor put on the case?" Mingus asked.

His brows raised, Ellington eyed his brother curiously. "Who told you about her?"

"You know they can't keep anything secret down at the station. Apparently, she's made quite the impression."

"Her name's Angela Stanfield. I like her," Ellington said with a slight shrug of his shoulders. "She wants the truth and hasn't automatically assumed that Parker is guilty. She seems like good people."

"She's got a solid reputation for being fair, so that's something."

"We'll see what happens."

"I need to go sweet-talk the coroner. See if she'll give me a sneak peek at the autopsy results."

"They took the body to the state lab."

Mingus chuckled. "I have friends there, too."

"You also have a wife. Don't let that sweet talk get you in any trouble."

"I think you forget who you're talking to," Mingus said. "Joanna would hurt me, and I don't like sleeping on the couch in my own home. That's not a good look."

Ellington smiled. "We're going to need a family vacation after this. Someplace tropical."

Mingus laughed. "Someplace far from each other, preferably."

Ellington laughed with him and opened the door. "Shall we?" he said, exiting the room.

Mingus followed on his brother's heels. "Is it selfish of me to hope that Mom cooked?"

Ellington chuckled warmly. "I hope not. I was just thinking the same thing."

The family was gathered around the dining room table. His mother had cooked, and they were eating heartily. All of them except Parker, who was pushing his food around on his plate as he half listened to the conversation. When Ellington called his name he jumped, the attention unexpected. Everyone else fell silent, turning to stare.

"I'm sorry. Were you asking me something?" he said softly.

Ellington nodded. "I thought it might be a good idea

for the whole family to go pay our respects to the Wyler family after we finish. I asked if you wanted to ride with me over there or if you wanted to ride with Mom and Dad?"

Parker shot his parents a look. "Dad, you're going?" There was no hiding the surprise that seeped like water from his eyes.

Jerome nodded. "Of course I'm going. Jonathan was important to you and even though I didn't know him well, that makes him important to all of us. I told you earlier, you won't have to go through this alone. We will all be right here to support you, son. Most especially, me. If you'll let me."

Tears misted Parker's eyes and he began to shake in his seat. Vaughan pressed a manicured hand against his forearm and squeezed gently. He was good until his sister touched him and then he couldn't hold back his tears. Their mother rose from her seat and scurried around the table to where he sat. She wrapped her arms around his shoulders and pulled him to her. As he sobbed, his family gathered around him, holding his hand, hugging each other as they hugged him. His father pressed a kiss to the top of his head, his hand heavy against his son's shoulder. Time stood still as they absorbed his pain, offering the comfort of their presence.

Parker sobbed until there were no tears left for him to cry and it was only when he'd taken a deep inhale of oxygen, beginning to compose himself, that they finally let him go.

Simone swiped the back of her hand across her own eyes. "Y'all are going to make me go into early labor," she quipped. "All this emotion is stressful!"

"Says the queen of drama," Davis responded as he pressed a cotton handkerchief to his nose.

The others wiped eyes, blew noses and hugged each other one last time.

Simone rolled her eyes skyward. "I need to go fix my makeup before we leave. Someone text me the address please."

"I'll send it to everyone," Parker answered as he reached for his phone and began to text in the group message chain they all shared.

"I'm going to go pick up Danni and we'll meet you there," Armstrong interjected.

"Neema's working tonight, so she probably won't be able to join us," Davis added. "I'll call her before I head in that direction. I need to make a quick stop at the office and then I'll meet everyone there."

"You all just be careful," Judith stated. She began to clear the dishes from the table, Vaughan stepping up to help her.

Parker turned to Ellington. "If you don't mind, I think I'll ride over with Mom and Dad."

Ellington nodded. "Whatever you want."

"I need to talk with them. To Dad." He shot his father a quick look.

The patriarch gave them both a warm smile. "Let me help your mother with the dishes and then we'll head over."

"Thanks, Pop," Parker said. He turned back to Ellington.

Ellington gave his brother the slightest smile. He said, "Before I forget, I scheduled your official statement for tomorrow morning. We should meet beforehand to go over your story and decide what you need to say."

"I plan to tell the truth. I didn't kill Jon."

"I know. We just want to make sure they can't twist or distort what you do say."

"Who's taking my statement?"

"Her name's Angela Stanfield. She's a special investigator with the mayor's office."

"I know her. We met once at a law enforcement conference. I liked her."

Ellington tried not to let his surprise at that bit of information show. Angela hadn't mentioned knowing his brother and he wondered why. "Well," he said, "she has a solid reputation. I've only heard good things about her. I don't get the impression she's here to try and railroad you."

Parker shook his head. "I never got the impression that that's her style. She plays by the rules. She's also smart. If she's gunning for me, we're not going to see her coming until she has her case airtight. And that might make her dangerous."

"Or an ally you want on your side."

Parker shrugged. "Maybe. Maybe not. Everything about this feels wrong. Someone's setting me up and they've done a hell of a job making me look guilty."

"We'll do a better job proving your innocence," Ellington affirmed. "You can trust that."

His brother nodded. "I do. More than you know."

Ellington fell into his bed feeling like it had been the longest day in his entire life. Paying their respects to Jonathan's family had been as uncomfortable as he'd imagined. Jonathan's mother had cried on Parker's shoulder and his father had sat in a rocker on the front porch of their home refusing to speak to any of them as he stared out into space. Family had milled around, everyone reminiscing about the past they'd all shared with Jonathan and in the midst of it there was an air of doubt hanging like a dark cloud over his brother's shoulder.

Ellington suddenly found himself reconsidering his

career options. Wondering what it might feel like to work a nine-to-five on a tropical beach serving fruity drinks to tourists who blew in and blew out with the wind. It sounded great in theory, but he knew that even that would wear thin after a while.

It had been some time since he'd last had a break. His plate was continually full and there was rarely enough time in a day for him to just sit back and relax. He knew that if Parker were officially charged with Jonathan's murder, then defending him would take every minute of every day and a break would literally be a thing of his imagination. As he lay there, both arms resting above his head, he found himself questioning if he was prepared for what might come.

Anyone else with a case the police thought was as cut-and-dried, and Ellington would have been trying to figure out a plea deal for his client, not trying to solve a puzzle with a few missing pieces. But Parker wasn't just anyone and nothing about what had happened made any sense. He suddenly thought about his lunch with Angela Stanfield. He'd been in awe of the beautiful woman, her restraint and calm a welcome reprieve. She'd made him laugh and her easy demeanor had been a nice change from the women he usually found himself spending time with. His last lunch date had been too high-strung and had talked incessantly about absolutely nothing. He appreciated that Angela had staunch opinions about police policy and procedures, and she didn't necessarily follow the status quo. He found himself appreciating how she planned to approach her investigation, most especially because his brother's future depended on it. His trust in her spoke volumes, because there were few people Ellington would even consider trusting with something so important to him and his family.

He rolled onto his side and adjusted the pillow beneath his head. Sleep was being elusive, and he desperately needed to sleep. But thinking about Angela had him reflective and he couldn't help wondering if the lovely woman was thinking about this whole mess, too, and maybe, also, thinking about him.

Chapter 4

Angela sat parked in front of Jonathan Wyler's home. Hours earlier a light had come on in the living room as the evening sun had begun to set. Apparently on timer, it was scheduled to welcome the residents back home. No one had gone in or come out since Detective Caswell had locked the door and cordoned off the property with the requisite yellow police tape. A patrol car and a uniformed officer were positioned in the driveway to keep an eye out for intruders. Angela had been watching him and the neighborhood, and spying through the home's open window blinds since she'd arrived.

The tree-lined street was relatively quiet. The occasional dog walker strolled the sidewalk and only one child had bounced a ball at the edge of a driveway until his mother called him inside. The initial police reports rested in her lap, a compilation of quickly scribbled notes and assessments that leaned toward Parker Black being their prime suspect. It always amazed her how no one ever considered other options when the answers seemed too easy.

There had been no signs of any forced entry into the home. A basement door that led out to the backyard had been locked and so had the sliding glass doors that opened onto a rear deck. Angela mused that if the police had to investigate whether someone other than Parker Black had murdered Jonathan Wyler, then they needed to consider how that person had entered the home and made their exit.

Angela closed her eyes and walked herself over the floor plan, recalling the space in her mind. The perpetrator would have had to possess a key, or someone must've let him inside. If Captain Black had been in the shower as he professed, then who had Jonathan opened his door to and why? Or maybe Captain Black had killed his friend, hoping if he denied the allegations loudly enough, someone might actually believe him.

Stepping out of the vehicle, she tossed the short stack of manila folders onto the driver's seat. She reached into the back seat for her digital camera, slipped it around her neck and then secured the car's doors. With her badge in hand, she walked to the patrol car, waving it and her hand toward the officer seated inside. The man jumped, startled from the game he was playing on his cell phone. His expression was contrite as he scrambled out of the vehicle, his cell phone falling to the floorboard beneath his feet.

"Sorry, ma'am," he muttered. "I wasn't expecting anyone…"

"At ease, Officer. I need to get inside the home. Did Caswell leave a key with you?"

"Yes, ma'am. It's in the mailbox, I think."

"You think?"

"No… I mean yes… I mean…it's there…yes…" he stammered.

"I'll let myself in," she said, stepping past him.

The young man stared after her and it was only after she'd let herself inside and closed the door that he resumed his position inside the car.

A search warrant had allowed Caswell and his team to totally disrupt the ordered neatness that she'd experienced earlier in the day. They had torn up the home, moving and scrutinizing every personal belonging. Drawers were left open, pillows had been shredded, closets emptied, and everything that wasn't nailed down had been dropped to the floor. It was chaos from one side of the room to the other. Angela blew a heavy sigh. She'd be willing to bet that the detective hadn't found anything useful. The destruction was more for show than anything else. Him wielding his power just because he could had put him squarely on the top of her dislike list.

She slipped on a pair of rubber gloves as she moved from the living room to the master bedroom. It, too, had been ransacked, the space looking like a home invasion gone awry. Mounds of debris littered the floor, and nothing remained where it apparently belonged. Shaking her head, Angela reached into the shower and turned on the water. Moving back to the bedroom, she found the remote for the flat-screen television mounted on the wall. She turned it on and ramped up the volume. Jimmy Kimmel was in the middle of his monologue, cracking jokes on the current White House administration and a president whose behavior had become fodder for many late-night talk show hosts.

She walked back into the bathroom and closed the door. She stood at the edge of the shower door, closed her eyes and listened. Water running down the drain echoed off the walls, and except for the spray of moisture falling out of the shower head, all else was quiet. The insulation in the room was above standards. She couldn't hear the television and she had maxed out the volume. Two people chatting on the other side of the door, their voices hushed, would never have registered on a sound meter. If you believed Parker Black had been in the shower, with his head beneath the flow of water, it was highly unlikely that he had heard anything, including the gunshots.

For a few good minutes she stood as still as stone. The room had begun to fill with steam, a thick layer of mist painting the mirrors and walls. When the water pipes suddenly creaked, disrupting the reverie she'd fallen into, she took a deep inhale of air. She turned off the water, came back into the bedroom and turned off the television.

Lifting the camera, she snapped a few select shots of those things that had caught her eye earlier in the day when she'd first walked through. In the kitchen, remnants of green rubber had littered the counter by the coffee-pot. Remnants from what looked like a medical grade glove. It was still there. Another piece of green rubber had been on the dresser in the bedroom. It was now on the floor, knocked off the wooden top. Whether they'd been dismissed or just not noticed by the earlier team that Caswell had brought in was concerning. Where was the glove? And what had it been used for?

She was about to exit the space when she noticed movement out of the corner of her eye. The window blinds were open, the windows facing the neighboring unit. Someone had been watching, standing in their own darkened space, their face pressed against the glass across the way. Thinking back, Angela remembered the window had been open during her first walk-through earlier that day. She had to wonder if whoever was being curious now had been watching then, too. And if they might have seen something in the early hours when Jonathan Wyler had died.

It was way too late to go knocking on their front door, but Angela made a mental note to pay the neighbors a visit first thing in the morning. With one last glance around the room, she shut off the lights, strode back through the living room and headed toward her car. As she pulled the sedan out of its parking space, she cast her eyes to the home next door. A woman stood in her front window, still watching what was going on. The light from a rear room illuminated her frame and Angela sensed that whoever she was, what she had seen would answer questions that hadn't yet been asked.

The mayor had put Angela up at the Chicago Lake Shore Hotel. Located in the Hyde Park neighborhood, it was clean, cozy, convenient to the downtown area, and the staff was pleasant.

Angela had made herself at home. The wall beside the king-size bed was adorned with sticky notes and pushpins as she had begun to lay out the case. She pulled the mysterious letter that had been left on her desk from the folder she carried and added it to the scribblings. Anyone else looking at her makeshift blackboard wouldn't have been able to decipher the hodgepodge of scraps. But they made sense to her, and until she solved the case, she thought, that was all that mattered.

Her gaze fell on a photo of the Black brothers. She had printed it from an online newspaper article about the family and had pinned it to the top left corner of her display. Thoughts of Ellington Black suddenly spiraled through her mind, a cavalcade of energy shooting through her body. Her temperature rose and she found the room warmer than normal. Kicking off her heels, she turned toward the bathroom and the shower, leaving a trail of clothes behind her.

The water was just cool enough, and she stepped into the shower, almost desperate for the spray of moisture against her skin. The palm of her hand soon trailed a soapy path from her shoulder, down her arm, to rest against her abdomen just below her belly button. A quiver of energy rippled through her midsection. Unable to get him out of her head, she allowed herself a moment of reflection.

Without knowing a lot about the man, she did know there was something special about Ellington Black. The short time they'd spent together would barely be considered long enough for her to pass judgment. But intuition told her he was not a man anyone should sleep on. He was intense and deeply committed to the greater good. He took his job seriously, believed in morality and fought a fair fight. And there was no denying his devotion to his family. He adored his mother, idolized his father and had immense respect for both his parents. He was also super protective of his siblings, the epitome of an elder-born big brother. Everything about him moved her and she knew that fawning over the man would not be a good look. But she felt herself feeling slightly schoolgirl-giddy and nothing about that made an ounce of sense to her.

There had been very few men who had been able to move Angela's interest meter. When she first discovered boys, she'd been ultra-picky about her choices. The few who did make her list then had to jump through hoops to prove themselves worthy of her attention. She never made it easy for any man and she didn't think she had to. They could either step up or not waste her time. Dating had never been problematic, but her career had always come first, any relationship with a man put on the back burner.

Her last relationship had ended after six months. His name was Derek and he'd been a New York City firefighter with flaming red hair and a mile-wide smile. Things between them had been okay until she'd wanted to come back to Illinois. There'd been no compromising and she had refused to bend her will to his. Getting what she wanted took precedence over all else, even her infatuation for a man with the body of a god and the prowess of a porn star. His good just hadn't been good enough.

Stepping from the flow of water she turned off the faucet with one hand and reached for a stark white towel with the other. Moving back into the other room, she dropped her naked frame onto the corner of the bed. Her skin tingled beneath the surface as she thought about Ellington's eyes and the looks he had given her as they talked. Had she stared back she would easily have fallen deep into their oceanic depths and gotten lost. It had been a struggle not to stare. She could get accustomed to a man looking at her like that, she thought.

She reached for the bottle of Aveeno lotion that rested on the nightstand. As she moisturized her skin, she let her hands linger sweetly against her flesh. Lying back against the mattress, her fingers danced a slow two-step over her body. They trailed across her breasts, teasing one protrusion of nipple and then the other. Easing past the flat of her stomach, they hovered over the apex between her legs, twirling through the curl of pubic hair. Her eyes closed, she let herself ease into the most sensual thoughts. As she lay on her back, pulling her knees back toward her shoulders, she let herself imagine what Ellington's touch might be like if their circumstances were different.

* * *

The murder case haunted her dreams. Angela had fallen to sleep in the spot where she'd lain back and closed her eyes. Her hand was still pressed tightly between her thick thighs. Over and over again she'd watched Jonathan Wyler being shot in the chest, a gloved hand pulling the trigger. Each time she turned to look in the mirror to see the face of his killer, the dream would rewind, and the shots would be fired again. It played out in slow motion and Angela kept trying to see what she was missing so that she could figure out who'd done it.

She'd woken up in a cold sweat, feeling like she needed another shower. She rose from the bed and headed into the bathroom, shaking away the early-morning reverie that clouded her thoughts. Minutes later, with a fresh, minty mouth, she felt ready to take on the world, or at least give it a run for its money.

Angela took the tourist route back to the Wyler home, diverting through the prestigious Streeterville neighborhood. Urban renewal had transformed the landscape, a multitude of high-rise buildings towering skyward. In awe of the architecture, Angela took her time maneuvering down North Michigan Avenue. The stop-and-go traffic on the street dubbed The Magnificent Mile allowed her a few moments of sightseeing as she sipped on a Starbucks caramel macchiato made with vanilla soy milk. When she finally arrived at the Wyler property, a different officer was parked in the driveway, watching the door.

Sitting in the quiet lull of her automobile, Angela finished her beverage as she listened to 103.5 KISS FM. Fred, the morning radio jock, was bantering back and forth with a colorful cast of characters, the conversation amusing as they compared dating horror stories. As she slurped the last sip of her drink, her gaze skipped over the landscape, noting the rise in activity on the block. Noticeably absent was the heavy police presence from the previous day. Detective Caswell hadn't arrived yet, nor had anyone else from his team. Just the lone patrol officer sitting reluctantly in the police cruiser.

The street was busy. People scurrying to the bus stop, walking small dogs or headed off to school. It was busier than she'd expected for the early-morning hour. Further inspection found a traffic camera on a pole at the intersection and at least four homes that appeared to have private video cameras, two of which were facing the street and the Wyler house. There had been no mention of the cameras in Caswell's notes.

As she stepped out of the car, the officer exited his own, looking toward her. His expression was stoic as he adjusted his uniform, trying to appear professional. He lifted his hand in a slight wave and called out to her.

"Good morning, Special Agent!"

Sauntering toward the man, Angela greeted him with a slight nod of her head. "Good morning, Officer. Where's your boss?"

"Detective Caswell said he would be here around ten to release the home back to the family."

Her eyebrows lifted, but she didn't comment. It was barely twenty-four hours after the murder and Caswell being ready to release the home didn't sit well with her. In fact, nothing about Caswell and his actions made sense. For a seasoned detective, his work was shoddy, and his efforts were minimal at best. Clearly, he needed to be reminded who was in charge of the investigation and who wasn't.

"Should you speak to Caswell before I do, please have him call me."

"Yes, ma'am."

She pulled her cell phone to her ear as she turned from the young man, putting a few feet of distance between them. She paused in front of the home next door as the call connected, going straight to voice mail.

"Detective Caswell, this is Special Agent Stanfield. Call me when you get this message. I'm at the Wyler property and I'm curious to know why you aren't." She hung up the call and dialed a second number. Detective Armstrong Black answered on the second ring.

"Chicago PD. This is Detective Black."

"Detective, good morning. This is Special Agent Angela Stanfield. I'm investigating the Wyler murder."

"Special Agent, how can I help you?"

"I need two forensic specialists to meet me here at the house. I need your best and brightest."

Armstrong chuckled softly. "Have you spoken to Caswell?"

"Not speaking to Caswell is why I'm calling you. Your father gave me your number in case I ran into any problems. My guy from the state lab won't get here until this afternoon. He's finishing up a case in La Grange and I'm not totally sold on the guy Caswell had here yesterday."

"I understand. Expect Paris Landry and John Mills. I'll have them there in the next thirty minutes."

"I appreciate that."

"I'd join them but under the circumstances…" His voice trailed off.

"…that's not a good idea," Angela finished.

"Don't hesitate to let me know if there's anything else I can do to help you, Special Agent. And I look forward to meeting you in person."

"Since you mention it, I'm interviewing Captain Black at eleven. But I'd like to speak with you before that if you have the time. Say ten thirty? I should be back at the station by then. I just have a few questions for you about your brother."

"I'll be here," Armstrong replied.

Angela dialed one last number. The woman who answered greeted her cheerily.

"Agent Stanfield! Top of the morning to you!"

Angela laughed. "Good morning, Sister! It's good to hear a cheery voice this hour of the day."

Sister-Gregg Donovan was one of the best forensic specialists in the state. She was also one of Angela's dearest friends. Years before her birth, her parents had been Catholic clergy, her father a priest and her mother a nun. Her name had been a nod to their hippie spirit and the time they'd served in the church before deserting the Pope for each other. Angela and Sister-Gregg had worked one of their biggest cases together, catching a serial killer who'd gone unnoticed for almost forty-five years. Their bond had been irrefutable ever since.

"All day, every day. Tell me you have something good for me."

"You should have received forensic evidence from a Detective Caswell with Chicago PD."

"It wasn't much considering this is a murder investigation. Who's on sight? Scooby-Doo and Shaggy?" she asked, referring to the cartoon from back in the day.

"They think they know who did it. They're not interested in the science."

"Well, someone should be."

"There's another team coming in a few minutes. The crime scene's been compromised by police incompetence but I'm hopeful."

"Do you know who they're sending?"

"John Mills and Paris Something."

"Paris Landry. I know her. She's good. Incredibly detail-oriented. If there's something to find she'll find it."

"I called Patrick as well. He's on another case but said he could get here this afternoon."

"You're good, then. Between them, if there's something to find, they'll dig it up."

"Let's hope so. I sent you some photos I took last night. I also need you to send me a copy of the inventory Caswell sent you."

"Are you looking for something in particular?"

"Just following a hunch."

"You got it. And I'll start processing what we got in, later this afternoon."

"Why this afternoon? I thought you were my best friend. I need that information yesterday."

"I have to testify this morning. I'm headed to court right now as a matter of fact."

"Ohhh! Sorry about that. I should have asked if you were busy."

"You've always been a little selfish like that."

"I'll own that."

Sister-Gregg laughed. "So, how's the eye candy in Chicago?"

"I don't know. I haven't been looking."

"I'm sure that's a lie. You've been looking. You're just afraid to taste the goods."

"Now I know you've fallen down and bumped your head," Angela chuckled. "You know better than anyone that I'm not afraid of anything."

"I know you like to pretend you're tough. But deep down…"

"I did not call so that you could psychoanalyze me," Angela said, interrupting the lecture she felt coming.

"Besides, I'm sure you're going to be late for court, so I'm not going to hold you up any longer. I have work to do."

Her friend's warm laughter echoed over the phone line. "We will finish this conversation later tonight. You're not getting off that easily."

"Fine. I'll call you when I get back to my hotel. After my dinner date. Then I can tell you about the man I met."

Sister-Gregg screamed into the receiver. "A man? When did you meet a man? And where is this man taking you on your dinner date?"

"Goodbye!" Angela chimed as she disconnected the call. She smiled, her expression smug as she imagined the look on her friend's face. It would be an interesting conversation when they did have it, she thought.

She moved to the front door of the neighboring home and rang the doorbell. As she took a step back, she noted the window blinds that shifted ever so slightly and she smiled, holding up her badge for the person peeking out at her. Before she could blink, the door opened and a portly woman wearing too much makeup and a bad wig greeted her brusquely.

"Well, it's about time," the woman said, annoyance vibrating in her tone.

"Good morning," Angela greeted politely. "I'm Special Agent Angela Stanfield. And I'd like to ask you some questions about your neighbor next door."

"Took you long enough. I told that man what I knew, and he said you'd be right on over to take my statement. That was a whole day ago!"

"I'm sorry, I think I've missed something," Angela said, confusion washing over her expression. "You spoke to a man?"

"That really pretty one. Said he was a friend of Mr. Wyler and his family. Didn't give me his name. Said he was from the neighborhood watch asking in an unofficial capacity. I'm sure he was just being nosy, but he was respectful. Men these days don't always treat women the way they should be treated. His mother raised him well," she said, finally pausing to take a breath.

Angela nodded, her eyes skating from side to side as she tried to fathom who that man might have been. She took her own deep breath. "Please accept my apology for the delay. There's been a lot going on. Again, my name's Angela Stanfield, and you are…?"

"Ray-Anne Harlow. But everyone just calls me Ray."

Angela tried to not let the surprise show on her face, reminded of the note that had been left on her desk. "Is this a good time to talk, Ms. Harlow?"

"As good a time as any," she said as she gestured for Angela to enter the home. "Can I get you a cup of coffee? I just brewed a pot. I make good coffee."

"Thank you. I'd appreciate that," Angela responded.

The home was welcoming, reminding Angela of her grandmother's Detroit cottage. Ray-Anne Harlow was a collector of knickknacks: an array of tchotchkes cluttered every surface of every table and shelf. The hardwood floors were covered with vintage Bohemian rugs. The furniture was well-worn, their fabrics frayed and stained and covered with pillows and blanket throws. Nothing matched but it all worked well together. Her father had called the styling a poor woman's shabby chic. Ray-Anne had taken her shabby to the nth degree. One more objet d'art and she'd be hoarding, the clutter falling into an abyss that would be difficult to come back from. And the entire space smelled like warm cinnamon.

Angela inhaled deeply and Ray-Anne seemed to read her mind. "I just took a tray of cookies out the oven," she said as she set a full plate and that promised cup of coffee on the kitchen table.

As Angela sat down, she saw that the kitchen's bay window looked out toward the home next door and right into the neighboring window. The blinds were wide-open, and light poured through the panes, casting a warm glow over the room. Peering through them, Angela could see that Detective Caswell had finally arrived: the officer stood in the other home's master bedroom.

"I tried to talk to that one, too," Ray-Anne said, as she dropped into the seat beside Angela. She gestured across the way with her head and scowled, her mouth twisting as if she'd bitten into something sour. "That one has serious attitude! His kind don't need a badge," she said emphatically.

"And he didn't take your statement, either?"

"No. Told me it wasn't needed. That they had caught the suspect. Then he called me a crazy bat. He thought I didn't hear him, but I heard it clear as day! And there is nothing crazy about me! I know what I saw! And I know what I didn't see. And I certainly didn't see their *suspect* shoot his boyfriend!"

Angela nodded. "Did you see who did shoot him, Ms. Harlow?"

"I didn't, but I did see that woman rushing out the house just after that detective right there pulled up, sitting in his car like he didn't have nothing to do. She rushed out, looked dead at him, and he didn't do a thing. He said something to her and then she jumped into her car and took off. A few minutes later the rest of them officers all showed up. That's when he finally got out of his car, suddenly acting like he wanted to do some work."

Angela sat analyzing the details being shared and filing them away like a superfast computer. "Have you ever seen this woman before?" she questioned.

Ray-Anne nodded. "About two years ago she lived there for a few weeks. I thought she might have been his sister, but he never said, and I never asked. I don't get in people's business like that. Then she was gone. But she came back last week, and they had an argument. The boyfriend—Parker Black—broke things up. It looked like he came home unexpectedly and surprised the two of them."

"Can you describe this woman for me?"

"Tall, blonde, average looks. But she had big boobs. My husband, Hank, had a lot to say about her boobs. But she was a hot mess if you ask me. Her hair needed a comb and she looked like she'd just rolled out of a Wood-stock commercial."

Angela smiled. "How so?"

"She was very bohemian. Always wearing mixed prints, gauzy blouses, ruffled skirts and Jesus sandals. And she had a thing about not wearing a bra. When she lived there, Hank almost lost his mind every time he saw her. I'm not abundantly blessed in that department and my Hank's a titty man, even if he does deny it. The bigger the better. She'd be bouncing all over the place and Hank would try to pretend he wasn't looking." Ray-Anne chuckled softly and took a sip from her coffee cup.

"What can you tell me about Mr. Wyler and his boy-friend?"

"They were a nice couple. Always respectful and overly polite. Too touchy-feely for Hank, though," she said with a shrug. "But then Hank doesn't do public displays of af-fection of any kind."

"So, she was arguing with Mr. Wyler?"

Ray-Anne nodded. "They were having a knock-down,

drag-out fight. Calling it an argument would be nicer, but it wouldn't be the truth. She actually threw a punch and hit him in the chest. She tried to hit him a second time and he grabbed her wrists. Before you knew it, they were tousling around like wrestling professionals. That's when Parker came in and pulled her off him. I didn't see her again until she was rushing out yesterday."

"Did your husband see her yesterday, too?"

"No, unless he saw her arrive. Hank had already left for work when she left. But you can ask him about her. He drives a bus for Chicago Transit."

Angela nodded, jotting notes into the lined notepad she'd pulled from her pocket. "Is there anything else you remember that you think I should know?" Angela questioned.

Ray-Anne's eyes shifted back toward the window across the way. "Them two were happy. Incredibly happy. They would never have hurt each other. Not on purpose. It's not often that you see a love like theirs. My husband didn't understand it, but there's not a woman alive who wouldn't want a loving relationship like them two had. It makes me sad," she concluded, "that someone would take that from them."

Ray-Anne's expression was thoughtful, her eyes misting slightly. After one final sip of the morning brew, Angela set her coffee cup back on the table. "Thank you for your time, Ms. Harlow. I appreciate you talking to me."

Ray-Anne gestured back toward the other window and Detective Caswell. "That one is crooked as hell. Trust me when I tell you! He's dirty and cops like him give all of you a bad name. I wouldn't turn my back on him if I were you."

Rising from her seat, Angela turned to stare where the woman stared. She didn't say so out loud, but she was already taking heed of Ray-Anne's warning. "One last question," she said, turning her attention back to the older woman. "I saw a security camera on the edge of your property. Have the police requested the video?"

Ray-Anne shook her head. "No," she said, rising from her seat and moving to the counter. She pulled a DVD from inside one of her cookbooks that rested in the corner. "I wouldn't dare give this to him," she said, pointing at Caswell. "I'm sure if I did it would conveniently disappear."

"Thank you," Angela said as she took the tape from the woman. "Someone from the department may come asking…"

Ray-Anne chuckled. "I can tell them that the cameras weren't on that day. I'll call it a technology malfunction."

Angela grinned. "I appreciate that, but you can tell them the truth. It's already been confiscated and then you can point them in my direction. I'll handle it from there."

Ray-Anne laughed loudly. "I like you. Straight to the point. I hope you catch who really did it."

"I will," Angela responded. "Thank you for your help. I may need to talk to you again."

"I'll be here!" Ray-Anne answered as she showed Angela to the front door.

Back out on the sidewalk Angela replayed the conversation over in her head, a lengthy list of questions rising that suddenly needed to be answered. *Had Detective Caswell been at the Wyler home before the 911 call? How was he connected to the woman Ray-Anne had seen him talking to prior to the police team arriving? Who was this exceptionally endowed mystery woman? And why was this case suddenly feeling like someone was trying to cover up something other than the murder of the district attorney?*

Detective Caswell grunted in greeting when Angela walked into the Wyler home. Her high heels tapped loudly against the hardwood floors. He was thoroughly disinterested in her presence and his annoyance showed on his face. The breath he took was visible, his nostrils flaring and his chest pushing forward as he inhaled deeply.

"Special Agent! We weren't expecting you!" His tone was dry, lifted a half octave as he feigned surprise.

"And why not?" Angela answered. "Did you not get my message that I was here wondering where you were?"

The man turned a brilliant shade of beet red. "I did, but there's not much here for you to do since we have our perpetrator."

"Do we?"

"I don't think there's any doubt that Parker Black killed his lover during a domestic spat. It seems pretty cut-and-dried to the rest of us. I'm just finishing up here and then I'll head back to the station to finalize my report. I'll personally bring him in and put the handcuffs on him."

"I'm meeting with him and his lawyer in an hour. I've also come into some information that precludes Mr. Black from being our perpetrator."

"What information?"

"Information I imagine won't be in that report you plan to prepare for me."

Caswell bristled, his entire body seeming to stiffen and swell. Confusion washed over his expression and perspiration suddenly beaded his brow. He stammered, "I… It's… How…" His jaw suddenly slapped closed, and his lips pushed forward in a deep pout. He went on the defense. "If you have information, I need to be in the loop…" he started.

"You need to remember that I'm leading this investigation," Angela said matter-of-factly. "I need your report before the end of the day. I also need your forensic guys out of here. I have another team on the way. Make sure that report includes a complete inventory of everything that's been sent to the lab thus far." Angela took a breath before continuing. "Have your officers canvassed the neighborhood? Interviewed the neighbors?"

Caswell nodded. "Yeah. We didn't get much. Crazy bat next door talked us to death about spaceships and aliens. That's about it."

"Spaceships and aliens?"

He shrugged. "I think there's some dementia going on."

Angela stood staring at him, her eyes narrowed just slightly. The bold-faced lie that had rolled off his tongue had her ready to snap, but she gave him a faint smile instead. She nodded. "I'd like to see you and your team in my office at three o'clock."

"Yes, ma'am," he snapped, attitude floating around each word. He turned from her, calling out to the officers in the room. "Special Agent wants to see us all this afternoon! Until then everybody out!"

As the last of his men exited the space, John Mills and Paris Landry stood in the doorway.

"Damn!" Paris exclaimed. "Was this a robbery gone wrong?" the woman asked, looking around the space. She barely stood five feet tall in heels. She was petite with large eyes, a pixie haircut and features that gave her an elfin quality.

Angela shook her head as she extended her hand to shake theirs. "No. This was police overreach."

"They've contaminated the crime scene," John said. He carried an oversize plastic toolbox.

It was on the tip of Angela's tongue to say that was

what they wanted to do, but she didn't. Instead, she said, "The state crime lab has a list of what was received, if that will help you."

"If there's anything here to find, we'll find it," Paris said.

After briefly detailing what she knew and sharing the photos she'd taken the night before, Angela watched as John headed toward the bedroom and Paris followed. Just the few minutes with them had her feeling that things were in safe hands. She trusted what Paris had professed and anticipated them finding more than she could begin to hope for. Making her own exit from the home, she headed to the police station.

Chapter 5

Ellington squeezed his brother's shoulder. Parker sat low in the chair, his arms crossed over his chest and his posture defensive. He had barely spoken ten words since Ellington had picked him up from their parents' home and those ten had been laced with frustration and rage. He wanted answers and Ellington didn't have any for him.

"Just remember what I told you," Ellington was saying. "Don't volunteer any information. Just answer the questions asked of you. Be straightforward and get right to your point."

"I know how to do this," Parker snapped. "I'm usually the one asking the questions, remember?"

"And be mindful of your tone," his brother responded. "Don't let them use your frustration against you."

Parker slapped his fist against the table. Ellington ignored the outburst of anger and then the door opened, as Angela entered the small interrogation room.

"Good morning," she said, greeting them both with a warm smile. She extended her hand to Ellington first and then Parker. "It's good to see you again, Captain Black."

"I wish it were under better circumstances," Parker said as they shook hands.

"As do I," Angela said. "First, allow me to express how sorry I am for your loss. I'll try to make this as brief as possible."

"Thank you," Parker responded, giving her a curt nod.

She took the seat facing the two men. Her body language was suddenly stiff and her expression staid. She flipped open a manila folder. A headshot of Jonathan was clipped to the inside flap. She reached into her pocket and pulled a small recording device from inside, setting it on the table between them. As she pushed the record button, she cleared her throat.

"Today's date is the fifteenth of August. I am Special Agent Angela Stanfield, assigned to case number 2765-A by the Chicago mayor's office. I am here with Captain Parker Black and his attorney, Ellington Black. Captain Black has invoked his right to self-incrimination. He is here to provide an official statement of the events that led up to the death of one Jonathan Wyler."

Angela sat back in her seat, folding her hands together in her lap as she looked Parker in the eyes. "Captain Black, would you please tell me what you know about the murder of Jonathan Wyler."

Ellington gave his brother a look and a slight nod of his head for him to proceed. He was comfortable that Parker was well prepped for any questions that might be thrown at him. He shifted his gaze toward Angela, noting the intensity of her stare as she studied his sibling. Her eyes flickered back and forth across Parker's face and for a split second it felt like she might be reading his mind, privy to thoughts that he didn't even know. But then he realized she was watching Parker like he was prey, and she were ready to pounce if he made one wrong move. It was disconcerting but he realized she was exceptionally serious when it came to her job. He took a deep breath as they both waited to hear what he and Parker had already agreed that his brother would say.

"It was a typical morning for the two of us. Jonathan had a deposition scheduled and had planned to head to the office early. He showered first and I started the coffeepot."

"What time was this?" Angela questioned.

"It was early. The alarm went off at six thirty and we both got right up. It was probably seven o'clock when he got out of the shower, and I got in."

Angela nodded, gesturing with her eyes for him to continue.

"I was in the bathroom for thirty, maybe forty minutes. When I came out, Jonathan was on the floor. My service revolver was lying on the floor by his right shoulder."

Angela shifted in her seat and jotted something down on the yellow-lined notepad that rested on the table before her. When she looked back up, Ellington was still staring at her. "What did you do then?" she questioned.

"I retrieved my personal revolver from the nightstand and checked the house for an intruder, but no one was there."

"You had the forethought not to pick up the revolver on the floor?"

"It was just police instinct kicking in. I knew not to contaminate the crime scene."

She nodded. "What happened then?"

"I went back to check on Jonathan, but he didn't have a pulse. Then I called for backup."

"Did you call 911 on your cell phone or did you use your service radio for dispatch?"

"My radio. After I called for help, I used my cell phone and called my brother."

"You called your brother?" She gave Ellington a quick glance.

"I knew the drill, Investigator. I knew I would be the prime suspect."

"What about your doors? Were they open?"

Parker shook his head. His voice cracked ever so slightly as he spoke. "No. They were secure."

"So, you would have us believe that someone entered your home, shot your boyfriend and disappeared while you were in the shower?"

"That's what happened," Parker answered, his tone dry as annoyance painted his words.

There was a pregnant pause as Angela seemed to be collecting her thoughts. She reached to turn off the recorder, dropping it back into her pocket. As she did, she gave Ellington the slightest smile before turning her attention back to his brother.

"How long were you and prosecutor Wyler in a relationship?" Angela's tone was soft, and her voice had dropped an octave.

Parker's bottom lip quivered slightly before he answered. Ellington pressed a large hand to his shoulder. Both men took deep breaths, one seeming to fuel the other. "We've been good friends for almost ten years," Parker finally answered. "It became romantic just over two years ago."

"Were there problems in the relationship?"

"No. Jon was the love of my life. We were happy. W-we..." he stammered.

"You kept your relationship a secret. If things were that good, why not share it with family and friends?"

Parker bristled at the question.

"Don't answer that," Ellington interjected. His gaze narrowed substantially as he stared at the woman. "The question is irrelevant and has no bearing on the activity that took place yesterday."

"No, it doesn't," Angela responded. "But some might say it gives your client a motive. If things weren't well between Captain Black and Mr. Wyler."

"We were very happy," Parker said. "And I should have..." he started, then caught himself, biting back his words.

"If you had heard the shots and confronted the shooter, I might be here investigating your murder as well," Angela said.

She jotted another row of notes onto her notepad before she continued. "A neighbor reported a woman leaving your home yesterday morning. The same woman argued with Mr. Wyler and you last week. Who is she?"

A flitter of surprise crossed Parker's face. He tried not to let it show, but Angela didn't miss the twitch that suddenly danced over his left eye, his gaze darting back and forth as he considered what she'd just shared. He shook his head, not bothering to respond with a comment.

Angela blew a soft sigh. "I know you don't trust me, Captain Black, but I really am here to help. I'm not passing judgment or jumping to conclusions. I'm here to put together the facts and find the truth. I'm good at that. *Really* good! And that, you *can* trust. So, please, let me help! Take me through your morning again and don't leave anything out. Even if it seems irrelevant to you, let me be the judge of that. Please."

Ellington and Angela sat studying each other. His eyes danced over her face, noting the hint of a scar along her jawline despite the meticulous application of her foundation. Her dark eyes shimmered, and as he found himself falling deep into the heat of them, something inside swept through his gut. He inhaled swiftly and held the air deep in his lungs. An easy calm washed over his spirit, feeling like a warm blanket around him.

A lengthy moment passed between them all. No one spoke until Ellington leaned in and whispered into his brother's ear. "Trust her," he said, his voice having dropped multiple octaves. "I do."

The two brothers locked gazes briefly and Parker nodded, clearing his throat before he began to speak. "It was supposed to be an average day. Jonathan woke before I did. When the alarm went off, he was already up and dressed."

"Was that normal for him?" Angela asked softly.

Parker shook his head. "No. Normally he'll press the snooze button once or twice before he crawls out of bed."

"What time was the alarm set for?"

"Six thirty. We had planned to go for an early-morning run. But he was already dressed for work. He said that something had come up and he needed to go into the office earlier than planned."

"Did he tell you what that something was?" Angela questioned, noting he'd omitted that fact from his *official* statement.

"He'd gotten a tip about a case he was hoping to prosecute. That was all he would say."

"Do you know anything else about the case?"

Parker hesitated, his eyes suddenly darting back and

forth. He looked up and met Angela's intense stare. "No," he said. "No, I don't."

Ellington shifted in his seat. He knew when his brother was lying, and a bold lie had just rolled off Parker's tongue. *So much for full disclosure*, he thought. If Angela had not been in the room studying them both so intently, he would have challenged him. For the moment he would have to hold off questioning why Parker had withheld the truth from Angela, and from him.

She continued her line of inquiry. "So, what happened after you woke?"

"We made plans for dinner. We were going to eat in. Jonathan had already prepped the Crock-Pot for his garlic chicken. I headed into the bathroom to take my shower and he kissed me goodbye."

"How long were you in the bathroom?"

"Thirty, maybe forty minutes."

"Was the water running the entire time?"

Parker scowled, then shrugged his broad shoulders. "I turned it on first thing to heat the water and then I brushed my teeth. But yeah, the water ran until I got out of the shower."

Angela gestured for him to continue.

"When I exited the bathroom, Jonathan was lying on the floor. Blood was everywhere." Parker's voice dropped to a loud whisper. "I knelt down to check his pulse and when I realized he was dead, I broke down. I don't know how long I held him in my arms, but then I thought I heard a noise in the other room. I reached for my service revolver, but it wasn't on the nightstand where I'd left it, and that's when I realized it was lying on the floor by Jon's body. I went for my personal revolver from the drawer and swept the house, thinking the killer might still be there. But the house was empty. The doors were closed and locked. That's when I called 911. After I called for backup, I called my brother." He sighed, seeming grateful that he could be fully transparent about all that had happened and it couldn't be used against him.

"How long did it take you to get there, Attorney Black?"

"Less than fifteen minutes. I was already on the road to my office when I got his call," Ellington answered.

"And Detective Caswell and his team were already there?"

Ellington nodded. "Yes, they were."

Parker's brow suddenly furrowed. "They were there within minutes of my call. Almost like they had been waiting for it," he said, the thought easing past his full lips before he could catch it. He lifted his eyes back to Angela and she was jotting notes, the information not seeming to surprise her.

Ellington read his brother's mind, speaking what he was thinking. "You knew that already, didn't you?" he questioned.

Angela locked eyes with the man. She didn't bother to answer, turning her attention back to Parker instead. "I appreciate your time today, Captain Black. I will have your statement typed up and forwarded to your attorney for his approval, and your signature. I may have additional questions for you later. Questions that will stay off the record and not be part of your official statement."

Ellington's eyes narrowed. "Questions like…?"

"Like, who was the woman seen leaving the home right before the police arrived that your brother was also seen arguing with last week?"

Ellington turned to stare at his brother. The two seemed

to be having a conversation that Angela wasn't privy to, their eyes dancing in sync. Parker suddenly heaved a deep sigh.

"Vivian Wyler. If the woman leaving the house was the same woman, then it had to be Vivian. She's Jonathan's ex-wife. She's an addict, and trouble. But I didn't see her yesterday morning and as far as I know she wasn't at the house."

"Unless she arrived and left while you were in that shower," Angela said curtly. "Do you know where I can find Mrs. Wyler?"

Parker shrugged. "She could be anywhere. I don't think she has a permanent residence here in the city."

Angela made a mental note to put an APB out on the woman. "What were you arguing with her about?"

Parker blew a soft sigh. "Jonathan," he said softly. "She's still hurt that he left her for a man. She was also angry that he wouldn't continue to pay for her habit."

"Angry enough to kill him?"

"What's that saying about a woman scorned?" Parker responded.

"Did she stand to inherit anything from Jonathan's death that you know of?"

There was a moment of pause as Parker reflected on her question. He shrugged his shoulders as he spoke. "He had a small insurance policy that still had her name on it. He'd purchased it before they separated and never changed the beneficiary after the divorce. You can check but it's only ten grand." His voice dropped an octave, quivering slightly. "Everything else we put in both our names so there wouldn't be any issues if something did happen to one of us."

Angela gave him a slight nod. "Well, thank you again

for your time," she said. She stood up, extending her hand to shake his and then Ellington's.

"Is seven o'clock good for you?" Ellington questioned, his voice low. Eagerness seeped from his eyes.

Angela smiled as she gathered her papers. "I can meet you. Just text me the details."

Ellington grinned. "See you then," he said.

Climbing into his brother's car, Parker shook his head. "Tell me you are *not* trying to date the woman trying to put me away?"

Ellington grinned. "She's not trying to put you away. She wants to get to the truth and that's what we all want. Our having dinner together is no big deal. I'm just getting to know her. That's all."

Parker rolled his eyes skyward. "I think it's a big deal. Your father might have a problem with it as well. Conflict of interest and all that."

"Which is why I didn't mention it to you, or him. Plausible deniability and all that." Ellington laughed and Parker tossed him the slightest smile that disappeared as swiftly as it had risen.

"Anything from Mingus yet?" Parker questioned.

Ellington shook his head. "I haven't heard from him."

"Why do I feel like no one's doing anything?"

"Because you're not able to do anything. And you're frustrated."

Parker sighed as his brother shot him a quick glance.

"Since we're on the subject," Ellington started. "What case was Jonathan working on?"

"Case?"

"The one you told Investigator Stanfield that you knew nothing about."

"I don't."

"And I know a lie when I hear it. You and Jonathan shared everything. You bounced work off each other all the time. There's no way in hell he was working a case you didn't have some knowledge about."

Parker sighed again, a loud gush of air blowing past his full lips. He hesitated a moment before he spoke. "He was following that police misconduct case and I think it was leading him down a dark rabbit hole."

"That's the officer charged with forcing a woman to have sex with him after pulling her over for speeding?"

Parker nodded. "They had him on malfeasance and third-degree sexual assault. Apparently, he'd been trading leniency on traffic tickets for sexual favors for some time."

"From all I know that case was pretty cut-and-dried. You had some twelve or thirteen women who came forward to testify against him, correct?"

"He was just the tip of the iceberg. It was bigger than that. We're talking extortion, intimidation, maybe even murder. And the number of officers involved is mind-boggling. A tip fell in Jon's lap, an audio tape of a meeting that some of Chicago's finest participated in, boasting about their crimes. I got the impression it wasn't pretty, and he was just about to get his hands on hard evidence that would have helped him to take them all down. But that is all I know. He was keeping it very close to the chest. He wouldn't reveal his sources. Not even to me. Most of what I know I got from overhearing him on the phone or things I was able to surmise from the few questions he asked me."

"Do you think he kept it from you because he thought you might be involved?"

Parker's eyes widened as he pondered the question. He finally answered. "I think he kept it from me because he wanted to protect me from any backlash when it hit the fan."

"And now he's dead and someone really wants you to go down for his murder."

"I couldn't tell the investigator. I don't know who in the department to trust other than Armstrong and Dad and I'm not putting them in danger, so you need to keep this to yourself until we can figure out exactly what Jon knew and had."

Ellington nodded in agreement, but in the back of his mind he wasn't so sure that keeping quiet would serve any of them well. There was too much they still didn't know that could easily come back to bite them. And as he thought back to their last hour with Angela Stanfield, he was willing to bet she knew far more than she'd been willing to share. Dinner, he thought, was going to be interesting.

Angela sat staring at the photographs taken from the crime scene. She scrutinized each one, searching for anything that seemed out of place. Something was amiss and at first glance she couldn't put her finger on it. And then just like that, it clicked. She stole a quick glance to the clock on the wall. She only had a few minutes before her meeting with Caswell and the officers who served him. As soon as the meeting was over, she needed to head back to the Wyler home to confirm what she saw in the photos. Or more importantly, what she didn't see.

She thought back to her meeting with the department's prime suspect and his attorney. Angela trusted her instincts and something in her gut told her Parker Black was no killer. The brothers had clearly been very protective of each other, and she admired Ellington's devotion to his sibling. She didn't get the sense that he was trying to cover for the man, nor did she take him for someone who lied easily or readily. She'd known plenty of men who fit that bill and that was not Ellington Black.

She settled back against the leather executive's chair, folding her hands together in her lap. She was excited to see Ellington again and looked forward to dinner. She also knew she needed to ensure their casual meal together didn't become a problem for either of them. Giving it some thought, she decided to mention it casually to the mayor the next time she was in his office and depending on how he responded, take it from there. There was no point in making something of it before they'd even ordered an appetizer. It wasn't like dinner was going to lead to dessert, she thought. Not that she wouldn't seriously consider it if the opportunity presented itself.

She reached into her desk drawer for her compact to check her face. She looked weary, she thought, dark circles beginning to form under her eyes. Angela had worked cases that barely raised her blood pressure. This case not only had her on edge but was beginning to take a physical toll. And she was only hours into her investigation. She took that as a sign that she was too close; everything about finding the truth had become personal. It was the second rule since meeting Ellington that she found herself breaking and that had her in her feelings. Shaking the thought, Angela turned her attention back to the photographs.

Three men sat around the conference room table. Detective Caswell, Detective Jeremy Pickings and Officer Leonard Polk. Their conversation stalled abruptly when Angela entered the room. She didn't miss the exchange of looks that passed between them, something being secreted away, out of her reach. She forced a smile onto her face.

"Gentlemen, good afternoon," she said softly.

"I hope this won't take too long," Caswell noted. "I have an arrest warrant to serve."

Angela moved to the seat at the head of the table. "And who might this arrest warrant be for?"

"Parker Black. We're fairly certain he's responsible for the district attorney's murder."

"Fairly certain? I'd think it's important that you be certain beyond any reasonable doubt."

Caswell shrugged. "I've already spoken to the mayor and the state prosecutor. We have more than enough evidence linking Captain Black to the crime."

"The evidence you have is purely circumstantial. And I haven't declared this investigation done and finished yet."

"I understand you want to make a good showing and all, but there's no reason to keep this case open."

"I believe finding the truth is a very good reason, Detective Caswell."

The man's gaze narrowed, and he was chewing the inside of his cheek. Angela knew he was fighting to keep from saying something he knew he would regret. But he also had an unfettered desire to put her in her place. She forced another smile to her face as she leaned forward in her seat.

"Why don't you update me," she said. "Lay out your case and everything you have thus far. Start with motive and then walk me through how you think the murder happened." She then sat back, her hands clasped together in her lap.

Caswell nodded his head at Pickings, who flipped open the manila folder that rested on the table before him. He began to speak, sounding like he'd inhaled a shot of helium, his voice high-pitched and raspy. "I think I'm coming down with something," he said, excusing his snuffles.

Angela gave him a polite nod as he continued.

"We have a witness who will testify that Captain Black and district attorney Wyler were having problems. In fact, Wyler wanted out of the relationship and had threatened to leave him multiple times."

"Who's the witness?" Angela questioned.

"Wyler's ex-wife. They'd discussed reconciling and Captain Black wasn't happy about that."

Angela's face was blank as she took the information in and processed it in her head. "And you have a written statement?"

"Not yet," Caswell interjected. "But we will. I spoke to her personally."

"I'd like to speak with her," she said, directing her comment at Officer Polk. "Bring her in for questioning."

The man nodded as she turned back to Pickings. "Can anyone else substantiate that allegation?" Angela asked.

His eyes widened and he suddenly looked confused. He shot a glance at Caswell, who answered for him.

"I'm sure we can find others to corroborate her claims."

"We will need to. I'm sure there are at least a dozen people who'll testify they were the happiest couple in Chicago, with no problems at all, and that would cast doubt on your motive that love drove him to it."

Caswell grunted but said nothing.

"How about their financials?" Angela asked. "Anything not kosher?"

"I'm still waiting for that info," Pickings responded.

"We're digging deep into Parker's pockets," Caswell

said. "There are a lot of rumors going around about him and his whole family being on the take."

Angela shook her head. "Rumors don't make a man guilty of murder. So right now, our motive is shaky at best. What about the evidence? What did you find in the home?"

For ten minutes Caswell sugarcoated the forensics, making assumptions that any good defense attorney would rip to shreds. The mediocrity of the work he and his team had completed was cringeworthy and Angela had no problems saying so. For ten more minutes she ripped him a new orifice, bullet-pointing every problem with his investigation and his conclusions.

Caswell sneered, his face a deep shade of beet red. "You can't talk to me like that!" he snapped.

"Please don't underestimate me, Detective Caswell. I've been doing this long enough to know when a man is being railroaded for a crime he didn't commit. You don't have enough to charge anyone with this murder. You'll need to do better and if you're not willing to hold yourself to a higher standard you best believe I will."

Angela rose from the table. "Text me when the former Mrs. Wyler is available for interrogation," she said.

As she moved to the door, Caswell muttered under his breath, "Bitch!"

Angela turned back toward him. The glaze across her face was steely, the look she gave him shooting daggers of ice. "Yes," she said, her tone even colder. "I can be. But not today, Detective. Today, you're my bitch. Now do your damn job."

This time when Angela pulled in front of the Wyler property there was no city-issued police car sitting in the driveway. Caswell had released the home back to the family and inside, a single light burned in the front window.

At the front door she rang the bell and waited. It was a good minute before Parker Black opened the door. His eyes were swollen like he'd been crying, and he looked fatigued. Behind him two oversize garbage bags were filled to their brims, holding remnants of the destruction that had covered the floor earlier and needed to be thrown away.

"Special Investigator!" There was a hint of surprise in his tone at seeing her.

"Captain Black. I apologize for disturbing you. Do you mind if I come in?"

Parker gave her a slight smile as he fanned his arm, gesturing for her to enter. "What brings you back?" he asked.

"If you don't mind, I'd like to take a look in your office for something."

Parker shrugged. "Not sure you'll be able to find anything. They really did a number on the house."

"I'm really sorry about that."

"It's not your fault. I expected worse. I have no doubt a few of the guys took this as an opportunity to settle some old grudges."

"Guys like Caswell?"

"Leader of the pack, I'm sure."

"He's definitely special."

"What can I help you find?" Parker asked as he led the way into the office he had shared with Jonathan.

The two of them stood in the doorway, eyeing the mess that was still scattered across the desk and floor. Angela stepped across the threshold and moved to the file folders that lay undisturbed on the floor.

"Attorney Wyler was very meticulous about labeling his folders, wasn't he?"

"Almost anal about it. Labeled, color coded and filed in its place."

"What about you?"

"I wasn't as organized. Jonathan kept me organized."

Angela pulled a pair of rubber gloves from her jacket pocket and slid them on her hands. She knelt, scanning the labeled folders. Most of the papers that had been inside them were scattered haphazardly around the room. The one folder that had caught her attention in the photos was still where it had been left and she reached for it, pulling it into her hands as she stood back up. She rested it on the desk. This folder was not labeled, and there was nothing at all to indicate what should be inside. At a random glance, it would have been missed, just one folder among many. Her trained eye had honed right in on it, the disparity standing out like a red flag. When she opened it, one sheet of paper still lay inside. The word *Phoenix* was printed in bold letters at the top of the page. Angela read the contents, then closed the folder. If anyone were looking for it and hadn't known where to search, they would have missed it.

"What is it?" Parker asked.

Angela turned, staring into his eyes. "A list of names. I'm sure once I check they'll all be police officers under your jurisdiction. Caswell's name was at the top of the list. What was your boyfriend investigating, Captain Parker? And I really need you to be honest with me."

Parker stared back, his gaze suddenly skating from side to side as he pondered her question. "Police corruption," he said finally. "But he never elaborated on what he had or didn't have. I suspected he was collecting evidence to build a racketeering case against them. But he didn't want me involved in the investigation and tried to shield me from the fallout he anticipated would come once it went public. He didn't want anyone saying I got a pass because we were involved."

Angela nodded. "I need to take this with me," she said, gesturing with the manila folder. The statement was respectful, but her tone let him know she wasn't asking for his permission.

Parker nodded. "Be careful, Angela," he said. "Jon stirred up a beehive. I don't want to see you get stung trying to help me."

Angela gave him the slightest smile. "Take care of yourself, Parker. I'll be in touch."

Parker escorted her to the front door. As she stepped back out, he called her name.

"Yes?"

"Ellington's a good guy. In fact, my brother's one of the best. You'll be hard-pressed to find better. I just wanted you to know that. In case you needed someone to vouch for him."

Angela gave him one last smile and turned, heading back to her car as he closed his front door after her. As she slid into the driver's seat, she noticed Ray-Anne Harlow staring out her front window. She lifted her hand in a slight wave and the old woman waved back before shuttering her wood blinds and disappearing from view.

She sat in the quiet for a few good minutes, pondering what she knew and, more importantly, what she didn't. What had Jonathan Wyler discovered about Chicago's finest and did what he learn get him killed, she wondered. That list of names was also telling. How far up the ladder did that corruption go in the police department? And who all was involved?

Angela's attention shifted as a dark sedan suddenly pulled out of a parking space a few yards back. It moved slowly, its lights off despite the evening hour darkness.

As the driver pulled slowly past, Angela realized it was police-issue. The driver was likely an undercover officer but, from what little she could see past the tinted windows, not anyone she knew or recognized.

She took a deep breath and held it for a quick moment, blowing it slowly past her lips. As she watched the car turn the corner, Sister-Gregg's alto voice suddenly rang in her head. As her bestie often said, things were about to get very real.

Chapter 6

Ellington stole a quick glance at his reflection in the full-length mirror that hung in his bedroom. He'd changed clothes twice, finally selecting a black-on-black ensemble that complemented his pale complexion. The classic cashmere silk turtleneck and velvet jacquard jacket had been a gift from his sisters, the two proclaiming his wardrobe boring. The satin-trimmed slacks had been tailored to fit, and with the addition of a black silk pocket square, even he had to admit that he looked good. He couldn't help but hope that Angela Stanfield would be equally impressed.

He was headed to his car when his brother pulled into the driveway behind him. Mingus honked his horn and eased out of the car. He sported the beginnings of a scraggly beard and mustache and looked like he'd been on a wilderness retreat.

"Don't you look pretty!" Mingus exclaimed, greeting him warmly.

The two men slapped palms and bumped shoulders in a one-arm embrace.

"You look like you've had a rough few days," Ellington responded.

"I've been working hard."

"I hope that's a good thing."

Mingus shrugged. "It has its moments. Where are you headed?"

"Dinner. With a date."

"She cute?"

"Cute is for teenyboppers. She is a stunning woman! Intelligent, driven and worthy of adoration."

Mingus gave his brother an exaggerated eye roll, his light orbs swirling skyward. "You do remember what your mother says about something sounding too good to be true, right? That it usually is."

"Something tells me this woman would pass any test Judith Harmon Black threw at her."

"For your sake I would hope so."

"So, what brings you here?" Ellington leaned back against his car, his arms folded over his broad chest.

"You need to ask Parker what he knows about Operation Phoenix. Let me know what he says and tell him to be specific."

"What is it?"

"I'm hoping he'll tell you. I hit a wall, but I think it has everything to do with whatever Jonathan was working on."

"And you know this how?"

Mingus shrugged his shoulders. "A little birdie told me," he said, saying nothing more. He turned back toward his own car and tossed up his hand in a slight wave. "Enjoy your date. Make sure you show Ms. Stanfield a good time. We have a reputation to uphold. Can't have you sullying the Black family name." The wide smile on his face was taunting.

Ellington laughed. "What do you know about Angela Stanfield?"

Mingus grinned. "Where do you want me to start?" he called back. "You know I'm thorough."

Ellington shook his head from side to side and just like that his brother was backing his car out into the roadway.

Ellington had made reservations for two at River Roast. The LaSalle Street restaurant was located right on the Chicago River and featured spectacular views of the city and the water. The atmosphere was lively and vibrant and that night one of his favorite small-town bands was performing. With its promising menu of contemporary American tavern fare, and a multitude of stellar reviews, he was confident about the choice and had high hopes that he and Angela would enjoy their evening together.

Angela arrived just as the hostess pronounced their table on the patio was ready for them to be seated. She wore a silk jumpsuit in a Versace-inspired print and chunky, five-inch heels, and she'd freed her lengthy braids, allowing them to flow down her back and over her shoulders. As she approached, Ellington couldn't stop the full grin that pulled wide across his face, and he was grateful that the one she wore was just as magnanimous.

"Agent Stanfield. I'm glad you could make it," he said. He gently squeezed her shoulder.

"I wouldn't miss it," Angela answered. "You said food and free. Two of my favorite words."

Ellington laughed and gently pressed his palm to her lower back as the hostess led the way to the outside seating area.

"This is beautiful," Angela said, her eyes wandering

over the landscape. She took a seat in the chair he'd pulled out for her. "Have you eaten here before?"

He shook his head. "No, my sister recommended it. She says the food is exceptionally good."

"I hope so. I should have warned you. I'm not one of those women who order a salad and then spend half the night pushing the tomatoes from one side of the plate to the other. My father blessed me with a healthy appetite, and I love good food as long as it's not too over the top."

"That's good to know. I like a woman who likes to eat." Ellington gestured with the menu. "Will you permit me to order for the both of us?"

"Only if you make sure to include a very cold bottle of beer for me. And you may need to keep them coming. It's been that kind of day."

Ellington nodded at the waiter who'd been standing beside the table waiting for their attention. He'd introduced himself as Carlos. "We'll start with two beers, Carlos. Whatever you have on tap, please."

The young man nodded. "Would you like to start your meal with an appetizer?"

"We would," Ellington said as Angela watched him, a wry smile on her face. "We'll have the charcuterie platter with finocchiona, calabrese and 'nduja."

"Great choices, sir!"

"And we're ready to order our meal. We'll do the whole roasted chicken with street corn, carrots and dirt, and cauliflower."

"Thank you," Carlos said as he gathered their menus and headed back through the dining room.

"A whole roasted chicken?"

"You're the one who said you liked to eat," Ellington responded. "You're not going to be able to say I didn't feed you well."

"You ordered carrots and dirt," Angela said with a soft chuckle.

Ellington laughed warmly. "It's carrots topped with pumpernickel crumbs, goat cheese and a balsamic vinegar. My sister says it's her favorite thing to eat here."

"And you trust your sister?"

"I trust this sister. Vaughan would never steer me wrong. You can never be sure with my baby sister, Simone."

"I'd be willing to wage that Simone wouldn't agree."

"And you'd probably win that wager."

Carlos soon returned with their appetizer and two frothy mugs of ice-cold beer. There was a moment of pause as they waited for him to set the food on the table, questioning if there was anything else they needed.

"This is good," Ellington stated. "Thank you."

"Your dinner will be up shortly," Carlos said before he turned his attention to a table on the other side.

Angela lifted her mug to her lips and took a sip. Their gazes met and her eyes lifted in a bright smile. "Perfection! That just hit the spot!" she exclaimed.

Ellington hummed in agreement, swallowing his own mouthful of brew. He set the glass mug back on the table. "So, tell me about the rest of your day, Agent Stanfield. Was it really that bad?"

"First, call me Angela. And second, business is off-limits. I have no desire to talk work, or any other police-related case tonight. Agreed?"

"You won't get any arguments out of me!"

Angela took another sip of her beer. "So, tell me all of your deep, dark secrets, Mr. Black." Her eyes shimmered as she sat forward, leaning her chin on the back of her hands, her elbows resting on the tabletop.

"Only if you call me by my first name, Angela. Mr. Black is my father."

She gave him a sly nod. "Any nicknames, Ellington?"

"Not any that I'd be willing to say out loud," he said with a hearty laugh. Amusement danced across his face, and hers. "Have you had any opportunity to enjoy the city? I always recommend people do the tourist track most especially if they've ever lived here. Chicago has much to offer if folks are willing to give it a chance and I'm always surprised when I discover a resident who's never explored the city."

"Chicago scares people. You always hear the horror stories, the violence statistics, and about the incompetence of its leadership, but next to nothing about the people and programs that have molded Chicago. But I really like Chicago. This city has great energy. From what little I've been able to explore this trip, I'd even consider living here again. The city is constantly growing."

"I can't imagine myself living anywhere else. I lived abroad for a few years. In London. But I never considered it home."

"London? Wow! What took you there?"

"Hertford College at the University of Oxford. I did my postgraduate studies there."

"Master's?"

"Doctor of Philosophy in Socio-Legal Studies."

Angela's eyes widened. "Doctor! In Oxford? Were you a Rhodes Scholar?"

The barest hint of a dark shadow flushed Ellington's face, Angela noting the change in his expression. He shook his head, the gesture nonchalant. "No, I just wanted to study abroad, and my parents afforded me the opportunity," he said, something in his tone hinting at a larger story.

Curiosity furrowed her brow. "What am I missing?" she asked.

Ellington shrugged. "As children we're taught that Cecil Rhodes, the founder of the De Beers diamond company in South Africa, is a hero and a statesman and if they study hard and do well in school, they may be eligible to win a Rhodes Scholarship. It's the oldest, most celebrated international fellowship award in the world. But they don't teach that Cecil Rhodes killed millions of Africans times ten. They don't mention that those scholarships are paid for with the blood of our ancestors."

"I didn't know that."

"Not many people do."

"I'm impressed, *Dr.* Black! What did you do your doctoral thesis on? I'm always curious what people choose to defend."

"I argued that the criminalization of sexuality and women's reproductive rights catastrophically impacts Black women and women of color physically, emotionally and financially, more than it does white women. It was something to that effect," he muttered softly.

Angela's eyes danced over Ellington's face, and she realized he didn't much like talking about himself. He was handsome, intelligent, humble and slightly shy, and she found that to be a desirable combination for a man. "I would love to hear your argument one day," she finally said.

"One day. But enough about me. Why aren't you married?"

Angela laughed. "That's direct and to the point."

"I learned that in lawyer school. I'm exceptionally good at it." He winked his eye at her, amusement twinkling in his eyes.

Angela's bright smile lifted slowly as she studied his

smug expression. "You are quite an interesting man, El-lington."

"Yes, I am! Now you're avoiding my question. Why aren't you married?"

"Who says I'm not?"

Ellington's expression dropped, shock registering across his face. Air caught in his chest and his cheeks reddened. He was visibly flustered and reached for his water glass, taking a big gulp.

Angela laughed, holding up her hand. "I'm not! That was a joke. I've never been married," she said, still gig-gling.

Drawing a closed fist to his chest, Ellington took a deep inhale of air. "Don't do that. You just shattered my heart. For a second there I didn't know how I was going to get up from this table and walk away."

She was still giggling. "So, you don't date married women?"

"The only married woman you will ever see me dat-ing is the woman I'm married to. No, I don't do that. Not now. Not ever."

Moral fiber, Angela thought, her eyes locking with his. "Good to know!"

Ellington continued. "Are you going to answer my question or not?"

She shrugged. "Most of the men I've encountered are looking for a mother to take care of them. I'm looking for a partner to share myself with, not someone I have to parent or babysit."

Ellington nodded. "I have a mother. A wonderful woman, as a matter of fact. I don't need another mother."

Her laughter rang sweetly through the space, moving the patrons seated near them to turn and stare. Angela shook her head. "So, let me ask you the same question.

Why are you still single? I imagine many women think you're a good catch."

"I am. For the right woman. Until recently, I hadn't met a woman who came close to fitting the bill."

"Until recently?"

Ellington grinned but didn't elaborate. He continued, not skipping a beat as he tooted his own horn. "I own my own home. Two, as a matter of fact. I have a beach house on South Padre Island. I have money in the bank and my pension plan will ensure me a comfortable retirement. I think it's important for a woman to know that I'm more than capable of taking care of myself and my family, but I'm very much a minimalist and I'm not the random ATM machine some women would like me to be. Most women run when they find that out."

"Touché," Angela responded. "Now, pray tell, where is South Padre Island?"

"Texas."

Angela blinked. "Texas? There's an island in Texas?"

"It's a resort town on the coastal tip of Texas. It's known for its beautiful beaches, the warm Gulf Coast waters and dolphins. I like to deep sea fish and it's a perfect location for getaways."

"I've never heard of it. I'll have to go explore it one day."

"I look forward to showing you around." That smug smile pulled full and wide across his face. He looked at her like he knew something she didn't, his gaze teasing her sensibilities. Angela heard herself gasp, felt herself falling deep into the possibility behind his eyes. Her body was responding as her mind raced to catch up.

Before she could comment, Carlos appeared at her side. He carried their meals on an oversize tray. Their conversation was paused as the man skillfully carved the whole chicken at the table and laid the individual pieces on a large platter.

"Is there anything else I can get for you?" Carlos questioned.

Ellington held up his hand. "Two more beers, please."

"And a shot of Jack Daniels," Angela added. She was feeling slightly froggy, unnerved by the energy that hovered between her and him. She hoped a shot of liquid courage would keep that rise of anxiety away.

Ellington locked eyes with the beautiful woman and held her gaze. "Make that two shots," he said, the comment for Carlos.

"I'll bring that right out," the waiter responded. He moved back across the room. Angela and Ellington continued to stare at each other.

"Would you like me to say grace?" he questioned, his eyes doing a slow two-step over her face.

A man who prays, Angela thought to herself, checking off another positive in her head. "Yes, please," she said aloud.

Ellington reached across the table and gestured for her hands. As she slid her palms against his, a wave of comforting warmth wafted between them. Angela inhaled the beauty of it, allowing it to fill her lungs and seep into every vein in her body. She lifted her eyes to stare as Ellington lowered his head and began to bless the food.

"Father God, we thank Thee for the food that has been provided and the hands that prepared this meal. We ask Thee to bless it that it may nourish our souls and strengthen our bodies. In the name of Jesus Christ, we pray. Amen."

She gave him her sweetest smile. "Amen."

Ellington smiled back. "How did you like the 'nduja?" he asked, moving the conversation back to the meal. Food was a safe topic. He took another bite of the spreadable pork salume that he had layered on a small wedge of Italian bread.

She nodded. "It's good. I don't know that I would have tried it if you hadn't ordered it. But it's better than I anticipated. It reminds me of the sobrasada that they eat in Mallorca."

"You've been to Spain?"

"I have. About three years ago I took a cruise with my parents. The food was interesting."

Ellington chuckled. "I take it you're not an adventurous eater."

"Actually, I'm quite adventurous. Sometimes. But I'm partial to what I put into my mouth." Her smile was mischievous as she met his stare, a hint of innuendo lifting the lilt of her tone.

Ellington responded with a laugh that sounded gut-deep. The conversation lasted through dessert. It was light and easy, peppered with laughter that rang easily through the room. She knew he liked to tease, and they both flirted shamelessly. When they'd taken their last bite, their meals finished, their banter continued over one final cup of coffee; she could tell neither wanted their time together to end.

"I've had a great time," Ellington said as he pushed his empty cup to the center of the table. "I'm so glad we did this."

Angela leaned forward in her seat. "So am I. Thank you. I hope we get a chance to do it again soon." Her bright smile was like a beam drawing him in.

Ellington leaned in toward her, the gesture feeling conspiratorial. His voice dropped an octave, sounding to her like warm caramel drizzled over vanilla ice cream. It was sweet and decadent and sexy as hell. "I'm free tomorrow. But we could also continue this at my place tonight. I see no reason to bring the evening to an end."

Amusement filled Angela. "You're trying to get me into trouble," she said, her seductive tone a loud whisper. Something bewitching sparkled behind her eyes. Her thick lashes fluttered, her coquettish gaze beguiling.

Ellington shifted nervously in his seat. "I promise it'll be the best kind of trouble. Or don't you trust me?"

"Trust has nothing to do with it," she answered. "If I didn't trust you, Ellington, I wouldn't be here right now."

"Then let me get you into really good trouble," he said, his tone teasing.

They sat studying each other intently. Something unspoken swept like a tidal wave between them. Something that had taken on a life of its own. It was sucking the air from the room, leaving them both panting slightly. Heat rose with a vengeance and perspiration began to puddle in places she never anticipated. Angela couldn't help but think the trouble they were both thinking of came with capital letters.

"What do you have in mind?"

A blush suddenly flooded Ellington's cheeks with color. He bit down against his bottom lip and lifted his eyebrows suggestively. Angela laughed, rolling her own eyes skyward. Laughing with her, Ellington shrugged, his broad shoulders lifting toward the ceiling. Neither said a word; not one was necessary. Their bodies were beginning to speak a language of their own.

Ellington gestured for the check. As the waiter moved to their table to collect his credit card, Angela excused herself from the table and headed to the restroom. She could tell he was watching the gentle sway of her hips as she walked away.

After a quick check of the stalls Angela pulled her cell

phone from her purse and dialed. Sister-Gregg answered on the second ring.

"And why are you standing in the bathroom calling me? I thought you were on a date?"

"Whatever happened to hello. Hello, Angela. How are you? Didn't your folks teach you how to answer a telephone? And how do you know I'm standing in a bathroom?"

Sister-Gregg laughed. "That was a lucky guess. So, why are you in a bathroom?"

"I'm calling you! Focus! I need you to talk me down. I'm on a ledge right now."

"This sounds interesting. Who is he?"

"His name's Ellington. Ellington Black. He's the attorney for, and brother of, the suspect in the case I'm investigating, and I really need you to talk me down. Because I like him. I really like him, and I've had just enough to drink that I'm seriously thinking about giving him some. Tell me why this whole thing isn't a good idea."

"It sounds like it's a little late for that. If you're ready to give up your cookies, it's serious. Mr. Black must be something special because you never drink that much."

"You're not helping."

"Wow! He is cute," Sister-Gregg said after a moment's pause. "He's really cute!"

"Why are you googling him?"

"Who said anything about Google? Not that you're wrong, but how did you know?"

"My lucky guess," Angela responded, sarcasm tainting her tone. "Are you going to help me out or not?"

"I'm not sure what the problem is. If you like the guy…"

"It would be highly unprofessional of me," Angela said, interrupting.

"There's that, but when has being professional ever stopped you from going after what you want?"

"You're not helping."

"Fine. We do not have sex with men we barely know and definitely not on the first date. At least not since you were twenty-four and dating that guy with the cocked eye."

"I did not sleep with him on the first date. Or the second, and there was no third date. He had issues that couldn't be resolved with therapy or a weapon. I still believe the man was possessed by some sort of demonic force."

"Exactly. That's why we don't do that anymore. Demon sex is a no-no, although I don't get a predatorial vibe from your friend. And he is definitely handsome! I'd do him! Plus, his bio reads like he might be fairly stable. Yeah, I would definitely do him!"

"Stop with the Google already!" Angela said, sounding like a petulant child. "You're not helping!"

"You're on your own, my friend. If you do the dirty deed and it turns out badly, you are not going to blame me."

"What if it turns out to be the best decision I ever made?"

"Then I'll tell you I told you so!" Sister-Gregg laughed. "Just trust your gut. That has never failed you. Now get out of the bathroom, go back to the table and have a good time. Call me in the morning and tell me how he was!"

Angela laughed with her friend. "Who says I won't call you back in an hour because nothing is going to happen?"

"Good night, Angela! Don't do anything I wouldn't do."

"Well, I guess that leaves the doors wide-open! Good night, Sister!"

She disconnected the call and dropped her cell phone back into her purse. Taking a deep breath, Angela stared at her reflection in the mirror. Her cheeks were flushed, the faintest hint of color warming her dark complexion. Her eyes were bright and except for the lipstick she'd eaten off, her makeup was still intact. She dug deep into her purse, then refreshed her lip color with a sweet shade of Scarlet Rouge Gold by Tom Ford. The vibrant shade of red was her favorite and complemented her skin nicely. She dug into her purse a second time for the atomizer lost in the bottom. A quick spritz of her signature perfume wafted past her nostrils and as she pulled a hand through the length of her braids, she smiled.

Her bestie knew her better than most. For Angela to be second-guessing her decisions, she was off-kilter, and any man able to throw her off her game was a man who needed to be considered with caution. Angela didn't need to say the words to her friend. Despite wanting to blame that last shot of bourbon for what she was feeling, Angela knew that it was all Ellington Black who had her wanting to toss her reservations, and her panties, aside. She wanted to be reckless and spontaneous and go with the moment instead of overthinking the ramifications of pursuing a man who should have been off-limits.

She stood with her eyes closed and thought about the kind of trouble she was earnestly considering getting herself into. The kind of trouble that would have gotten her expelled from school, arrested if she did it in public and disowned by her Baptist father if he were to ever find out. She wanted to manhandle the man until she brought him to his knees and had him begging. She wanted to be touched in intimate places, held like she was the most beautiful woman in the world and loved until she couldn't walk straight. She wanted Ellington Black, in his bed or hers, buck naked and sweaty. She needed that more than she would ever be able to explain, and that need was suddenly holding her hostage and making her question what the hell she was getting herself into.

Ellington was nervous as hell, and he couldn't begin to explain why. Female companionship had never been an issue for him. There were women who fell over themselves to get his attention. Since he'd been fourteen and had discovered the opposite sex, there had been a few beauties he'd pursued, enjoying the chase if given one. But Angela Stanfield had him tongue-tied and anxious. He'd had a visceral response to her, every nerve ending in his body vibrating like a tuning fork gone awry. Every muscle below his navel had tightened with a vengeance and he couldn't stop thinking about her. He wanted her with a carnal desire so intense that he was having a hard time focusing on anything else but touching her. How she might feel against him, skin to skin, body heat melting into body heat. Where he wanted to put his tongue. The intensity of it was like nothing he had ever experienced before. He suddenly felt like he was sixteen again, when he'd fallen head over heels for Stacy McCoy, before Stacy had broken his heart. When he was giddy, and excited, and energy pitched through his abdomen like a marching band. When he imagined him and Angela together, he felt all that on steroids.

He suddenly stood as Angela returned to the table, gliding across the room like she was floating on air. He thought her even more stunning. Everything about her had his heart singing. And then she blessed him with a smile and Ellington instinctively knew getting the woman out of his system would be next to impossible. Everything about Angela Stanfield had gotten under his skin.

He reached for her hand, tangling her fingers between his own. When she pressed her palm against his palm and squeezed his hand back, the anxiety he was fighting lifted like a morning sunrise in search of a bright blue sky. He was suddenly calm, his confidence at an all-time high. In that moment, if anyone had asked, he would have had to tell them that dreams really did come true. Instinctively, he leaned forward and pressed a gentle kiss against her forehead.

Minutes later Angela's lips still smoldered, the sensation of Ellington's mouth burning against her skin. So lost in the memory of his lips atop hers, she could barely drive as she followed behind him, headed toward his home. One damn kiss had ignited a flame in the core of her feminine spirit and the fire burning was suddenly raging out of control.

They had exited the restaurant still holding hands. As they walked to her car, there had been a brief debate about whether she should leave her car and ride with him in his or drive herself and follow him. She'd opted to drive herself, wanting to ensure she had her own transportation in case things went south between them. In case she ended up doing that morning walk of shame back into her hotel room for a fresh change of clothes before starting the day. Having her own vehicle allowed her a semblance of control when she was feeling as if control was completely lost.

As they'd stood closely together, Ellington making a case why she shouldn't drive, she'd been compelled to kiss him, reaching up to press her mouth to his. That kiss had stalled his words. She'd giggled softly and then he'd eased an arm around her waist and had pulled her tightly

toward him. His touch fanned that lit flame and heat billowed in thick swells. She'd eased her tongue past his full
lips, and he had tasted of his last sip of wine and a breath
mint. She had lingered in that one kiss until her legs had
begun to wobble and she'd been ready to strip naked in
that parking lot. Now her lips smoldered, and she could
still feel the heat of his hands pressed against her skin.

Angela took a deep breath and then a second. This
was happening too fast to be any good for anyone. She
shook her head, wanting to wave the reverie away and
make sense of the moment and what she was doing. She
slowly depressed the brake pedal as they neared an intersection, a red light turning green as they approached.
Ellington engaged his turn signal and made the right.
Angela hesitated for a split second and then turned left,
heading off in the opposite direction.

Ellington had gone to sleep with Angela on his mind.
He woke still thinking about her. He reached across the
bed for his cell phone, wanting to reread the single text
message she'd sent hours earlier. I can't. I'm sorry, the
only words. To say he'd been devastated was putting it
mildly. It felt as if someone had snatched his kidney with
a pair of rusty pliers and replaced his favorite strawberry
ice cream with vinegar. His feelings had been hurt, and
for the first time in forever he was having a difficult
time reconciling the wealth of emotion that cradled him.

When they left the restaurant together, he'd been excited. When she initiated that first kiss, tasting of strawberries and mint, he'd been beside himself with joy. He
had wanted her to ride with him in his car, but she'd refused. He understood her wanting her own transportation, but he hadn't wanted her to leave him. Then he'd

turned onto Division Street and her car's headlights had disappeared from his rearview.

For a moment he thought she might have been caught at a red light, so he'd slowed his car, pulling over to the side of the road to wait. Then her text message came, and his excitement sank like an anchor into the pit of his stomach. He had called, determined to change her mind, but she hadn't answered. And now he was feeling like a lost dog that had been kicked. Waking up alone was not how he'd wanted to start his morning.

Ellington read the message one last time, checked his emails and his calendar, then he tossed the phone aside. He rolled himself to the edge of the bed and moved his long legs off the mattress as he sat upright. As he stretched his arms toward the ceiling, he took a deep inhale of air.

If his schedule was any indication of what was coming, he was in for an exceedingly long day. Back-to-back meetings first thing, court later in the day and establishing a plan for his brother's case well into the evening. He thought about Angela and considered the possibility of another date with the beautiful woman. But since he wasn't even sure she would talk to him, he figured that idea was null and void. He also didn't want to risk being disappointed if he did ask her out and she turned him down. He didn't think his heart could take another gut punch. He paused, trying to remember the last time he felt so discombobulated over any woman, then realized he'd been in his teens and uncertain about life in general.

Rising, Ellington took one last deep breath and headed toward the shower. He left a trail of clothes from one room to the other, a white tank top and navy boxer briefs tossed to the floor. As he stepped into the spray of warm water, the energizing flow falling over his head, he was still thinking about what might have happened between them if Angela hadn't changed her mind.

Chapter 7

Angela started her new day with an hour of yoga, doing a full *vinyasa* flow before her shower. Yoga was her new thing to do, added to an exercise regime that included daily runs on a treadmill and a pole dancing class that Sister had pushed her into trying. She wasn't particularly good at any of it, but what she lacked in skill she tried to make up for with enthusiasm. But this particular morning she was too lost in thought to be excited about much of anything.

She had tossed and turned for most of the night. She wished she hadn't changed her mind about following Ellington home. She'd gotten into her head, allowing doubt and uncertainty to jockey for position in her brain. It wasn't often that Angela second-guessed herself, and those few times when she had, she almost instantly regretted it. Thinking about Ellington was giving her a bucket of compunctions to contend with and she hadn't even had breakfast.

She reached for her cell phone to check if he'd responded to her last text message. There was nothing. Just a single call that had come immediately after she'd sent her apologies and then nothing. Not one other call to try and change her mind. His silence also had her in her feelings. Was he that easily dismissive of her? Had he not been as interested as she'd thought? And why was it bothering her as much as it was? Most especially since she'd been the one to run from him.

The cell phone vibrating in the palm of her hand surprised her. In all honesty she wasn't expecting anyone to call her at that hour of the day. Not even Ellington Black. She answered on the third ring, immediately recognizing the number on the caller ID.

"Angela Stanfield!" she answered cheerily.

"Good morning, Ms. Stanfield. This is Aubrey from Mayor Perry's office. The mayor would like to meet with you first thing this morning. If you would please be here at nine o'clock sharp."

"Do you know what this is about?" Angela questioned.

"I'll let the mayor know you'll be here on time," the woman said, ignoring the question.

"You do that," Angela said snidely, instantly irritated by the polite aggression. Annoyed that a whole hour of yoga had done nothing but give her a pulled muscle from a badly executed downward dog. Because she was no longer feeling relaxed or centered.

She disconnected the call, pausing to consider what her being summoned to the boss's office might mean for the case and what she needed to do to prepare for the questions she fathomed were coming. Mayor Perry was as anxious for her to close the investigation as the detectives who'd been assigned to the case. Maybe even more so. She knew that he was preoccupied with his reelection prospects, not wanting anything to interfere with him keeping his seat and the perks that came with the job. Singularly focused, he couldn't have cared less about the truth or the innocence of a man who might be wrongly accused of a crime. Angela had to question how much of that had to do with the mayor being a selfish bastard and whether or not His Honor might be protecting someone or something. Had he hired her just because he needed the optics to seem like he'd done his due diligence? He would be better served by looking like he'd gotten it right despite the questions that still plagued the case. She suddenly had as many questions for Mayor Perry as she imagined he would probably have for her. Which meant Ellington Black and all thoughts of him would have to wait.

She grabbed the matching silk jacket to the gray tailored dress she wore and exited the room. As she crossed the carpeted floor of the hotel lobby the desk clerk called her name, greeting her warmly. She'd become a familiar face to the staff of regulars who kept the hotel up and operational.

"Good morning," Angela responded, her face lifting in a warm smile.

"Good morning, Ms. Stanfield," the young woman said, in an island accent thick and melodious. "You had a delivery this morning." She passed Angela a sealed, legal-sized mailer.

"Thank you," Angela said as she eyed the manila envelope. Her name was printed in black ink, and she recognized the handwriting. It was distinct, bold and identical to the handwriting on the message she'd found on her desk days earlier. The message that had put Ray-Anne

Harlow on her radar. She gave the clerk a bright smile. "Did you by chance recognize the delivery person?"

"No, ma'am. I wasn't on duty when it arrived. Someone left it on the counter as we were changing shifts."

Angela nodded. "Thank you," she repeated, gesturing with the mailer. She turned toward the door and exited the building. When she reached her rental car she paused, glancing over the landscape. For a moment she felt as if someone was watching her, the sensation disconcerting as it flitted like a cold breeze up the length of her spine.

Traffic was beginning to pick up on the main road as people headed out to their respective jobs. At first glance nothing appeared out of the norm and then she noticed the dark sedan in the far corner of the hotel's lot. Its windows were tinted, preventing her from seeing inside. She couldn't say with any certainty that it was the same car she'd seen the night before when she sat parked in front of the Wyler home, but something about it was unnerving. As she continued to stare in the car's direction, someone inside started the engine and pulled out of the space. The vehicle drove slowly, then paused, someone watching her as she watched them, and then it turned out of the lot and onto the main road.

Angela took a deep breath. Under different circumstances, she might have been fearful. If someone hoped to intimidate her, they were in for a huge surprise. In that moment she was pissed and ready for a fight if someone wanted to bring one. She opened the car's door and slid into the driver's seat. After locking the car's doors, she tore open the envelope's seal. A compact audio cassette rested in the bottom of the container. It was the kind that fit into a small portable recorder. She cursed. Loudly.

Angela's curiosity was piqued but finding a device to play it on would take time she didn't have. Listening to the cassette would have to wait until after her meeting with the mayor. Tucking the unit into the pocket of her jacket, she started the car's engine and shifted the transmission into Drive. She stole one last glance around the parking lot, then turned toward City Hall, headed in the same direction as the sedan that had turned onto the main road before her.

At 9:45 a.m. Angela was still waiting in the lobby of the mayor's office for that early-morning appointment that had been so important. The assistant named Aubrey, a petite woman with mousy features and a perpetual frown, had twice offered her coffee. No one had bothered to apologize for wasting her time. She looked at her wristwatch, then blew an audible gust of air past her glossed lips.

"I have someplace to be," she said, directing her comment at Aubrey. "Do you expect Mayor Perry to be much longer?"

"I'm sure he'll be with you shortly," Aubrey answered. "Can I offer you something while you wait? Coffee, tea, water?"

Angela shook her head. She muttered under her breath, her frustration palpable. "You can put me out of my misery. You can do that!"

"Excuse me?" Aubrey said, her expression questioning.

Angela pulled her lips into a half smile. "I apologize. I was talking to myself, letting my frustration get the better of me for a moment." She stretched that smile a tad bit wider, her eyes bright as she took an inhale of breath and blew it out slowly before continuing. "But no, thank you. I don't want coffee, tea or water," she said, the faintest hint of snark still in her tone. She rolled her eyes as she folded her arms over her chest.

The door to the office suddenly swung open and Angela watched as Mayor Perry and Detective Caswell stepped across the threshold, the two men pausing to shake hands. There was an air of camaraderie between them, a level of familiarity that spoke volumes. Angela would have bet their two families vacationed together, babysat for each other's pets and children whilst the other was away for holiday, and met for backyard barbecues once per month during the summer. It was that old-boy network in play, and she was excluded by virtue of the hand dealt to her at birth. Being Black and female kept that door closed and locked to her.

Angela stood as the two men turned in her direction. Caswell sneered, his mouth curling unnaturally as her eyes met his. He gave her a nod of his head, turned to shake the mayor's hand one last time and then swept past her toward the elevators. The mayor gestured with a wave of his hand.

"Angela, good morning. I'm glad you could make it."

Angela smiled. "I wasn't aware I had a choice, Mayor Perry."

He laughed heartily and ushered her into his office. As he rounded his desk, he pointed toward an upholstered chair. "Have a seat. This won't take long."

Angela took a deep breath as she sat down, crossing one leg over the other. She blew the air that filled her lungs out slowly. The atmosphere in the room suddenly painted the walls a murky shade of gloomy.

"I'll get right to the point," the mayor started as he took his own seat. His eyes flitted over a stack of papers on his desk. "We no longer require your services, Special Agent Stanfield. Detective Caswell and his team have enough evidence to press charges against Captain Black and I am satisfied they have successfully closed this investigation. I'll need you to file your final report and pass that on to my office at your earliest convenience. We appreciate your services and will definitely call on you in the future if the need arises."

Angela watched him as he fiddled with a paper clip and refused to look her in the eye. Sweat beaded across his brow and his cheeks had turned a brilliant shade of coward red.

She shook her head slowly. "You're wrong. Captain Black did not kill his partner. He was not responsible for Mr. Wyler's death. I assure you, the most incompetent attorney in the world would have no problems shutting down Detective Caswell's case. I have no doubts that Attorney Black will tear it and the police department to shreds if you proceed."

The mayor shrugged. "I also have to point out that your relationship with Ellington Black has proven to be problematic. I'm sure our attorneys will find it to be a flagrant conflict of interest in this case and perhaps even a violation of the morals clause you signed."

"Except I have no relationship with Ellington Black."

"Did you not have dinner with him last night?"

"Did I? Are you having me followed?"

"Let's not play games, Angela."

"No, let's not. Who I dine with on my personal time is my private business and since I have never violated my oath to this office or my professionalism in this case, you and your attorneys will be hard-pressed to prove otherwise. So, let's you and I not play *that* game."

The mayor bristled. For a moment he seemed to ponder her comment, then he took a gulp of beverage from a ceramic coffee mug that bore the city's emblem. He swallowed hard before he spoke. "If you have evidence that contradicts Captain Black's guilt, I'll appreciate you making sure the detective and his team have it. Again, thank you for your service. Now, if you'll excuse me, I have another appointment."

Angela stood, nothing else needing to be said. She'd been dismissed without cause, as if she hadn't done her job and done it well. Removed because she was getting too close to the truth and becoming a threat to whatever they were hoping to keep hidden. The mayor had fired her, hoping she would just slink away and disappear. Obviously, he didn't know her, she thought. He didn't know her at all.

Aubrey called her name as she slammed the office door after herself.

"Yes?"

"Human Resources need you to sign some papers. Ask for Carol and she'll be able to help you."

"I'll do that," Angela said. "You have a good day."

"You, too," the other woman said. "And the best of luck to you."

"Have you finished your report yet?" Angela questioned, her cell phone pressed tightly to her ear.

Sister-Gregg responded on the other end. "I did. But I received an order this morning that all the evidence and information was being transferred back to local jurisdiction. They're sending someone to collect it. I was told you're off the case."

"That was quick. The mayor just fired me."

"That didn't take long at all. You must have pissed off a long list of people."

"When you're good, you're good," Angela said facetiously.

"What can I do to help?"

"I need a copy of everything you have, and I need you

to keep it just between us. Don't let them know you released any information to me."

"You want me to put my job at risk and get fired, too?"

"I want you to help me prove that their prime suspect is innocent because he is. That information could also help me take down some really bad cops."

Sister-Gregg sighed. "Check your email," she said. "It's a good thing I sent you everything I had last night. Now if I go down, I'll go down in a blaze of glory!"

"Thank you. That's why you're my BFF. I know if I needed to bury a body you'd come with a shovel and never ask a question."

"No, I'd ask lots of questions! And I'd bring sulfuric acid along with that shovel."

Angela laughed.

"Just remember, if anyone asks, you received that report before I found out you'd been taken off the case. That's my story and I'm sticking to it."

"Anything I need to pay particular attention to?" Angela questioned.

"We got a partial fingerprint off that green rubber glove fragment that caught your attention and a hit in IAFIS. It belongs to a woman named Vivian Wyler."

The familiar name gave Angela a moment of pause. IAFIS was the Integrated Automated Fingerprint Identification System, a computerized criminal history database maintained by the FBI. Vivian being in that system meant this wasn't her first run-in with the law. It could also mean they'd gotten their first real break in the case against Parker. She took a deep breath and blew it out slowly. "You're certain about that?"

"Very. You'll have to figure out the why and when of her being there wearing gloves. That I can't help you with. I also can't explain why there are no fingerprints on the murder weapon. Just that it appears to have been wiped clean. You would presume your suspect's prints should have been on the gun, but there's not a single print on it. I'm not sure the rest of what we found has any relevance to you being able to find the culprit, but you'll need to decide that for yourself. Your victim was definitely shot at point-blank range. Six of the seventeen shots that were fired hit him directly in his chest. Two of those bullets tore right through his aorta, killing him instantly. He was also shot in his arms, legs and groin. There was bruising against the length of his arm, too, like he'd been punched. And besides the beginnings of an ulcer, he was in excellent health. But everything's in the file I sent you."

Like snapshots from an instant camera being pinned to a board, Angela filed it all away in her head. It was good information and more than she had hoped for. "Thank you," she said, her mood shifting considerably.

"Thank me when you catch your killer. This was excessive and took the term *crime of passion* to a whole new level. What are you planning to do now?" her friend asked.

There was a moment of hesitation as Angela pondered the question. "What I should have done the moment I realized what I was dealing with," she said softly. "I'll call you later."

"Be careful, Angela. I'd like to be at your wedding!"

Angela laughed, the random comment bringing a smile to her face. "The day that happens I'd like to be there, too," she answered.

When Ellington entered the office conference room, Parker and Mingus were seated at one end of the oversize table. The two were poring over stacks of paperwork that littered the tabletop. Neither looked happy to be there.

"Is there a reason we had to be here at the crack of dawn while you got to sleep in?" Mingus questioned, tossing his brother a look.

Ellington laughed. "I just said be here early." He stole a quick look at his wristwatch. "Nine o'clock was hardly the crack of dawn. And I had to go to court this morning."

"How'd that go?" Parker asked.

"The case was tossed out. I have another satisfied client."

"Good to know. I was beginning to think I might need to hire someone else to represent me," Parker said, his tone sarcastic. "You might actually be as good as people claim you are."

"I'm better than good. Don't you ever forget it."

"You could have brought breakfast," Mingus muttered.

Ellington laughed. "There are fresh bagels in the break room. You better run before Simone finds out they're there. She's been eating anything that's not nailed down lately."

Mingus stood. "You want one?" he questioned, pausing to give Parker a look.

His brother shook his head. "No thanks. That last cup of coffee filled me up."

With a nod of his head, Mingus exited the room.

Ellington moved to the chair that faced Parker and took a seat. "How are you doing?" he asked, as they stared at each other.

Parker shrugged. "I'm still standing. I guess that counts for something. And Mingus has been hovering over me like a personal bodyguard. It's creepy."

"It's Mingus," he said matter-of-factly. "You up to some questions?"

"If it'll help us find Jon's killer, I'll head to hell, commune with Satan and bring you back a report."

"Sounds like we're getting somewhere, then." Ellington smiled.

Parker changed the subject. "How was your date last night?"

"What date?"

"Don't play dumb, especially after I put in a good word for you."

Ellington rolled his eyes, his brow furrowing as he thought back to his evening with Angela. "I crashed and burned."

"Damn! How'd you manage to do that after I talked you up and gave her a laundry list of your exceptional skills?"

"That's probably why I crashed. Her expectations were high."

Parker laughed, shaking his head. "Well, you know what your mother used to always say. If at first you don't succeed, try, try again!"

"She never said that."

"She said it to me all the time."

"You were special."

"I was exceptional. You were special."

Ellington shrugged. "Well, now that you know my date ended on a high note, what were you and Mingus doing?"

"Trying to decipher some paperwork I found in Jonathan's files. Mingus thinks this might be a list of his contacts that he wanted off the record. He recognized a few of the names and they don't necessarily run in polite circles."

Mingus moved back into the room, one bagel hanging from his mouth as he took a bite and another resting on a paper plate propped over a coffee cup. "What are we talking about?" he asked as he sat down.

"That list of names," Parker answered.

He nodded. "I'll check them out this afternoon. See if anyone's willing to talk to me. Most are high rollers. Some are in the drug game. I know one or two personally and they owe me a favor."

Ellington nodded. "Were you able to come up with anything else?"

"Not enough to keep him out of jail. Did you ask him what he knew about Operation Phoenix?"

Parker raised his hand, his eyes wide. "I'm sitting right here. You two are talking about me like I'm off somewhere on the other side of town."

"Just waiting for you to join the conversation. Jump in whenever you're ready." An amused smirk pulled at Ellington's full lips.

Parker shook his head slowly. "What's this Operation Phoenix?"

"Something Jonathan was working on. His secretary said the day before he died, she overheard him in a heated conversation with someone and that he mentioned Operation Phoenix."

"You talked to his secretary?" Parker asked.

"Bought her a drink or two. She's very perky when she's excited. Too high-energy, though, if you get my drift."

Ellington and Parker shot each other a look. Laughter suddenly rang warmly between them.

"I swear! I can't with you," Ellington said. "When Joanna finds out, do not mention my name. I will not have your woman angry with me because you're out here buying drinks for perky women."

"Someone's got to do your dirty work. Joanna knows that woman is just a means to an end."

"Did he really just say that?" Parker questioned.

"That's your brother," Ellington responded. "But I bet

if I asked Joanna, she might not agree with that state-ment."

"That's why this conversation remains between us and only us," Mingus said, a broad grin spreading across his face. "I am not trying to die anytime soon."

Ellington changed the subject, shifting the conversa-tion back to business. "So, do you know what Operation Phoenix is?" he asked, turning to look at Parker.

Parker shrugged. Before he could answer, a female voice rang from the doorway.

"I think I do," Angela said, suddenly moving into the space. "I think I know exactly what Operation Phoenix is and we don't have a whole lot of time to put all the pieces together."

Angela found the receptionist who'd come running after her slightly annoying. She understood the young woman was only trying to do her job, but the fact that Angela had gotten past her without breaking a sweat in-dicated she might not be as good at it as she wanted her boss to believe. Now she was whining to Ellington as if Angela had committed some heinous crime.

"I tried to stop her, Mr. Black!"

Angela nodded, folding her arms over her chest. "She did. She did try to stop me. But I explained that it was a matter of life and death that I speak with you."

"I told her you were in an important meeting, sir!"

Shock and surprise painted Ellington's face. He wanted to jump from his seat and wrap his arms around Angela in a deep bear hug, the sight of her suddenly bringing him immense joy. He managed to contain his excitement, acutely aware that his brothers were watching them in-tently. He took a deep inhale of air instead, filling his lungs. "It's fine, Leslie. Just hold any further interruptions, please!"

Leslie was not amused as she gave Angela a torrid side-eye. "Yes, Mr. Black. I'm very sorry, sir."

"I apologize as well," Angela said, smiling sweetly at the other woman. "Now, if you'll please excuse us." She stood with her hand on the doorknob, gesturing with her head for Leslie to leave.

Leslie's gaze narrowed considerably as she tossed Ellington one last look. He gave a quick nod and she turned, stomping back to the reception area as Angela closed the door after her.

Angela made a face, turning her attention toward Ellington. "Sorry about that! She's a little sensitive, isn't she?" She eased to his side and gently squeezed his forearm as she stepped past him.

He chuckled softly, his cheeks tinged a bright shade of red. "What's going on, Angela? I didn't think I was going to see you today."

Moving to the table, Angela took a seat. She slid the briefcase she carried onto the tabletop. "They've issued a warrant for Parker's arrest. They're coming for him, and we need to make sure they don't find him."

Ellington's brow furrowed. "I don't understand."

Angela shot Parker a quick look before lifting her eyes to meet Ellington's. "Someone in the police department has put a hit out on your brother."

For the next hour Angela told them everything she'd discovered since walking into the Wyler home days before. She repeated her conversation with neighbor Ray-Anne. Passed along the home security tape that Ray-Anne had given her. Filled them in on the forensics and her questions about the ex-wife and how she might be involved, then told them about the car that had been following her. When she was finished, she finally told them the mayor had terminated their professional relationship, sending her packing so fast that if she had blinked, she would have missed it.

"None of this makes an ounce of sense," Ellington said, his expression skeptical. "Why hire you only to fire you?"

"Because she won't play their game," Mingus interjected. He winked an eye at Angela. "I'm Mingus Black, by the way. The prettier one out of this lot."

Angela smiled. "Nice to meet you."

"So, what's your theory about Operation Phoenix?" Mingus continued.

"When I was visiting with Parker yesterday, I found this list labeled Phoenix," Angela said, passing the document to Parker.

He scanned it quickly, then lifted his eyes to hers. "They're all police officers in my unit."

She nodded. "A few of them were suspended for a number of sordid reasons. Two are currently under investigation for using excessive force. All of them have had complaints filed against them and were disciplined by you. And at the top of that list is the man initially assigned to investigate your case."

"Caswell." Parker shook his head slowly.

"Mike Caswell," Angela repeated. "And his investigation is plagued with problems. Sloppy doesn't begin to describe his work. He has manipulated evidence, blatantly lied about who he's interviewed and the content of those conversations. And his burgeoning friendship with the mayor feels wrong for many reasons."

"He's in line to get my job when I'm convicted," Parker said, his words dripping with sarcasm.

"That's if you're convicted. This—" she waved the audio tape that had been left for her earlier that morning "—says they're planning to make sure you never make it to trial."

The brothers all shot a look around the table. Ellington reached for the intercom on the table and depressed the talk button. "Leslie, please bring me a tape recorder from the supply closet."

"No need," Angela said, reaching into her briefcase for the player she'd swiped from police headquarters when she'd gone to pack up her belongings.

"Cancel that, Leslie," he said.

"Yes, sir." The intercom clicked silent and Ellington double-checked that it was turned off, not wanting to risk anyone overhearing their conversation.

"Where did you get that cassette tape?" Ellington questioned.

Angela shook her head. "Someone left it for me at the hotel's front desk this morning." She handed him the envelope it had come in. "As well as the note about Ray-Anne, which I found on my desk in the precinct. Someone's leaving breadcrumbs," she said. "The bigger question is why and are they friend or foe?"

She inserted the audio cassette into the player. After a quick adjustment of the volume, she pushed the play button before setting it in the middle of the table. Two clear and distinct voices rang out from the speakers. The men instantly recognized Caswell's voice. The other, a low baritone with the faintest hint of a Midwestern accent, wasn't familiar to anyone in the room.

"Where are we with that problem?" Caswell questioned.

The other man responded, his tone nonchalant. "It's being handled as we speak."

"It had better be. I can't afford to have this blow back on me. I have too much to lose."

"Just hold up your end of our agreement. The sooner you arrest your captain, the sooner all of your problems go away."

"I want him incinerated," Caswell spat. "He needs to be so far gone not even his family will remember who he was."

"Oh, they'll remember. I need them to remember, and I need it to hurt." The man's tone was ice-cold, every one of his words laced with venom.

Angela eyed Ellington, who winced as if someone had hit him with a gut punch. His brow furrowed as he pondered the comment. She watched as he shot his brothers a look but said nothing.

Caswell continued. "You never did tell me what he did to you."

"That's not your concern. Just know he's more than earned what's coming to him. Now, what about that woman?"

"I have that handled. She's already messed up, wiping the gun clean. She knew Parker's fingerprints needed to be the only ones on that weapon. It was stupid!"

"You trusted a junkie with the most important task. What did you expect?"

"Well, we can't risk her making any more mistakes. She's getting cold feet and would out this whole operation for an ounce of crack. I'm sure she's already blown through the money we paid her."

"Take care of her. We don't need any loose ends and if she's a liability then she needs to go, too. I want her and Parker Black dead before this week is out."

There was the sound of two glasses clapping against each other, the tinkling of glass and ice feeling out of place for the moment. Time passed and then a chair scraped against a floor, followed by a heavy door slamming harshly.

Caswell suddenly spoke one last time, his voice raised. "Danube, move your ass. You're still on duty, newbie!"

Angela reached across the table and depressed the off button. The quiet in the room was stifling, each of the men falling into thought as they replayed the conversation over in their heads.

"Danube? Wasn't that the patrolman Dad assigned to you the morning of the murder?" Ellington asked.

Parker nodded. "The kid's still wet behind the ears, but he's got heart. Wanted to be a police officer since he was a boy. Mom was actually the one who helped him get on the force. He had appeared before her on a juvenile charge when he was still in middle school. He straightened his life out and when he graduated from high school, he reached out to thank her. She recommended him for the police academy. And Dad liked him well enough to hire him. Thought he was good people."

"Is it possible he's still good people?" Angela asked. "Someone in that room made this tape and sent it to me."

Parker shrugged. "Anything's possible."

"One way to know for sure is to ask," Ellington said, rising from his seat.

"Or let it play out," Mingus interjected. "If the rookie is the one feeding Angela information, then let him keep doing that. If you start interrogating him, he may change his mind."

"He's right," Angela added. "If it is him, and he's trying to help, then let him keep doing that. Because if he's trying to help on the down low, then he's also trying to stay alive. They'll kill him, too, if he knows too much."

"We definitely don't want to put him at risk if he's one of the good guys," Ellington said.

"Assuming he's one of the good guys. I don't know if we can trust it," Parker muttered.

"Who's the woman they're talking about?" Ellington asked.

"I think it's Vivian Wyler," Angela answered. "Jonathan's ex-wife. Her fingerprint was found on a surgical glove in the home. That fact didn't make the final evidence list Caswell handed over to the district attorney."

"Then we need to find her," Parker said. "She's not safe. She's not one of my favorite people but I don't want to see something happen to her."

They all nodded in agreement.

Angela removed the recording from the player and slid it toward Ellington. "I trust this will be safe with you?"

He slid the tape into the interior pocket of his suit jacket. "I'll guard it with my life," he said.

"Do you have a dollar?" Angela questioned.

Confusion washed over Ellington's face. "A dollar?"

"Yeah, do you have a dollar?"

"I have one," Parker said, reaching for his billfold.

She shook her head. "Sorry, it needs to come from him."

Ellington pulled his wallet from his back pocket and pulled a dollar bill from inside. He slid it across the table and watched as Angela folded it in half and slipped it into a folder in her briefcase.

"We'll take care of the paperwork later," she said, "but I'm officially on your payroll for the duration of this case. I have no doubt the mayor will pitch a fit, but there's nothing in the contract between myself and the city to keep me from continuing to work this case for the defense team."

"I'll need to see that contract, please, just to make sure there's nothing in the fine print that could have them coming after you or after me."

"I'll make sure to leave a copy with Leslie." She winked her eye at him, the slightest smile on her face.

"So, what now?" Mingus questioned.

Ellington gave his brother a nod. "Take Parker someplace safe. Somewhere he can't be found and arrested. I'll try to negotiate a surrender and stall them for as long as I can. If anyone asks, he's taking some time away to mourn. I'll update Dad because I'm sure there's going to be some blowback toward him when Parker doesn't turn himself in and they can't find him. Then I need you to run down that list of names and see what you can find out. We need to figure out who else was in on that conversation with Caswell."

"What do you plan to do?" Parker asked his brother.

Ellington met Angela's intense gaze. "My new associate and I need to find Jonathan's ex-wife. Then we need to go knock down some big doors."

Angela grinned. "A sledgehammer moment. You've got a girl feeling all kinds of warm and fuzzy!"

"I'm glad something works," Ellington mumbled.

Angela felt her face warm with color and she bit down against her bottom lip, holding back the quip on the tip of her tongue since his brothers were in the room.

Parker laughed, he and Mingus exchanging a look. "You two are funny," he said.

Mingus moved toward the door. As he eased past Angela, he extended his hand to shake hers. He grinned. "It's been a pleasure."

Angela's entire face seemed to lift with joy as he pumped

her arm up and down. "The pleasure's been mine. Your brother has told me a lot about you."

Mingus shot Ellington a look. His expression was smug and teasing. "He's been keeping you a secret," he said. "He hasn't told us anything about you."

Ellington shook his head, not at all amused by his brother's teasing. "Don't do that." He turned to Angela. "Forgive my little brother. Giving me a hard time should be the national pastime, according to him. He's been doing it since we were boys. Every time I think he's outgrown it, he simply reinvents the wheels and starts over again."

"Ellington can be a little sensitive," Mingus said as he winked his eye at her, the gesture moving Angela to chuckle softly.

Parker had stood with his brother and the two men headed toward the conference room door. "Once I get wherever I'm going, I'll call you," he said.

Ellington shook his head. "Don't. Plausible deniability. I don't need to know anything. Mingus will keep me updated if there's something I need to know."

Parker nodded. "Thank you," he said, his eyes scanning Angela's face.

She shrugged. "I'm just doing what's right," she said. "Bringing a semblance of normalcy back to your life will be all the thanks I need."

"I like her," Mingus said to Parker as they exited the room. "Wanna take bets on how long it takes him to mess it up?"

Laughter rang warmly through the air behind the two men.

Ellington shook his head, his cheeks a brilliant shade of embarrassed. Amusement danced across Angela's face.

"If you'll excuse me while I show those two out," he said. "I should be right back."

Angela blessed him with a smile. "I'll be here waiting for you."

Chapter 8

Ellington stood outside the conference room door for a brief moment to quell the nervous tension that rippled through the pit of his stomach. He was excited to have Angela there despite his brother's efforts to toss him under a bus. She seemed unbothered by how things had been left between them although he was feeling out of sorts and his heart was beating a drum line in his chest.

When he pushed the door open, he found Angela seated at the table. She leaned back in the executive chair and her legs were propped up on top of the mahogany wood and crossed at the ankles. She was perusing one of the files Mingus had left on the table, singularly focused on what she was reading. And she was simply beautiful, Ellington thought.

Her braids had been pulled back into a ponytail. Her expression was studious, her eyes dancing back and forth across the pages. There was an aura of light that seemed to radiate from the warmth of her skin, and she bit down against one side of her lush lips as she focused. He found the sight of her mesmerizing, wanting to sweep her into his arms and hold her close. Instead, he took a deep breath and clinched his hands into tight fists.

"You're staring," Angela said, a slight smirk pulling across her face.

Ellington smiled. "I was. I couldn't help myself."

She closed the folder in her hand and placed it back where she'd taken it from. She sat forward in her seat, resting her elbows atop the table as she folded her hands together in front of her face. "I'm sorry," she said softly.

"For what?"

"For running away last night."

"Is that what you were doing? Running away?"

"Not really, but I was avoiding you and what I knew would happen between us."

"And what was going to happen between us?"

Angela smiled, noting the smug expression across his handsome face. She chuckled softly. "I imagine," she answered, "that you were going to show off your best boxer shorts and those scrawny legs of yours. I didn't want you to embarrass yourself."

Ellington laughed heartily. "There is nothing scrawny about my legs!" he said as he moved around the table to stand beside her.

Angela sat back in the upholstered chair and lifted her eyes to his. They stared at each other for a moment and then Ellington leaned down to press his mouth to hers. One of his hands rested on the table and the other on the back of her chair as he cradled his body into the embrace, his mouth eagerly searching hers. The kiss was warm, her lips like plush pillows that Ellington felt himself sinking into, his whole body falling against hers. As his tongue eagerly searched out hers, the moment felt surreal.

Ellington slipped his arm around her waist and pulled her to him, lifting her from her seat. Her arms slid around his neck, her fingers pressing against the back of his head. He spun her around and laid her against the conference table, as their kiss heated quickly.

The moment was suddenly interrupted when the door swung open, revealing Ellington's sister in the doorway. The couple jumped, startled from their furtive ministrations and looking like they'd been caught red-handed committing a crime. Ellington felt his cheeks become warm and he could only begin to imagine the deep shade of red that painted his expression.

"You could knock, Simone."

Simone stood staring, her expression smug as she looked from her brother to the woman and back. Amusement danced out of her eyes as she crossed her hands over a very pregnant belly. "You seem to forget that this is a professional office. You should not be feeling up strange women in the conference room." She took a step forward and extended her hand. "Hi, I'm Simone Black-Reilly, Attorney Black's sister."

Angela refastened the top button on her blouse, then extended her own hand in greeting. "It's nice to meet you, Simone. I'm Angela. Angela Stanfield. I'm the new hire."

Simone's brow lifted, curiosity piercing her gaze. "New hire?" she said with a slight nod of her head. "That's interesting."

"It really isn't, Simone," Ellington interjected. "Angela is going to help us prove Parker is innocent."

"And Angela has superpowers, to be able to do this?"

Angela laughed. "As a matter of fact, I do. I'm faster than a speeding bullet. More powerful than a locomotive, and able to leap over tall buildings in a single bound. I'm a Black woman with no tolerance for BS and a take-no-prisoners attitude! I can be your best friend or your worst enemy and you will always know where you stand with me. I'm also damn good at what I do and what I do is search out the truth that others don't want to come out."

Simone blinked, her expression blank.

"No?" Angela said. "How about, when I come to town, all the brothers gather round, 'cause I can really shake 'em down. I'm a one-hit chick squad!" Angela continued to paraphrase the lyrics to the theme song from the 1974 *Foxy Brown* movie. "A chick with drive, who don't take no jive!"

A slow grin pulled Simone's lips upward. "She's got jokes!" She shook her head. "Okay! I like you!" she proclaimed. "Now I need to know what's going on with you and Mr. Straight-and-Narrow over here. Because him making out with a woman at his day job is totally out of character for him."

Angela laughed. "So, he only does things like that at his night job?"

Ellington rolled his eyes skyward. "Excuse me, but I'm standing right here."

"I'm just trying to assess the situation," Simone quipped.

"And I'm helping your sister assess the situation," Angela said. She winked an eye at him, her bright smile like a warm blanket over the room. "I also want to know more about this night job where you make out with women."

Simone laughed, then suddenly grabbed her belly and winced. "Ouch!"

Ellington's eyes widened. "What's wrong?"

His sister shook her head. "Nothing. Your niece doesn't like my sense of humor."

"My nephew is a smart boy!"

Simone made a face at her brother. She turned her attention back to Angela. "I *really* like you, and my brother will tell you I don't like many people, most especially the women who are sleeping with my brothers! But let's do lunch. I've got plenty of stories I can tell you about this one," she said, pointing at Ellington. "And I look forward to getting to know you."

Angela gave her a nod. "Just say when and where. I'm sure it'll be a good time."

Simone moved back toward the door. "Attorney Black, I came to tell you that I'm headed to the courthouse for the Benson hearing and then I'm going home to put my feet up. I also settled and closed the Whitmer case. Did you need anything else from me before I leave?" she asked Ellington.

He shook his head. "No. Get some rest, and please, don't have that baby in Judge Murphy's courtroom."

"Wouldn't that be something," Simone said with a hearty giggle.

"You'll give that old man a heart attack, Simone."

"We should be so lucky!" she responded, the snark in her tone as thick as sorghum molasses.

Angela laughed. "I take it the judge isn't a favorite of yours?" she mused.

"Our mother beat him out of a federal appointment. He's been resentful and vindictive ever since. Landing on his calendar is like navigating a minefield. You never know when he's going to blow. Fortunately, I have an agreement on the table with the attorney handling this case. It shouldn't take long for Judge Murphy to snarl in my direction before he slams his gavel down."

Angela nodded. "Good luck. Sounds like you might need it."

"I'll be fine," Simone said, heading out the door. "I have that Black family magic on my side." She closed the door behind her, the sound of her heels fading in the distance as she headed down the hall.

"I like your baby sister," Angela said. "Something tells me she and I are going to be great friends." She gave Ellington a smile.

The man groaned, shaking his head from side to side. "Don't let that winning personality fool you. She's being nice but I'd bet my last dollar she's trying to decide how best to cut you to shreds and not have you bleed out on her good shoes."

Angela laughed. "Well, that sounds intimidating."

He shrugged. "I'm just giving you fair warning. Now, enough about Simone. Where were we?" He reached to pull her back into his arms, the gesture rejected as she sidestepped out of his reach.

Angela shook her head. "We need to find Vivian Wyler. But if we keep doing what we were doing, we're not going to be able to find our way out of a brown paper bag."

He laughed. "What were you planning to do?"

"What I planned would have your head spinning. And right now, I need you coherent and on top of your game."

"You do know I rarely leave the office to do any leg work, right? That's what I have my brother Mingus for. And I employ a team of paralegals to do my research. So, this is a first for me."

"You're a virgin investigator! I like that. I promise I'll be gentle."

Ellington laughed again, the wealth of it gut-deep and moving a tear to rain from his eye. He leaned to press one last kiss against her lips. "I'm really happy that you're here," he whispered when he pulled himself from her.

Angela nodded. "So am I," she whispered back. "But for the moment we need to get to work. Lives are depending on us."

He nodded. "You drive. I'll navigate."

"Isn't this your city?"

"It is, but since I won't be able to take my eyes off of you, this will make things easier."

Angela smiled, the slightest eye roll skating toward the ceiling. "Easier for who?"

Vivian Wyler had a drug habit and no verifiable address. Ellington reasoned that a woman living her life on the streets wouldn't have many places to rest her head without being harassed by the police. He also knew that only a select few places would cater to her habit or the kind of debauchery that could come with that lifestyle.

He pointed Angela to Roseland and that area known as the "wild 100s" between 103rd and 115th Streets. Cottage Grove Avenue lay to the east and State Street to the west. The area they called the "ho stroll" sat between the two, down Michigan Avenue. He'd often driven by and wondered about the community there: the women who waved for attention, their eyes devoid of emotion, and the men who seemed to always be scurrying to and from their cars, hoping not to be seen. It wasn't a world he walked in; everything about it felt foreign to him. But he understood the dichotomy of it all—the times of feast versus those of famine, the saved and the righteous pontificating against the ghosts and demons, the prey challenging the predator. It was an uneasy balance, a vicious cycle with no ending in sight.

He took a deep breath as Angela pulled the car into a parking space and shut down the engine. It was still too early in the day for many of the regulars who probably ran in the same circles as Vivian, but they reasoned that showing her picture and asking about her whereabouts would be a start. They hoped that if they threw out a line, they'd get lucky, and something would bite. Neither said anything as they stepped from the car and moved from point A to point B, questioning everyone who stepped in their path. Ellington took one side of Michigan Avenue and Angela took the other. Periodically, one would cross the street to walk alongside the other.

"One of us should have brought some snacks," Ellington declared as they strolled past Victory Centre, pausing at the bus stop on the corner of 105th Street.

Angela laughed. "One of us?"

"This was your idea."

She grinned. "I'll treat you to a bag of chips and a bottle of pop if it'll make you feel better," she said as she pointed to Rose Ridge Foods, a small convenience store across the street.

Ellington shook his head. "No, thank you. It's too late. I'll just starve." He feigned a pout, giving her his best puppy dog eyes.

Angela laughed heartily. "Is that your idea of a tantrum? Because if it is, I don't see you getting your way anytime soon."

Ellington laughed with her and shrugged his shoulders. "I thought I'd give it my best effort and maybe you'd buy me a candy bar with that bag of chips. Milky Way bars are my favorite."

Angela rolled her eyes skyward, amusement painting her expression. "That's so not cute, Counselor." She looked left and then right before stepping off the curb and crossing the street.

"Cute enough," Ellington mumbled under his breath. "It's getting me a candy bar!"

"I'm not buying you a candy bar!" Angela shouted back over her shoulder. She laughed heartily as Ellington stood with his hands on his hips, shaking his head.

The moment between them suddenly stalled as a police car whizzed past, sirens wailing and lights blazing. It was the second and then the third vehicles that followed that gave the two pause. Angela crossed back to the other side of the road, moving to Ellington's side. "Let's get the car and see what's going on," she said.

Ellington hesitated, considering a protest, and then four more police vehicles, including the superintendent's car, sped past. Any thoughts he'd had of debating the suggestion dissipated into thin air. He did an about-face, and they hurried back down the street to where they'd parked.

"I saw my father, so whatever is going on, it's serious," he said.

"Just considering the number of officers answering the call, I was thinking the same thing. It might not help our case, but it never hurts to know what's happening."

Ellington nodded his agreement as he pulled his car onto the roadway, following behind one more patrol car headed down the street.

The police presence at the intersection of Michigan and 111th Streets looked like a blue wave convention on steroids. More patrol cars than necessary filled the parking lot of the Dollar General store on the corner. Most were parked behind the black iron fence that bordered the property and uniformed officers milled around as a crowd of spectators gathered in front of the check cashing business on the other side of the street.

"Active shooter, maybe?" Ellington questioned, his eyes skating back and forth.

Angela shook her head. "No, I don't think so. There's no SWAT team." She pointed toward an older model

Hyundai Accent. The car's vibrant red color had faded substantially, and two spare doughnuts had replaced the rear tires. A side window was shattered and the license plates were missing. A couple of officers were stringing yellow crime scene tape to cordon off the area around the vehicle. The coroner's van had pulled behind it and three or four detectives stood with their hands in their pockets, their expressions mournful. Detective Caswell was front and center, pacing back and forth. He looked like a kicked dog ready to attack. Between the pacing he stood still, shaking his head in disbelief as an occasional tear ran down his cheek. The wealth of frustration in the air was palpable, feeling like the beginning of a tumultuous storm.

"Looks like there might be two bodies inside," she said as she strained to see around the officer who stood guard at the fence.

They had parked and exited their own car, crossing the road to stare past the fence. A burly officer with a balding head shouted for them to move along just as Ellington's father noticed the two of them standing there. Jerome called his son's name and gestured for the two of them to round the corner toward the entrance. He motioned for the officers standing guard to let them pass.

Ellington shook the patriarch's hand.

"What are you two doing here?" Jerome questioned. He tossed Angela a slight nod of his head.

"We were actually looking for someone," Ellington answered. "A woman who might have information that could help us with Parker's case. When we heard all the sirens, we came to see what all the commotion was about."

Jerome nodded. "We've got three bodies. Two of my officers and a local prostitute known as Viv."

Ellington and Angela exchanged a look. "Viv?" Angela questioned.

Jerome shrugged. "That's what I'm told. Apparently, she's a regular around here. We're working on IDing her now."

"Do you mind if I take a look, sir?" she asked.

Jerome hesitated for a split second before nodding his head. "Go ahead. It can't hurt to get another eye on the scene. Just stay out of the way," he ordered, his tone terse.

Angela responded with a quick shake of her head. She tossed Ellington a look and the faintest of smiles before moving swiftly toward the team of officers and the red car.

"Who are you two looking for?" Jerome suddenly questioned.

Ellington met his father's stare. "A woman named Vivian Wyler."

"Vivian?"

He nodded as his father's eyes darted from side to side. Ellington could see his father considering the similarities with the names of his victim and the woman they were searching for. His expression showed a mixture of surprise and confusion tossed over frustration and disbelief, emotions very like the ones he and Angela had felt moments earlier.

"You don't think…" Jerome started. His words stalled as he took a step closer to his son. His voice dropped an octave. "Where's Parker? They've issued a warrant for his arrest."

Ellington whispered back. "We know. Mingus has him until we can get this mess fixed."

Jerome nodded, the weight of everything furrowing his brow. "What's going on with you and Ms. Stanfield? The mayor sent notice that he'd fired her."

"He did. She's working for me now. There's a lot I need to catch you up on, but Parker's case isn't a slam dunk for the prosecution. Apparently, the work that investigative team did is questionable. It's why we were looking for Vivian Wyler. She may have information that would clear Parker, but it looks like someone might be trying to keep us from it."

"What else is new?" Jerome muttered, tossing up his hands in frustration.

Ellington took a deep breath and blew it out slowly. He turned his attention to Angela, who had moved to the other side of the yellow police tape and stood in conversation with the coroner. She didn't seem at all bothered by the bodies going rancid inside that little red car and she was oblivious to the officers who were eyeing her with contempt, questioning her presence in what they deemed their space. Her expression was tense, her jaw tight as she seemed to be clenching her teeth tightly. She wasn't happy and Ellington suddenly found that slightly disconcerting.

"Your brother is going to have to turn himself in," Jerome was saying.

Ellington shook his head, shifting his gaze back to his father. "Someone's put a hit out on Parker. We have it on tape. He can't come in until we can figure out who and why."

Shock rained across Jerome's expression. He clenched his fists tightly against his sides, trying not to let that emotion spill out of his eyes. He shot a look over his shoulder and around the parking lot, suddenly annoyed by all the officers milling about as if they didn't have a city to protect. He turned back to Ellington. "Do we have any idea who?" he whispered loudly as he shifted his body until he was standing shoulder to shoulder with his son.

"We know Detective Caswell is involved. But until we figure out all the players, we can't risk him knowing that."

Jerome nodded, clearly trying to make sense of it all. His head waved ever so slightly from side to side.

"Who were the two officers?" Ellington asked as he gestured with his head toward the red car.

"Detective Pickings and Officer Polk," Jerome answered, his mouth pulled in a deep frown. "Both were on the Jonathan Wyler murder investigation with Caswell."

"I don't know about you," Ellington said, "but I don't believe in coincidences."

His father grunted. "Neither do I and that concerns me."

"Why?"

"Because if I were putting two and two together, I might look at your brother for these murders, too."

The two men were still staring at each other when Angela moved back to their side.

"I believe we've found Vivian Wyler," she said, her expression grim. "She and Officer Polk took a single shot to the back of the head. Detective Pickings was sitting beside the shooter in the back seat. He got two bullets in the chest and a third in the face."

Ellington winced. "This is feeling like someone's cleaning up loose ends."

"And Detective Caswell is already trying to use Parker's disappearance against him. Caswell is liking him for this crime."

Jerome grunted, the look he tossed his son saying "I told you so."

"Did he say that?" Ellington questioned, ignoring his father's expression.

She shook her head. "He didn't have to. He mentioned that Vivian was a key witness in Parker's case and Pickings and Polk were bringing her in to testify against him. The lead detective here is already asking where he is and why he hasn't been picked up yet."

Their attention was suddenly diverted to four men in black suits as they flapped their badges and pushed their way past the guards at the parking lot's gated entrance.

"You two should probably take off," Jerome quipped. "It looks like the Feds have arrived to take over this investigation."

"Feds?" Ellington questioned.

"It's all about optics," Superintendent Black muttered in a bad impersonation of the mayor. "And right now, it's looking like I don't have control of my police department. The mayor is hedging his bets that with the help of the FBI, he can take me down. With Parker's arrest and now this scandal, if they can get a conviction, he'll have me out of here."

Ellington and Angela exchanged glances, but neither said anything.

Jerome blew a heavy gust of breath into the warm air. "I'm going to play along with this game the mayor is playing. I plan to be as helpful and accommodating as I can be. Then I plan to hit him where it's going to hurt him the most. Until then, you two find your brothers and figure this mess out. Solve this case and clear Parker's name. Is that understood?"

Ellington nodded his head. He and Angela watched as Jerome turned and walked toward the federal agents, extending his hand in greeting as he reached their side. Ellington continued to watch his father. Angela's gaze swept the landscape, eyeing the bystanders, the officers and the cars rubbernecking through the intersection, hoping against all odds that they might see something.

Her eyes lingered on the throng of people who lined

the other side of the street. Most held cell phones in their hands, videotaping in case something of interest happened. A few held their phones to their ears, conversing about what they were seeing. Others looked bored, patience beginning to wear thin. And then she saw him, his own gaze seemingly focused on Ellington and Jerome.

She stared and then his eyes shifted in her direction. A smile pulled at his thin lips, and he winked an eye at her as if he held a secret that only she was privy to. Both held their gazes until Ellington calling her name pulled her attention away.

"Hey, do you know that man over there?" She turned back to the other side of the street, pointing her index finger.

"Which one?" Ellington asked, looking from her to the other side and back.

Angela's eyes darted back and forth. The man in question was gone, having disappeared in the blink of her eye. She frowned, her brow creased with confusion.

"What does he look like?" Ellington persisted.

Angela met the intense look he was giving her. A shudder slid up and down the length of her spine as she finally answered. "He looks like you."

Chapter 9

Ellington wasn't sure how to feel about having a doppelganger randomly roaming the streets with his face. He found the thought ludicrous at best and, under different circumstances, would have been amused by the idea. But Angela's insistence that he had an identical twin stranger who'd been randomly spying on him and his father was suddenly unnerving.

"It was eerie!" Angela was saying. "He looked like he could be related to you except he was white-white with auburn-red hair."

"White-white?"

She rolled her eyes skyward. "You know what I mean. He wasn't biracial and definitely not African-American. But he was your mirror image. He could have stood between you, Parker and Mingus and been mistaken for another brother, or maybe a cousin. But definitely related. The resemblance was that deep."

"You never know," Ellington said with a shrug. Although his tone was jovial, he was only half kidding. "My father and my uncle were rolling stones back in the day, most especially my uncle, my father's half brother."

Ellington blew a soft sigh as he navigated his car back to the office. He suddenly drifted into thoughts about the man who they had recently discovered was kin to them. Alexander Balducci was renowned on the streets of Chicago, his philanthropic efforts belied by his criminal enterprises. The Balducci name was synonymous with every felonious element in the city. One of the oldest crime families in Chicago history, the Balduccis were notorious. His father and Alexander had a longtime friendship that many didn't understand. For years, the two had walked on opposite sides of the law. Their children also had a lengthy toe-to-toe history with fatal outcomes. His brother Armstrong had gone up against Alexander's two sons and both Balduccis had lost. One his freedom and the other his life. But through it all, Jerome had maintained a relationship with the man others publicly distanced themselves from. Their long-standing alliance was why many questioned the police superintendent's credibility, assuming he had to be a dirty cop. Only their respective families knew the truth of their kinship—that they were brothers who shared the same father and both men wanted to keep it that way.

Ellington shot Angela a look. "My uncle has children only he knows about. You never know when they might show up for a family reunion."

"And your father?" Angela asked, her brow raised and curiosity dancing across her expression.

"As of today, he's only claimed the seven of us. Tomorrow may be another story!"

The two chuckled. Ellington would have previously

found such a thought absurd but with so much having happened with his family in the last year, he didn't think there was anything at all that could surprise him now.

He pulled his car into his reserved parking space. It had been a long afternoon and he was ready for the workday to end. Unfortunately, he knew there was a pile of folders stacked a mile high on his desk needing his attention. But something felt unsettled deep down in his core. He couldn't put his finger on it or find the words to describe the feeling, but it had him out of sorts. Paperwork was the last thing he was interested in doing. He shifted the transmission in Reverse and backed the car out onto the roadway.

"Where are we going?" Angela asked.

He pulled into the intersection, bringing the car to a full stop at the red light. He took a quick minute to type a message on his phone, his thumbs skating easily over the screen. "Is there someplace you need to be?" he asked, shooting her a quick glance.

Angela shook her head. "No, but I also don't like to feel like I'm being kidnapped."

"Kidnapping is harsh. Let's just say you're being whisked away on an adventure."

"Kidnapped. Whisked away. It's all relative, so we'll not argue semantics. Bottom line, we still need to figure this case out. Our only good lead is now dead, and I don't know where you're taking me."

"I know, and we will, but at the moment I can't think. I'm hungry."

Angela laughed.

"What's funny?"

"You're serious? You're hungry?"

"You never got me that bag of chips and candy bar you promised me. So yes, I'm hungry."

Amusement danced across Angela's face, tangling with the faintest hint of annoyance. She shook her head and muttered. "Unbelievable!"

Ellington chuckled softly. "Not really. But I'll be able to think better on a full stomach. Sorry!"

"Don't apologize to me. Save it for your brother. Parker may take issue with you being so nonchalant about clearing his name."

"My brother would have made sure I had something to eat. He knows I need to keep my energy up to function. Hang around long enough and you'll learn how to keep me functional, too." Ellington winked an eye in her direction before shifting his focus back to the road.

"Why did that sound like it had nothing at all to do with food?"

"No, it has everything to do with food. Dessert, mostly! Really, really good dessert!" Ellington laughed again, his tone cocky and teasing.

Angela shook her head. "That's so not cute, Counselor!"

"It might not have been one of my best lines, but it wasn't that bad. Give me a little credit."

"That went beyond a crash and burn. That was a total decimation."

"Now you're just being plain mean."

Angela laughed. "I get that a lot," she said as Ellington laughed with her.

The banter eased the tension and frustration that had waffled between them. Both knew they were no closer to resolving the case, but the nearness of each other and the laughter gave them a brief moment of reprieve from the severity of the situation.

They both blew a sigh of relief simultaneously and that led to another round of laughter.

Ellington gasped. "I swear, if we keep this up, soon we'll be..."

"...finishing each other's sentences!" Angela concluded with the warmest giggle. Ellington smiled as she laid her hand against his forearm and squeezed it gently.

A moment of pause swept between them. Dropping into reflection she thought about their current situation. Angela was genuinely surprised by how comfortable she was with the man. Ellington made her laugh and not many men had been able to do that successfully. She knew he was stressed but he didn't let it show, seeming unflappable when dealing with a taxing situation. He was steadfast and calm. Almost too calm. Which made her wonder what could push his buttons and make him snap.

Ellington drove the rest of the way lost inside his own thoughts. Angela was staring out the passenger-side window and he fought the urge to trail a finger along the profile of her face. Imagining the devilment they could get into if the circumstances were different was proving to be a distraction. He couldn't stop thinking about how she felt in his arms, her body pressed gently to his. He wanted to taste her, to feel his mouth against hers. The fantasies that raced through his head had become disconcerting. He wanted her and he sensed that she wanted him. And in spite of the desire that surged like its own energy source, he had to stay focused on the task at hand.

Angela was clearly doing a better job of keeping her emotions in check and he was impressed with her fortitude. She had no intentions of stopping until the job was done. She was efficient and determined and she reminded him of himself before he'd allowed her to be a distraction. He found himself genuinely annoyed that they couldn't just revel in the newness of their relationship. He wanted moments of silliness where they simply focused on entertaining each other, where there were no worries in either's world. When this was finished, he thought, his brother would owe him big-time, and he had every intention of collecting what was due.

Ellington pulled his car into a parking space on a street that appeared to be deserted. Most of the buildings on both sides of the street were boarded up, many of the brick structures tagged with spray paint. It had the vibe of an old warehouse district that had seen better times.

Angela was still checking out her surroundings when Ellington exited the vehicle and rounded the front of the car to open her door. He extended his hand and when she took it, he entwined his fingers between hers, squeezing gently.

"So now are you going to tell me where you've brought me?" she asked, tossing a quick glance over her shoulder as they crossed the street.

"Peace Row," Ellington answered. "My brother's nightclub."

"Parker has a nightclub?"

Ellington shook his head. "My brother Armstrong. It's a membership-only establishment for law enforcement officers. The boys in blue hide out here when they want to unwind. My siblings and I also meet up here when we need to figure out our lives."

"Interesting…" Angela muttered softly.

Ellington gave her a look, his expression smug, but he didn't respond. He led the way to a building that had no significant markers save the oversize black door with a large brass knob. Once inside, he guided her down a flight of carpeted stairs to a second door that had been painted a vibrant shade of glossy red. He lifted a heavy gold knocker to announce them, and they stood waiting for someone on the other side to allow them access.

The senior citizen who answered the knock gave Ellington a nod of his head as his eyes skated the length of Angela's lithe frame. He turned back to Ellington. "Good to see you again, young man! And what did you do to be accompanied by such a beauty?" He gave Angela a wink of his eye, a toothless grin spreading full across his face.

"Aren't you a charmer!" Angela responded, giving him a bright smile back.

The old man chuckled. He gave Ellington a gentle push and took a step closer to Angela. "Back in the day I would have given this young buck a run for his money. If he don't treat you right, you know where to find me. The name's Mack. Mack Henry. But you can call me Sugar Daddy!"

Angela laughed as Ellington stepped back between them. "Glad to see you're doing well, Mr. Henry!"

"Ain't nothing wrong with me, son. I'm just reaching my prime."

"Mr. Henry, you saw your prime almost twenty years ago. Stop trying to hit on my date."

"I'm just being friendly. We don't get too many pretty faces down here in this dungeon." He lifted his bushy eyebrows in her direction.

"Mr. Henry, I do believe you're flirting with me," Angela teased.

"Pretty lady, I'm too old to flirt. These days I have to throw out a line and hope something bites. At my age there's no guarantee I'll see tomorrow."

"Something tells me your best days are still ahead of you."

The old man chuckled. "I do like you! Say my name and I'll put you in my will."

Ellington shook his head. "At the rate you're going, Mr. Henry, the women you keep adding to your last will and testament will barely get a penny of inheritance."

"It's the thought that counts, young man!"

The trio laughed heartily as Ellington guided her through the door into the inner sanctum. Angela stared in awe as the glossy red door closed behind them. She suddenly felt like she'd been transported back to another time and place. The ambience was grown and sexy, and there was a nice crowd of faces but no one either of them recognized. Music resonated out of speakers strategically positioned in the walls. There was a deep bass thumping with horns and strings and a songstress whose voice sounded like melted butter. It was a comfortable space and almost instantly relaxing.

The walls were oak-paneled, polished to a high shine and looking like an expensive old library. Round tables were artfully arranged around a dance floor and full bar.

Armstrong waved them toward the back of the room and the newly constructed event room. A one-way wall of glass gave those inside a view of the outer room but allowed the inner area to remain secluded. With the door closed it was a wild guess what was going on inside. Ellington guided her to that back room, where his family was seated inside. A waitress dressed in black slacks and a matching turtleneck was circling the table taking drink orders. Armstrong and Mingus waved in greeting. Simone jumped from her seat to give Angela a hug. She pulled the woman to the seat beside her and introduced her to her sister, Vaughan, who was eyeing her cautiously.

"This is Angela, Ellington's new friend."

"It's nice to meet you," Angela said, extending her hand toward Vaughan.

Vaughan gave her a nod. "You're the special investigator."

"Something like that."

"And now you're dating my brother?"

Ellington interrupted the conversation. "Isn't this new! It's usually Simone giving people a hard time."

"Vaughan's been in a mood since Davis told her he wasn't planning a senate run," Simone said.

"I have not!" Vaughan muttered.

Simone nodded. "You really have."

"Well, it just doesn't make any sense. His popularity is at an all-time high. He needs to run while he has a chance of winning."

Angela turned toward the youngest brother. "Hi, I'm Angela. I know Mingus and Armstrong, so you must be Davis."

The two shook hands. "It's nice to meet you, Angela," Davis Black said warmly. "Ignore my sister. She hates it when people tell her no. But she'll get over it."

"I thought this was a family meeting?" Vaughan said, the snark in her tone thick with venom.

Angela gave her a shrug, tossing Ellington a raised brow.

"I invited you all to dinner," Ellington snapped. "The guest list was my choice. Now act like our mother raised you with some home training, please. Or I'm going to tell Daddy!"

Vaughan snarled, then pouted, and everyone around the table laughed.

Simone grinned. "Usually they're all yelling at me! I kind of like this!"

"Shut up, Simone," Vaughan said. She sat back in her

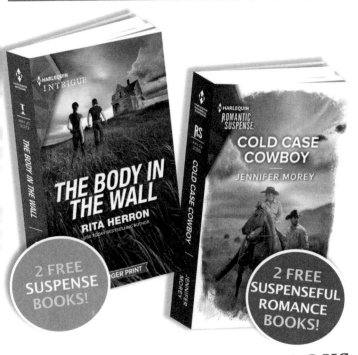

YOU pick your books –
WE pay for everything.
You get up to FOUR New Books and TWO Mystery Gifts...absolutely FREE!

Dear Reader,

I am writing to announce the launch of a huge **FREE BOOKS GIVEAWAY**... and to let you know that YOU are entitled to choose up to FOUR fantastic books that WE pay for.

Try **Harlequin® Romantic Suspense** books featuring heart-racing page-turners with unexpected plot twists and irresistible chemistry that will keep you guessing to the very end.

Try **Harlequin Intrigue® Larger-Print** books featuring action-packed stories that will keep you on the edge of your seat. Solve the crime and deliver justice at all costs.

Or TRY BOTH!

In return, we ask just one favor: Would you please participate in our brief Reader Survey? We'd love to hear from you.

This FREE BOOKS GIVEAWAY means that your introductory shipment is completely free, <u>even the shipping</u>! If you decide to continue, you can look forward to curated monthly shipments of brand-new books from your selected series, always at a discount off the cover price! <u>Plus you can cancel any time</u>. Who could pass up a deal like that?

Sincerely

Pam Powers

Pam Powers
For Harlequin Reader Service

Complete the survey below and return it today to receive up to 4 FREE BOOKS and FREE GIFTS guaranteed!

FREE BOOKS GIVEAWAY
Reader Survey

1
Do you prefer stories with suspensful storylines?

◯ YES   ◯ NO

2
Do you share your favorite books with friends?

◯ YES   ◯ NO

3
Do you often choose to read instead of watching TV?

◯ YES   ◯ NO

YES! Please send me my Free Rewards, consisting of **2 Free Books from each series I select** and **Free Mystery Gifts**. I understand that I am under no obligation to buy anything, no purchase necessary see terms and conditions for details.

❑ **Harlequin® Romantic Suspense** (240/340 HDL GRNT)
❑ **Harlequin Intrigue® Larger-Print** (199/399 HDL GRNT)
❑ **Try Both** (240/340 & 199/399 HDL GRN5)

FIRST NAME   LAST NAME

ADDRESS

APT.#   CITY

STATE/PROV.   ZIP/POSTAL CODE

EMAIL ❑ Please check this box if you would like to receive newsletters and promotional emails from Harlequin Enterprises ULC and its affiliates. You can unsubscribe anytime.

HI/HRS-122-FBG22_HI/HRS-122-FBGVR

seat, her arms crossed over her chest defiantly. She reached for the shot glass that rested on the table in front of her and tossed back the dark liquor.

Ellington gave his sister a look, noting the tears that misted her eyes. He made a mental note to find out what was bothering her. Clearly, something was amiss, because Mean Vaughan rarely made an appearance in front of strangers.

He shifted the conversation, turning his attention to Angela. "I hope you're hungry. The food here is some of the best in the city."

"I was able to wrangle the best chef in the state," Armstrong interjected.

"I'm excited," Angela responded. "That sounds very tempting!"

"What's on the menu?" Ellington asked.

His brother chuckled. "Whatever the chef puts on the table. We're eating family-style. You know how Ms. Francis does."

Minutes later, the family sat chatting among themselves. The conversation was casual and easy. Parker was the one sibling not there, and even though he wasn't mentioned, Angela could feel his absence was a major void in their cohesive little unit. Trying to maintain some levity around the table, no one spoke Parker's name. Instead, they peppered Angela with questions about herself and her family, and Ellington enjoyed watching how easily she interacted with them. He also appreciated that everyone seemed to be taking a liking to her as well. Even Vaughan, who'd finally relaxed and seemed to be enjoying herself.

Some twenty minutes later the famous Ms. Francis, a

robust Jamaican woman with waist-length, salt-and-pepper dreads, personally delivered platters of stewed chicken and curry goat, stew peas, white rice, fried plantains and a basket of coco bread. The decadent aroma scented the room and had them all salivating for a taste. They ate heartily, savoring every forkful until they were stuffed and ready to be rolled home.

When the staff came to clear away the dirty dishes, Ellington passed his brother his credit card. "Add a generous tip," he said.

Armstrong smirked. "How generous is generous?"

"Mom generous, not Dad generous."

"Dad's not a big tipper," Simone said. "And Mom over-tips."

"Exactly," Ellington said, pointing his finger at his sister.

They all chuckled. The conversation continued as the siblings bantered back and forth, catching up on each other's doings.

"Why haven't you and Neema set a date yet?" Simone was asking, her eyes locked on Davis, who'd recently asked a star reporter with the *Chicago Tribune* to be his wife.

"Because Neema and I will set a date on our own time, no one else's," Davis responded. "Why are you in such a hurry for us to be married?"

"I'm not in a hurry, but I'm sure your girlfriend would appreciate the commitment."

"My *fiancée* appreciates that I allow her to do things in her own time. She knows she's loved and that she has my heart on lock. Besides, you were mean to her, so she definitely isn't interested in your two cents about our relationship."

Simone tossed up her hands. "I apologized! How long

are you going to hold a momentary lapse of judgment against me?"

A round of laughter circled the table. Ellington shook his head as he turned to Angela and whispered, "Simone eviscerated Neema at a family dinner. It wasn't pretty. Her momentary lapses usually leave people in shambles. She's mean. Mean-as-spit mean!"

Angela laughed. "No wonder she and I get along so well!"

His eyes widened. "Should I be scared?"

"You should tread carefully."

"I'll consider myself warned."

Angela laughed and Ellington laughed with her as he winked an eye in her direction.

"What's so funny?" Vaughan questioned, her gaze bouncing from one to the other and back again.

Both sensed that she had been watching them intently. Ellington felt his cheeks warm.

Angela gave her a wide smile. "I was just telling your brother that strong, opinionated women are a gift. He should not take us lightly."

"I know that's right!" Simone interjected, giving Angela a high five.

"Looks like you're going to have your hands full," Armstrong said with a chuckle. "Glad I don't have that problem."

"Because you have your hands full with your wife and these renovations," Ellington quipped.

"And Danni is opinionated about what he can and cannot do with this new space," Davis added. "I've seen her in action!"

"Danni just wants to make sure things are done right. She's been great with the contractors."

"What other renovations are you planning?" Ellington asked.

"We've already knocked through the wall of the building next door for the additional event space. I'm also planning a public club along the same lines as Peace Row on the upper levels."

"So, you own the building next door as well?" Angela asked.

Armstrong smiled as Ellington answered for him. "My brother owns the entire block."

"I *co-own* the entire block," Armstrong said. "Ellington and Mingus are my partners. Our goal is to rejuvenate the neighborhood."

Angela cut her eye in Ellington's direction. "That's interesting."

"Not really," Ellington said, shaking his head. "This is all Armstrong. I just nod and sign checks. Eventually, we'll get to the last building on the corner, where I hope to move my law firm. But that's going to involve a lot of money and a lot of time that I don't have right now."

Mingus chuckled. "I know I don't have it," he muttered. "But don't let Ellington fool you. He's the wealthy brother."

"Keeping secrets from me already!" Angela said teasingly.

"You might be a gold digger," Ellington said. "I can't be too careful."

"She might have more money than all of us put together," Vaughan said. "I'll let you know after I run that background check."

Angela laughed. "Save yourself the trouble. I don't."

Vaughan laughed with her, sending them all into a fit of guffaws.

"As you can see, we try not to take ourselves too seriously," Ellington said as he leaned in to kiss Angela's cheek, the others nodding their agreement.

"I love the camaraderie between you all. It's really heartwarming."

"We're always here for each other," Mingus said. "And not to put a damper on this party but I need to take off in a few minutes." He leaned back on his chair legs, his expression stoic. "I hit a dead end. A few old heads are saying there's a new player in town, but no one knows anything about him. Balducci has put the word out for information, but nothing's come back yet. He says when he hears something he'll let me know."

"Someone's tying up loose ends," Angela said. "Our one good lead was executed along with two police officers."

Mingus's brow lifted in surprise. "Jon's ex-wife is dead?"

Ellington nodded. "Yeah. Whatever she knew, someone couldn't risk it getting out. And now they're gunning for Parker." He updated the others on the audio tape and their concern for Parker's safety. Angela told them about finding Vivian's body and the cops trying to link Parker to the three additional deaths.

"Our brother is safe, right?" Simone asked.

Mingus nodded. "He's probably doing better than we are. It helps to have family with a private jet, unlimited security and property all around the world."

"I guess Uncle Alexander is good for something," Simone muttered.

"What are you going to do now?" Vaughan questioned.

The room went quiet, everyone looking toward Ellington. He finally shook his head. "I don't know. I can easily build a case to show reasonable doubt, but they're not interested in Parker making it to trial. It means we need to find Jon's killer."

"We need to figure out who's holding a grudge against Parker. If we can identify that voice on the audio tape it may lead us right to our killer," Angela interjected.

"Sounds like you're looking for a needle in a haystack," Vaughan said.

"Finding a needle would be easier," Ellington responded.

Silence filled the space a second time, everyone falling into their own thoughts. No one needed to say anything. Angela could tell by the expressions that crossed their faces that the Black family would not be defeated by what seemed impossible.

Mingus jumped from his seat. "If I hear anything from Alexander, I'll let you know. I've got to run. Thanks for dinner."

Ellington nodded. "Be safe out there, please."

The two men slapped palms and Mingus leaned to kiss his sisters as he rounded the table.

"Who needs a ride?" Davis questioned, standing as well.

"Vaughan was giving me a ride home, but since you're going in that direction she doesn't need to go out of her way," Simone said. She rose from her own seat, her palm pressed tightly to her bulging belly.

"When are you due?" Angela asked.

"Not soon enough. This kid is killing my insides."

"Boy? Girl?"

"We're waiting to be surprised, although the general consensus is that it's a boy."

"It's a girl," Vaughan interjected.

"Boy!" the Black brothers all chimed at the same time. Angela laughed.

Simone shook her head. "He or she is well loved. That's all that matters to his father and me." She reached to give Angela a hug, then headed for the door.

The family began to file out of the room one by one. Ellington paused to have one last conversation with Armstrong as Angela stood politely off to the side to allow them a moment of privacy. It had been a good time and she had enjoyed visiting with his family. In the main room the DJ was spinning old-school R&B tunes—slow, bass-rich songs that spoke of good times and even better love. Couples were dancing close on the dance floor, the music thumping out of speakers that circled the room. Angela was bobbing her head and swaying slowly to the song "White Horse" by the Danish group Laid Back, her hips moving with a mind of their own. She jumped ever so slightly when Ellington suddenly stepped in behind her, an arm wrapping around her waist as he pulled her back against him. He pressed a kiss to the back of her neck.

"I should probably get you back to your car," he whispered in her ear.

Angela leaned back against his chest, reaching her right arm up to cup his face in the palm of her hand. "You need to dance with me," she answered, gently shimmying her buttocks against his groin.

Ellington chuckled. "I should forewarn you that I have two left feet."

"That's not a problem. I only need you to use one of them," Angela responded with the slightest giggle. "You just hold me close, and I'll do all the work. You use that good left foot to keep yourself standing upright."

"Now I'm really scared," he said as he nuzzled his face in her hair, inhaling the scent of coconut oil that coated the strands.

"You should be!" she quipped as she grabbed his hand and pulled him along behind her. On the dance floor she spun around to face him, wrapping her hands around his neck, her fingers laced together behind his head. She pressed her body tightly to his, her hips still moving of their own volition. It was an erotic, side-to-side shimmy that lengthened every muscle below Ellington's waist and had him sweating profusely beneath the cool lights on the stage. His hands trailed across her back and shoulders, down the length of her arms, his fingertips resting against the curve of her backside. She teased him unmercifully, dipping slightly then rotating against him until he thought he might explode in his pants. Each time he took a step back, needing to put a wisp of air between them, she moved against him again. They danced through four, maybe five songs, never losing the connection that had them both hot and bothered.

Anita Baker was singing sweetly in his ear when he suddenly felt like he was being watched. He looked up to see Armstrong standing in the back of the room, eyeing the two of them. A Cheshire-cat grin pulled from ear to ear. His brother gave him a thumbs-up and nodded his approval. Ellington shook his head ever so slightly.

He leaned to whisper in her ear. "I'm thinking we should get out of here."

"Your place?" Angela asked softly.

"If you'd like. You're always welcome. But don't get my hopes up and disappoint me again, Angela. My heart couldn't take it!"

She giggled, still swaying from side to side in obvious enjoyment of the music.

Movement at the door pulled at Ellington's attention. He was surprised when Mr. Henry escorted Officer Danube through the door, the uniformed officer moving to a table in a corner to whisper in another officer's ear. The exchange seemed tense as the two men appeared to argue. Even Armstrong stood focused on the conversation, prepared to intercede if necessary.

Ellington suddenly spun Angela around. Her eyes widened as his body went rigid, every ounce of relaxation having dissipated like air from a popped balloon.

"What's wrong?" she asked.

"Twelve o'clock," he said, gesturing with a toss of his head. "Do you know the officers at that table? Officer Danube is talking to them."

Angela stared. She recognized two faces but didn't have names to put to them. "Ask Armstrong," she said as she stepped from him and off the dance floor. "Then meet me at the car."

Ellington called her name, but she moved with the swiftness of a cheetah on the African plains. Danube had moved through the door. He and the other man made their exit as Angela followed after them, weaving her way through the crowd of revelers and the tables spaced just so far apart. Off-duty law enforcement were a rowdy bunch, eager for her attention and visibly disappointed when she pressed on, barely giving them a nod.

An open palm and a shake of her head stalled Mr. Henry from saying anything to her as she finally hurried down the length of hallway after the two men. When she reached the outer door, stepping out onto the sidewalk, she was instantly struck by how dark it had turned. The sun had set, and the barest hint of a quarter moon sat high in the black sky. A single streetlight barely illuminated the block and the high temperature from earlier had dropped to a comfortable level of cool.

As Angela got her bearings, Danube and his friend were getting into a dark sedan that sat in the middle of the street. Neither man looked in her direction. Caswell sat on the front passenger side, turning in his seat to berate the two men. He clearly wasn't happy about something. She wasn't able to see who was driving, the man's face obscured by the darkness and Caswell's oversize head. The car pulled off, leaving Angela to stare after it. When Ellington finally found his way to where she stood, its taillights had turned the corner and disappeared from view.

"I'll have Armstrong run the license plates," Ellington was saying. "And you're positive it was the car that's been following you?" They sat in his living room. Or rather Angela sat as Ellington paced back and forth across the hardwood floors.

"Yes, it's the same car but don't waste your time running the plates. I'm fairly certain it's police-issue," she said. She shook her head as she kicked off her shoes and pulled her legs up against the sofa cushions.

"Still, we can find out who it was issued to."

"I'd put my money on Caswell or Officer Danube. But since we don't know where they went or what they were up to, we still have nothing."

Ellington shook his head. His frustration was palpable. "I hate this case! I can't keep Parker hidden forever and even if we can keep him alive long enough to go to trial and win, this will destroy his reputation. He'll never work in law enforcement again. The sordid details of this damn case will haunt him forever. Even if we win, we can't win." He threw his hands up in frustration, moving to stare out the floor-to-ceiling windows.

Angela rose from her seat and moved to the bar. The iconic Lake Point Tower condo was impressive, an affirmation that Ellington had exceptionally good taste and liked the finer things without being boastful about his wealth. He'd purchased three units, gutting them all to renovate the space into a spectacular home. There were panoramic views of the lake and city from every room in the four-bedroom, three-bath design. The decor was minimalistic, and he attributed that to his mother and sisters. The bar was an amazing cherrywood structure that had been handcrafted specifically for the space. It was fully stocked, and Angela reached for an unopened bottle of bourbon, pouring shots into two glasses.

She moved to stand beside him, handed him one glass of dark liquor and downed the other. When he was finished with his she took the glass from his hand and placed it on the table. They still stood staring, neither saying a word. Angela leaned into his side, staring out into space with him. When he wrapped both arms around her, she allowed herself to settle comfortably against him, feeling completely at ease.

The city below glowed, lights illuminating the night sky. It felt like a wonderland, the twinkling feeling magical. Angela stared out with childlike wonder, in awe of how much the moment felt like home. She imagined the daily sunsets could steal your heart if you weren't prepared to protect it, and hers was feeling exposed.

Behind her Ellington breathed a heavy sigh. "My confidence is shaken," he said suddenly. He took a step back, turning from her. He moved to the sofa and sat down.

There was just enough vulnerability in his tone to make Angela want to wrap her arms tightly around him and hold him close. "Why?" she asked, moving to sit down beside him.

"I don't like to lose and right now I'm not sure I can save my brother. That's not a loss I'm prepared to handle."

"Parker doesn't need you to save him," she said. "He needs you to support him more than anything."

"Perhaps, but at the moment, I don't feel like I'm doing a very good job of that."

"You're doing the best you can, considering what you have to work with."

"Right now, though, my best isn't good enough, and I have people depending on me to do better."

"I get it, but this case isn't over yet."

"Unless you know something I don't, I don't see it going much further." He shrugged his broad shoulders and lifted his feet to the coffee table. He settled back against the sofa cushions. "You have to admit none of it makes any sense. We now have four dead bodies, a team of dirty cops, an unidentified suspect and no clue where to turn next."

Angela reached for his hand and lifted his arm around her shoulders. She settled into his side, her head on his chest. Her mind raced as her fingers teased the buttons that lined his shirt.

"We need to think like a criminal," she said. "We've been approaching the case like police."

Ellington nodded. "Okay, I'll play. I murder a district attorney, but I need to put his death on a third party."

"Why?"

"To maintain my credibility or my anonymity. Or both."

"Motive?"

"The attorney knew something or had something that could take me down."

"That's one theory. Now think about that tape." She shifted against him, and he pulled her closer and fell into thought.

Moments later it was as if a lightbulb had gone off in his head. His body stiffened. "Jon wasn't the target. He was a means to an end."

"How do you know?"

"The vitriol in our unknown suspect's tone. He's gunning for Parker. My brother is the target."

"Why?"

Ellington sat forward, his eyes shifting back and forth. "Because he's a Black. Whoever it is wants to hurt my entire family," he said as he reflected back on the taped conversation. *I want him incinerated. He needs to be so far gone not even his family will remember who he was. Oh, they'll remember. I need them to remember, and I need it to hurt.*

That one comment played on repeat in Ellington's head. *I need them to remember, and I need it to hurt.*

"So, if we know anything, we know that recording exonerates Parker for the shooting. But right now, we still don't know who we can share the tape with and trust it won't disappear. You could easily argue the case that Vivian was motivated to shoot her ex-husband for the insurance money. But Vivian's dead because she wiped the gun clean of all fingerprints. Even Parker's. Which was a mistake on her part because Caswell needed Parker's prints on the murder weapon for solid evidence. I'm thinking she probably panicked and wanted to make sure it couldn't come back on her. She was only another means to an end, and she'd become a liability."

Ellington nodded, beginning to make a sliver of sense out of the chaos.

Angela continued. "Now we just have to figure out who hates your family so much that they're willing to kill anyone in their way to get to you all."

Thinking about his family, his siblings and all of their career choices suddenly had Ellington even more on edge. As he thought back to the numerous cases they'd worked over the years, that short list of suspects increased ten-fold. He reached for the bottle of bourbon and poured them both another shot.

After downing his, he slapped the shot glass onto the coffee table. "Well, how much time do you have? Because that list suddenly got miles long."

Angela smiled, slapping her glass down beside his. "As much as you need."

Chapter 10

The harsh knock on his front door startled Ellington from a deep sleep. His eyes flew open, and he jumped slightly. His head lay in Angela's lap, his body stretched the length of the sofa. She rested with her legs extended atop the coffee table, her torso leaning to the side against a mound of pillows. One hand was beneath her head and the other was draped around his waist. She snored ever so softly, not at all disturbed by the loud tap-tap-tap against the door. She slept like a rock, not even budging when Ellington eased himself off her and the sofa to open the door.

He pulled the door open to find Mingus standing on the other side, a tray of Starbucks coffee and a bag of doughnuts in hand.

"What time is it?" Ellington asked, ringing his fingers around his bare wrist and wondering where he'd laid his wristwatch.

"Late. Why are you still sleeping?" Mingus pushed his way inside. As he moved toward the kitchen, he caught sight of Angela on the living room sofa. He tossed Ellington a look. "What were you doing last night?" he questioned, amusement furrowing his brow.

"It's not what you think," his brother answered. "Did you get my text?"

"Which one? You sent me at least a dozen messages last night."

"You didn't answer any of them."

"That's because I was in a warm bed with my hot wife. It would have taken an act of God to pull me away and you ain't God!" Mingus pulled a chair up to the kitchen counter and took a seat as he continued. "But because I like you, I did run a check on those names you sent me and came up empty. No one on your list could have been responsible for Jonathan's death. And none of them are coming for the family."

"Angela and I worked on this most of the night. We kept coming up empty, too."

"Maybe it's not about the family?" Mingus said with a shrug.

"Maybe." Ellington blew a soft sigh. He reached for a cup of coffee as he continued. "Right now, though, it's the only thing that actually makes the most sense."

"We need to get our hands on all the threats that have been made against Mom, Dad, Parker, any of us."

Ellington nodded in agreement. "I imagine there's a big file down at the FBI office. I'll reach out to my contacts."

A voice vibrated from the other room. "We need to speak with Caswell."

Both men turned to find Angela standing in the doorway, her body propped against the wall as if she might fall down. Her braids cascaded over her shoulders and her cheeks were flushed a brilliant shade of deep red.

"You okay?" Ellington asked, concern pulling at his expression. "You look like you might be ill."

"I'm fine. I just feel slightly hungover and my body's stiff." She stretched her arms up and outward as she arched her back.

Mingus laughed. "All that action you and my brother were getting last night. Lifting all that paper and those folders will do it to you."

"So, he's the comedian in your family," Angela said as she moved to Ellington's side, relieving him of the beverage in his hands. She took a sip of the coffee and purred, a look of satisfaction crossing her face.

"Had I known you were still here, I would have bought you one," Mingus said.

"It's no problem," she answered as she took another sip, then passed the cup back to Ellington. She lifted her face to his and kissed him on the lips. "Good morning," she whispered softly.

He kissed her back and smiled as he pulled her close and hugged her tightly. She swiped his cup of coffee a second time and moved to sit down beside Mingus. "Caswell's hands are dirty in all of this, and I think we need to put some pressure on him to get the answers we need. At the moment, he's the best lead that we have."

Mingus grinned. "What do you have in mind?"

"You ever play bad cop, bad cop?" she asked, grinning back.

"Why does that not sound legal?" Ellington questioned, moving to the refrigerator. He poured himself a glass of orange juice and came back to lean across the marble countertop, facing the two of them.

"It might cross a line or two," Angela answered with a shrug.

"Or three or four," Mingus added, meeting the stern look Ellington was giving him. "It's not something you should do, but it's what I do all day, every day."

"So, you'll back me up?" Angela asked.

"Whatever you need, I got you!"

"Do I have some say in all of this?" Ellington questioned.

Angela chuckled. "No," she answered. "You don't."

He gave her and his brother another look, his eyes darting back and forth between the two. The smirk on Mingus's face reflected his amusement and he seemed to be liking the exchange a tad too much.

Knowing he'd been vetoed, Ellington shook his head slowly, finally responding with a hint of attitude in his tone. "Okay, then. I just thought I'd ask." He moved to her side and kissed her lips gently. "And please," he concluded, "don't let my brother get you in trouble."

Angela laughed. "I don't think that's what you need to worry about," she said.

"Something tells me you need to be worried about me!" Mingus exclaimed.

Angela was grateful for the few minutes alone to gather her thoughts and figure out her next steps. Mingus had given her a ride to her car so she could return to her hotel room and change her clothes. He'd also given her a time to be downstairs in the lobby, ready to roll out. She hadn't had an opportunity to say so, but she appreciated the chance to shower and freshen up.

The late-night work session with the occasional nap had left her brain functioning on 100 percent, but her body was barely operating at fifty. Her muscles were tired, the sinewy tissue begging for a few hours of deep, uninterrupted sleep. She knew the onslaught of soap and hot water, and a strong cup of black coffee, would temporarily cure their problem and give her until the early afternoon before her energy level depleted completely. She was hopeful that by then, Caswell would be located and made to answer the questions she had for him. And she had questions for him. Starting with who he was working for and ending with who he was working for and why he had done all he'd done to harm the Black family.

Stepping into the shower, she grabbed a clean washcloth and the small jar of bath product that she'd rested on the counter. She'd chosen a whipped body scrub of coconut, almond and olive oils mixed with shea butter and sugar and enhanced with an aromatherapy blend of lavender, eucalyptus and peppermint essential oils to nourish her skin and revive her senses. It would leave her emotionally balanced and give her the pick-me-up she needed. It was one of six blends she'd packed to get her through until she returned home.

She massaged the creamy mixture onto her body. It began to lather ever so slightly as the sugar began to exfoliate her skin. She'd been using an organic beauty regime for years and often made her own beauty products. She considered herself somewhat of a veteran natural beauty alchemist. Mostly she just liked mixing oils and scents together to make pretty creams and scrubs.

Standing beneath the flow of hot water, she thought about Ellington. Another night between them gone awry. Admittedly, she'd gone to his home in want of his full and undivided attention. She'd had every intention of wrapping every inch of herself around him, maybe even throwing both legs around his backside, or draping them about his neck. She had planned a few dirty deeds she'd never done before, hopeful that her sexual skills would impress him to want more. Hopeful that he had the prowess and fortitude to keep up with her and maybe even throw out her back. She'd had every intention of leaving with her needs met, feeling slightly trashy and a lot satiated. Getting hers and then worrying about his had been her full intention, mutual consent giving them both whatever it was they needed. But with their focus on the case, his attention, and hers, had been everything but undivided.

The alarm on her phone suddenly rang from the counter. She had less than thirty minutes before Mingus would be back, expecting her to be ready. It was time to get to work. She blew a heavy sigh as the water rinsed the last of her sugar scrub from her skin.

Maybe it was for the best, she suddenly thought. Maybe their timing was off because they weren't meant to be. Maybe Ellington Black wasn't meant to scratch the itch that had the vivacity of Southern kudzu or English ivy. But for the life of her, Angela couldn't figure out why not. That itch was only there because he'd gotten deep under her skin, refusing to let go and let her be.

Finding Caswell had been easier than Angela had anticipated. She attributed the ease of their efforts to Mingus and his many resources in the Chicago streets. They found him on break from his policing duties, enjoying an early lunch at a local Vietnamese restaurant. He sat alone in a back booth, slurping noodles and chicken from a bowl of pho. They slid into the seats with him, Angela across from him and Mingus sitting beside him. Mingus carried a cordless nail gun that he dropped onto the table, the construction tool out of place and intimidating. When he draped an arm around Caswell's shoulders, the man's face dropped into his bowl, and he looked like he was about to be sick.

"What...what's going on?" he sputtered, his eyes darting around the room in search of a helping hand if one was needed. But the room had cleared, no one to be found.

"Let's just cut to the chase," Angela snapped. "We don't have time to waste. We know Vivian Wyler killed her ex-husband and we know that you talked to her just minutes after the murder. We also know that you're working with someone who's put a hit out on Parker Black. We need his name."

Mingus picked up the nail gun and pointed it toward Caswell's crotch. His eyes were narrowed and the smirk on his face was daunting.

Caswell's eyes widened substantially. "I don't know what you're talking about!" he snapped.

Bang! The nail gun firing was loud, sounding like a vibration of air and a hammer hitting the wooden seat. Caswell jumped, Mingus's fingers digging into his shoulders.

"Oops!" Mingus said, his grin widening.

Angela smiled sweetly. "My friend here has a nervous finger. Considering where he has that thing pointed, the next shot might not be pretty."

"You're going to regret this!" Caswell shouted.

Bang! The second shot landed inches from the first, catching the edge of Caswell's pant leg.

Mingus shook his head. "The next one won't miss. Threaten her again and you'll be the one who regrets it."

"What do you want from me?" he said, his voice a loud whisper.

"His name," Angela repeated. "I want to know who you're working with. Who's behind this?"

Caswell was shaking, his face ashen as if he'd seen a ghost. He fought back tears, his eyes misting with saline, and he chewed nervously on his bottom lip. He looked like his life had just flashed before him as he grabbed his chest and began to sputter. "You can't do this! I will have your ass for this," he muttered under his breath.

"He did warn you about those threats. He might hit a testicle next time," Angela said matter-of-factly. "I imagine that might really hurt." She shifted forward in her seat, lacing her fingers together atop the table. "Now, I'm going to ask you one last time. Who's behind this?"

Before Caswell could respond, the door to the restaurant swung open, someone calling Caswell's name from the entrance.

"Danube, back here!" Caswell shouted. "Help me!"

Angela rose from her seat, shaking her head. "I guess we'll have to finish the conversation another time," she said, annoyance like bad makeup across her face.

"I'm coming for you!" he snapped, pulling himself from Mingus's grasp. "I'm coming for you both."

Mingus tucked the nail gun into the oversize pocket of his trench coat. "Good luck with that," he said as he followed Angela toward the front door.

The two met Officer Danube near the front counter.

Angela smiled sweetly. "Officer Danube! It's good to see you again."

"Investigator."

"Detective Caswell is in the back," she said, gesturing with her head.

The young patrolman nodded. His gaze shifted to Mingus. The duo seemed to have a silent conversation that she wasn't privy to, and Angela sensed that the two men knew each other well. She didn't bother to introduce them.

She turned to Mingus. "You ready?"

He hesitated for a moment. "Give me a quick minute," he said as he turned an about-face and headed back to where Caswell still sat. Angela gave Danube another smile.

Bang! The harsh slam of that nail gun and the screams that followed echoed off the four walls. Caswell cried and cursed, babbling words that didn't make an ounce of sense. Mingus sauntered back to where she and Danube stood.

"Was that necessary?" Danube questioned, the two exchanging another look between them. "I'll have to answer for that."

With a shrug of his shoulders, Mingus offered no words of explanation, dismissive of his actions and clearly not caring what either of them thought.

Danube shook his head, seeming outranked by the man who was clearly a stark contrast to his older brother. Watching the exchange, Angela sensed a power dynamic that she hadn't expected, and she had questions that needed to be answered.

"Does he need an ambulance?" Danube asked.

Mingus shook his head. "Nah! I only hit muscle. He'll probably be sore for a few days, but he'll live. You might need to call for help to get him off that bench, though. I'm thinking the fire department might have a nail puller."

Danube nodded. "Did I see you?"

"Not this go around," Mingus said as he pointed Angela toward the door. "Just say we were gone by the time you got here. Or not. It's your call."

Danube nodded a second time. "I guess I need to go check on him."

"Or not," Mingus repeated. He grinned sheepishly.

In the distance, Caswell still hadn't stopped cursing, the litany of profanity like a sacred mantra. He swore and moaned and occasionally cried like a baby, cursing his predicament. Angela watched as the officer slowly moved to where the man still sat. He began to swear at Danube, his ire raging.

She shook her head as she turned her attention to Mingus. "What am I missing?" she questioned.

"What do you mean?" Mingus replied as he moved through the door to the sidewalk outside.

Angela followed. "What's up with you and Danube?"

Mingus cut an eye in her direction. "We have mutual interests."

"What kind of mutual interests?"

"The kind that's none of your business."

Angela's brow lifted. "That's cool but you're going to have to give me a little more than that. I need to understand all the dynamics in play. Here we were, trying to decide if he was friend or foe and you already had the answer. That's not cool. Is that why you warned us off him? You said let it play out because you already knew what game he was playing and whose side he was on."

Mingus seemed to drop into thought, his eyes darting back and forth over the landscape. In the distance sirens sounded, headed in their direction. "That's fair," he said as he headed toward the car.

"I don't need fair," Angela responded as she followed after him. "I need answers." She slid into the passenger seat, turning to face him.

Mingus shrugged but said nothing, his expression blank as he started the engine.

"You can give those answers to me now or you can give them to me later," Angela continued. "But I'm not going to let it go until I get them."

Not bothering to even look in her direction, Mingus pulled the car into traffic just as the first patrol car pulled onto the street, coming to a screeching halt in front of the restaurant. Angela could have been talking to a brick wall for all the response she got back from him. He was radio-silent the entire drive.

Ellington had just stepped out of the shower when his front door opened, Mingus using his spare key to let himself and Angela inside. Throwing on a T-shirt and a pair of gray sweatpants, he dragged a towel quickly over his wet hair, then tossed the towel to the floor. As he moved into the front room he was instantly aware of the tension between the two, the air around them feeling thick. He instinctively knew that something his brother had done had Angela frustrated.

"What's wrong?" he questioned, looking from one to the other. "What happened?"

Angela cut an eye in Mingus's direction. She found his smug expression doubly annoying. She shook her head. "Maybe your brother will tell you because he's not being very forthcoming with me!"

"Dude! What now?" Ellington questioned, turning his attention back to Mingus.

"Your woman is asking questions I'm not at liberty to answer. She's getting all I can give her and apparently it's not enough."

Angela tossed up her hands in frustration. "Is it too early to start drinking?" she muttered as she moved to his refrigerator and snatched open the door.

The two brothers exchanged a look and Ellington shrugged. "What's this about?"

"Officer Danube. He came in as we were questioning Caswell. He and I had an exchange and now she's obsessed." Mingus dropped down onto the sofa, extending his long legs outward.

"They know each other. I want to understand the relationship because Danube was taking direction from your brother," Angela interjected as she poured orange juice into a crystal goblet.

Ellington looked confused, his eyes darting back and forth as he took it all in.

"Exactly!" Angela exclaimed, noting his expression. "I just want to understand."

"How do you know Danube?" Ellington questioned. He sat down in the chair that faced his brother, leaning his forearms over his thighs.

"We've worked together previously," Mingus said nonchalantly. He eyed his brother with a raised brow.

There was a moment of silence and then Ellington slowly nodded his understanding. "How long has he been undercover?" he asked.

"Since he got here."

"Does Dad know?"

Mingus shrugged his broad shoulders. "Mom knows. She provided the backstory to get him in the door."

"Undercover?" Angela sat down against the arm of the chair Ellington was sitting in. She leaned into his side. "Who does he work for?"

Mingus stood. He shook his head, chuckling softly. "Like I told you, Special Investigator Stanfield. I'm not at liberty to say. My brother, however, does not have to abide by the same rules." He winked an eye at her.

Angela shot Ellington a look. "What the hell is going on?"

Ellington held up his hand, briefly stalling the conversation. He asked, "Did Caswell give you any answers?"

Mingus shook his head. "Nothing that would help us close this case."

"Not even when your brother shot him with a nail gun!" Angela interjected.

Mingus laughed. "You're such a tattletale! No wonder you and Simone get along with each other."

"A nail gun? Are you trying to get yourself arrested?" Ellington asked.

"It's a minor flesh wound. He'll live. And he won't come for me."

"Not legally," Angela added. "But trust and believe he's coming. You just gave him another reason to want you all gone."

Mingus nodded. "That's what I'm hoping for." He moved to the entrance. "I've got to run. I'll check in with you later," he said as he pulled the door open.

"Please, be careful out there," Ellington called after him. "These streets are dangerous!"

Angela moved to the seat Mingus had just vacated. The door still vibrated from the soft slam of it closing after the man. She and Ellington exchanged a look as she crossed her arms over her chest, attitude like a warm blanket wrapped around her shoulders. "So, are you going to shed some light on what's going on? If Officer Danube is undercover, who is he working for and what is he investigating? And why is your brother such a pain in the ass?"

Ellington smiled, his lips lifting warmly. "Mingus has been a pain since he was two and started walking and talking. It's in his DNA. With respect to Danube, I'm assuming he works for the Feds."

"FBI? He's working undercover for the FBI?" A wave of surprise crossed her face. "Are you sure?"

"No, but if I'm going on what little Mingus gave me, it just makes sense."

"I'm going to need a little bit more than that."

"Long story short, my brother was once a police officer. Before he left the force, the Feds came in and recruited him to assist them in a case. He had ties to some people they had their eye on and was able to get them into an inner circle they were having trouble infiltrating. Since then, he's helped them a few times, so if he knows Officer Danube, and Danube is undercover, they may have worked together previously. But this is all conjecture on my part. I don't know anything for certain."

"So, what is he working on now? And why was your brother keeping it a secret?"

"Mingus might not know the details of their investigation. Clearly, he's not a part of it and he'd never blow an agent's cover to ask. My brother might run in some shady circles but he's loyal to the law and his family always comes first. I guarantee, though, if there is something to find out, Mingus will have the details before the day is over."

Angela nodded. "I like your brother. But he's still a pain in the ass!"

Ellington laughed. "I've said that myself a few times!"

Chapter 11

Ellington was cooking. Angela was impressed as she watched him prepare eggs Benedict with sautéed spinach, sliced pears, sugar-glazed strawberries and pineapple mimosa. Their conversation was casual, both avoiding all talk of the case, his brother or anything else that would raise their anxiety.

"Where was the last place you traveled for fun?" Ellington asked.

"London. I have a friend who moved there last year, and I went to check out her new apartment. What about you?"

"It feels like forever, but my brothers and I stole away to Vegas for a few days when Simone got married. It was a good time."

"Anything planned for the near future?"

Ellington looked up to meet her gaze. There was a moment of pause as an idea seemed to dance through his thoughts. He blessed her with a warm smile before he spoke. "I would love to explore Greece. Or maybe Tuscany. But I'm open to letting you pick the location."

Angela laughed. "It's nice to know you're flexible about certain situations."

"Some. Not all. But I'm typically easy to work with. Besides, you can learn a lot about a person when you travel with them, and I want to learn everything I can about you."

She laughed again. "Traveling with me might not be the best way to do that. I'm finicky when I travel. I also tend to be mean when I can't have my way."

"You? Mean? I can't imagine such a thing!" he teased. "Liar!"

Ellington chuckled. "I was trying to be nice."

Angela shook her head as she watched him begin to prep the hollandaise sauce. He melted butter in a small saucepan. In a separate bowl he whisked egg yolks with a tablespoon of lime juice, heavy whipping cream, and salt and pepper. When the butter was melted, he slowly added a spoonful at a time to the egg mixture, tempering the mixture so it wouldn't curdle.

"The Canadian bacon is warm. I just need to poach the eggs and toast the English muffins. Once I assemble them, we can eat."

"It smells good," Angela said. "You know a man who can cook is worth his weight in gold, don't you? At least that's what my grandmother used to tell me."

"I don't know about all that. I just know it comes in handy."

"Is there anything I can do to help?" Angela asked.

He shook his head. "Not a thing. Had our night gone the way I planned, I would be serving you breakfast in bed. Right now, I'm just improvising."

Angela bit down against her bottom lip, her eyes narrowing as she eyed him keenly. "If you just need me to be in bed, I can certainly oblige," she said, her voice a seductive whisper.

Ellington cut an eye in her direction, then turned to give her his full attention as she rose from her seat and slipped her arms from the sweater she was wearing. She stood in a white lace bra that contrasted beautifully against her dark complexion. She dropped the sweater to the floor and moved in the direction of his bedroom. As she rounded the corner out of sight, her jeans dropped to her ankles and she stepped out of them, leaving them where they landed on the floor. Ellington felt every muscle below his waist harden, an erection blooming abundantly in his slacks. He took a deep inhale of air, holding it deep in his lungs as he prayed the sudden rise of nature would stall and flounder before he had to move.

His hand was shaking as he plated their meal, layering the English muffin with the bacon, then the poached egg, and ladling a healthy spoonful of hollandaise on top. He poured pineapple juice and champagne into two flutes and topped the mixture off with a hint of triple sec. When everything sat neatly on a wicker tray, a single plastic flower bloom in a petite vase as decoration, he headed toward the bedroom, trying not to skip with excitement the whole way.

Angela was certain she had lost every ounce of good sense God had blessed her with. She lay naked in Ellington's bed, the lush blue sheets wrapped around her torso. She'd released her braids and they hung down past her shoulders, framing her face. He was still puttering about in the kitchen, and she was suddenly second-guessing her decision to strip down to her birthday suit in invitation. They still had work to do and a case to solve. Instead, here

In the Arms of the Law

she was, spread-eagle against his Posturepedic pillow-top mattress, wanting to feel his large hands against her girl parts. Her forefathers would not have been amused.

Angela couldn't begin to explain the anxiety tying some serious knots in the pit of her stomach. It was worse than it had been the night when she'd changed her mind. Instantly regretting that decision was why she was naked now. She had always owned her sexuality proudly, and with the ferocity of a pit bull with a bone. She had mastered the art of one-night stands and could toss a man out of her bed and her life with sugar-coated precision. She could bring the most virile man to his knees and have him begging for more. She had never yearned for any long-term attachments and never gave anyone access to her goodies unless it was about her wants and needs first and foremost. She was known to be selfish in bed and she didn't often care.

But this felt different to her. This had her feeling insecure and needy, twisting with excitement that surprised her. This had her praying that Ellington Black wouldn't be disappointed. Now, waiting for him had her as nervous as a virgin bride on her wedding night. Doubt was clawing at her with jagged nails, leaving her to question everything she'd ever been certain about. What if she couldn't pleasure him? Would he want to come back for seconds or maybe even thirds? Would he be bothered by the cellulite on her thighs or the oddity of her inverted nipples that didn't harden or protrude like nipples were supposed to?

Angela suddenly wanted to find her clothes and run. Just as that thought ran through her head, Ellington stepped over the door's threshold, a food tray in hand and the most endearing smile on his face. He filled the room with his presence, like a warm blanket on a cold night. As he stared at her, Angela wanted to see what he saw, what fueled the light that glowed in his pale gaze. Because he was looking at her like she was the next best thing since sliced bread or the cherry on top of some seriously sweet cake or the chips *and* the cellophane bag! She took a deep breath and then a second, allowing that look to wash over her and fuel her next steps. She reached out her arms and beckoned him to her.

Ellington felt his legs begin to shake, his knees suddenly feeling like jelly. Angela lying in his bed was a dream come true. She was sunshine at the end of a dark tunnel, and he felt immensely blessed to be graced by her light. She was more than he could have imagined, looking like a ray of gold shimmering beneath a host of dark clouds. She was exquisite and in that near-perfect moment, he knew beyond any reasonable doubt that she was all his.

"Brunch is served," he said, the faintest smug smile on his face.

Angela smiled back. "It smells delicious, but I can't have brunch in bed all alone." She bit down against her bottom lip, her eyelids narrowing.

That smug smile widened. "And what might you be suggesting?"

"That you take off all your clothes and join me...for brunch, that is."

"Just brunch?"

Angela shrugged her narrow shoulders. "That's all going to depend on how good a cook you are. If the meal is good, I'll definitely want to taste a little dessert."

"But I didn't make any dessert."

Angela reached for a strawberry that decorated one of the plates. "Then I guess we'll have to make our own dessert." She took a bite of the fruit, her eyes locked tightly with his.

Ellington grabbed the back of her hand and pulled it to his lips. He took a bite of what was left of that strawberry, then he leaned in and kissed her mouth.

The meal was barely a sweet memory as Ellington laid the plates and tray on the nightstand. All he could focus on was Angela's lips and the sugary sweetness of the fruit they'd eaten. She tasted of those strawberries and mint and a longing that was wrapped around his name like a satin bow. He eased a large hand around her waist as he moved his body above hers. That kiss became energized by the hands that skated down the length of his back, fingertips tapping against the curve of his buttocks.

She'd had only to ask one time and he had stripped down to his boxers, crawling into bed with her. Her opening her arms to him had been everything, feeling like Christmas in July, as he'd answered the invitation. He'd fed her eggs Benedict and strawberries as they sipped on mimosas, the two of them laughing at the impracticality of their midday rendezvous. But everything felt right, time feeling like it had paused to allow them to fall into sync. She was giddy with glee and her laughter billowed like a warm breeze through the room.

The food had been just enough to leave them feeling satiated, the mimosas had them giddy, and then a different kind of hunger took hold, the two giving in to their yearning for each other. He kissed her sweetly and then she pressed a hand to his bare chest, pulling at his boxers with her other hand. Rolling himself above her, he braced the bulk of his weight on his arms, hovering over her as his mouth danced a sensuous two-step against her lips. She wrapped her arms around his neck and back and pulled him to her, pushing her pelvis forward to meet his. His penis was hard, needing attention as the length of it pressed anxiously against her leg.

Their kisses were furtive as he pulled her leg up against his side and settled himself against the apex of her feminine spirit. He left a damp trail of kisses down the side of her face, against the curve of her neck. He slowly eased himself down the length of her body, leaving kisses against bare skin until he reached her most private space and then he feasted, savoring the taste of her until she arched her back and screamed his name, her fists clutching the bedsheets. She orgasmed twice more before he found his way back up her torso and eased himself back between her legs.

She had no clue when he'd taken a moment to sheath himself with a condom. One seemed to magically appear in place as he tapped at her labia, seeming to ask for permission before he pushed forward, stretching the folds of her inner lining. He'd been immensely blessed, richly endowed with length and girth that Angela instinctively knew would test her own endurance. His touch was gentle, and he moved with the grace and precision of a premier danseur performing on the stage of a world-renowned theater. She arched her back and met him stroke for stroke as her body responded in perfect sync to his. The sensual acrobatics had her on her back one minute and her knees the next. He pushed and pulled and folded her body in position with an ease that was both surprising and exciting. Her body pulsed and tightened around him, gripping him with a vise-like hold. He nuzzled her neck, nipped at that spot beneath her chin and licked every crease and crevice that graced her body. Time stood still as he loved her and loved her well and Angela loved him back with equal vigor.

He rolled her from one side of the massive king-size bed to the other, sometimes landing on top and sometimes the bottom. Her on top quickly became his favorite position. Angela had skills that kept him hard and left him desperate for more. She rode him like a prized stallion in a million-dollar rodeo, her bump and grind the stuff of fantasies. She had thighs of steel, knees that didn't quit and she could clap her ass cheeks, shimmy her shoulders and twerk with precision that was damn near lethal.

His climax surged like a tsunami, giant waves of sheer bliss rolling over him with a vengeance. He rolled her back onto the mattress and pushed and pulled himself into her, his hips like a piston in overdrive. She gripped him tightly, her body pulsing around his male member like a marching band at a halftime show. He came, whimpering softly as he whispered her name, and then she screamed, loudly, falling with him into an abyss of pure, unadulterated pleasure.

The midday hour soon turned into the late afternoon and then suddenly it was early evening. Ellington had lost track of time and could no longer remember how many times Angela's body had been wrapped around his own. The last orgasm had sent him over the edge. There was a dull ache between his legs and for a brief moment he thought she might have broken him. He knew recovery would require a hot shower, a hotter meal and a modicum of distance away from the beauty snoring softly beside him.

He leaned to kiss her shoulder, pulling at the covers tangled around their feet. When she was adequately covered, he rose from the bed, grabbing his cell phone as he moved into the bathroom. He had silenced the device earlier and now saw that he had missed a half dozen calls from Mingus and just as many from his mother. The calm he'd been feeling just seconds earlier suddenly dissipated into thin air. He hit the redial button for his brother first.

Mingus answered on the second ring. "It's about damn time! Where are you?"

"I'm home. I dozed off."

"I assume Ms. Stanfield dozed off with you?"

Ellington grinned into the receiver, but he didn't bother to answer. "What's up?" he asked, changing the subject.

"Open your front door. We've got a problem!"

Ellington took a deep breath. "What now? And how long have you been outside my door?"

He moved to the front foyer and pulled open the wooden structure. Mingus was leaning against the outside wall, looking like he'd lost his best friend, his home and his dog. His expression felt like a punch to Ellington's gut. It wasn't often that Mingus showed his hand, not even when criminals were purposely gunning for him, bullets flying past his head. His expression was telling, and Ellington knew his brother was genuinely scared.

"I had a private conversation with Danube. He said the man pulling the strings goes by the name of Harmon. George Harmon. He can tie this George Harmon to the meetings with Caswell, but he wasn't privy to any orders that Caswell was given. The Feds don't have any record of a George Harmon affiliated with the case they're working. Danube just knew that after each meeting Caswell would say they had work to do. He's sending you a full statement with specifics."

Ellington's brow furrowed in thought. "George Harmon? But that's..." He paused, processing the information suddenly being thrown at him.

Mingus finished his thought. "...our maternal grandfather's name," Mingus said. "And according to Danube, there's a strong family resemblance. He said he looks like he could be our brother."

Ellington suddenly thought of Angela's near close encounter with his doppelganger and her assertion that they could pass for twins. "It can't be…" he muttered, confusion still painting his expression.

"I would have agreed with you, but I did some digging, and it seems that our half brother seems to be on hiatus from his former life. The school he was teaching at says he turned in his resignation a few months ago. He is no longer a resident in his rental apartment and none of his friends have heard from him. They think he's trekking his way through Europe, writing his doctoral thesis."

Ellington's mind was racing as he scrambled to put the pieces together. His little brother suddenly had him discombobulated as he tried to make sense of family turning on family. Particularly his family. And whether they were willing to acknowledge it or not, their mother's *other* son was still blood. Clearly, *that* son had done his own research. Their grandfather's name was not the name he'd been given and his knowledge of that connection to them spoke volumes. Now, he was doing far more than anyone had anticipated.

It was only recently that he and his siblings had learned of Judith Harmon Black's eldest child. A son she'd given up for adoption when she'd been in her teens. He had been the product of a violent sexual assault and his existence had been a secret their mother had hoped to take to her grave. Being pushed into a corner by someone hoping for a big payday had forced her hand. Telling them her secret had made her vulnerable in a way Ellington had never seen before. Her decision to walk away from her son a second time, not wanting a relationship with him, had left them all looking at her differently. And now it looked like it all may have caught up with her anyway.

He shook his head. "But it doesn't make sense. Why would he be coming after Parker? Why not me, or you, or all of us?"

"Parker's the eldest. Mom's second-born. What if all this is to hurt Mom? If he takes down Parker, we may just be next on his list, and he plans to hurt each of us one by one? That would destroy Mom!"

Ellington thought about the brother who shared half their bloodline. He'd been problematic even before they knew about him. His mother's secret being blackmail fodder had put her firstborn child on their radar, the family collectively circling the wagons to protect the matriarch from scandal. Now it seemed that he might be a bigger burden than they'd initially anticipated.

"But he didn't want to be found. He wasn't on the adoption registry, and we never made contact after Mom decided she didn't want to pursue a relationship with him. How would he even know about us? The adoption agency was given implicit instructions to contact me if he ever contacted them for his adoption information."

"About that…"

Ellington's eyes closed as he shook his head slowly. "Please tell me you did not…" He paused, the look he gave his brother questioning.

"You know I didn't, but Simone and Vaughan may have sought him out."

"Unbelievable!" He threw up a hand in frustration. "Mom told them to leave it alone."

"Has either one of them ever done what they were told?"

"So, what the hell? Did they just show up on his doorstep to introduce themselves?"

"Vaughan swears they only followed him to work and then to a coffee shop. She says they never spoke to him. Not once."

"And what did Simone say?"

"Nothing. She went into defense mode."

"Which means they spoke to him."

"You know your sisters!"

"I do. They probably gave him an engraved invitation to Thanksgiving dinner to surprise us all." Ellington drew his hand over his face, frustration like a fresh itch he couldn't scratch. "We need to find him."

"I'm already on it. If he's here in the city, my people will track him down."

"I think we already know he's here." Ellington was shaking his head. "And I think Angela saw him." He told his brother about her seeing the person she claimed could have been his white twin. "At the time, I honestly didn't give it any serious thought," he concluded.

Mingus nodded, understanding washing over his expression.

"Mom's been calling me. Does she know?"

"I didn't tell her. She's probably wanting to know where we are with Parker's case. I haven't been able to give her the answers she's looking for, so it's your turn."

"Let's just keep this to ourselves until we know for certain."

"Keep what to yourselves?" a voice questioned from the doorway.

Both men turned to stare. Angela's eyes shifted from one to the other and finally settled on Ellington, the faintest smile trying to pull at her lips. She wore one of his dress shirts and nothing else. The crisply ironed cotton fell nicely around her body, the stark white coloring contrasting well with her skin. The collar was turned up and she had only buttoned enough buttons to keep her private parts hidden. The length of her bare legs peeked from the shirt's hem. That hint of a smile was stirring, and heat began to simmer in Ellington's limbs.

"On that note, I need to get back to work," Mingus said. He gave his brother a slap on the back. "I'll let you know the minute I have something."

Ellington nodded as Mingus winked his eye in Angela's direction and headed toward the door.

She tossed up her hand in the slightest wave as Mingus made his exit. She turned to stare at Ellington. "What did I miss?"

He hesitated. His mother's secret wasn't his to tell, but if Mingus was right and their half brother was gunning for them, that secret no longer mattered. He also trusted Angela and knew she'd never use whatever he told her against him or anyone else in his family. He moved to her side and eased his arms around her waist. Pulling her to him, he kissed her mouth, allowing his lips to dance sweetly with hers. When he finally stepped from her, hating that he had to let her go, a single tear rained down his cheek.

"Wow!" Angela was shaking her head in disbelief as Ellington filled her in on everything he'd just learned, throwing in their family history for good measure.

"My mother's son is named Fabian Scott. He was adopted at birth, but it looks like something, or someone, has pointed him in our direction. Apparently, he's calling himself George Harmon, after my mother's father."

"The police need to put a BOLO out on your brother."

"My mother's son," Ellington said with a hint of attitude. "And I'd rather not bring my father or law enforcement into it until we know for certain how Mr. Scott fits into all this."

"Mr. Scott? You make it sound like he's a complete stranger."

Ellington shrugged his shoulders. "He is a stranger. I don't know him or anything about him. And if he's responsible for Jonathan's death and everything Parker and my family are going through, then he's also made himself an enemy. Blood relative or not."

There was something in his tone that Angela found disconcerting, and it showed on her face. She could tell Ellington instantly regretted the words he'd spoken. The emotion that had spilled out of his eyes without him actually expressing himself shone a spotlight on the disdain he felt for his mother's other son. Emotion he hadn't come to terms with or wanted anyone else to be aware of. Emotion that was telling, because despite the staunch exterior of his public persona, Ellington Black was still a man, flawed and imperfect.

"Mingus has his team out looking," Ellington continued. "If anyone can find him, he can."

Angela nodded. "So now that we know *who* might be behind it all, we need to tie him to the evidence. You don't have a case if the evidence doesn't make sense."

He nodded. "Let's get to work, then!"

She smiled, her hands latched firmly to the sides of her hips. "Yes, sir!"

For a quick moment they stood staring at each other. Ellington shook his head, his lips pulling into a wry smirk. Finally, he said, "I'm going to need you to put some clothes on first."

Chapter 12

Ellington found himself out of sorts. He didn't have the words to express what he was feeling, although he sensed that Angela had read his mood and just hadn't commented on it. He appreciated the level of space she'd given him. She seemed to understand that he needed time to make sense of it all. If his mother's son, his half brother, was capable of doing the horrific things they suspected, then what else was he capable of? And how would his mother take the news? It was Judith Harmon Black that he worried about most. Every decision she'd been forced to make since her child's conception had been a challenge, pushing her past her comfort levels. She'd been able to make peace with those decisions and now it seemed that karma had come back on her with a vengeance.

He blew a heavy sigh, the weight of all that he worried about feeling like a herd of elephants sitting on his shoulders. He pretended not to notice that Angela was giving him a look, her brow creased with concern.

Angela Stanfield! Sweet, beautiful, vivacious Angela!

If only he could carry her back to his bed and make love to her, over and over, stopping only to eat a meal, rest and then feast on the beautiful woman until his stomach rumbled for nourishment to do it all yet again. He didn't want to deal with the drama of his family, or the legal cases that still required his attention. He only wanted to hold Angela, to feel her naked flesh pressed against his own. To hear her laugh ringing through the air and those admonishments when she and he didn't necessarily agree with one another. She gave him a level of ease and comfort that he hadn't often known. And as he pretended not to watch her while she watched him, he knew that she'd gotten way under his skin, and he had no desire to ever let her go.

As if reading his mind, she reached out her hand and drew the length of her fingers down the side of his face. He slid his own palm against the back of her hand and kissed her fingers. Another soft sigh blew past his full lips.

"Do you want to talk about it?" Angela asked.

Ellington shook his head, his smile strained. His words caught deep in his throat, so he said nothing, his head still waving from side to side.

She nodded, then changed the subject. "We're going to need Caswell to confess. He's the only one that can tie Fabian Scott, or George Harmon, or anyone else who might be involved, to this case. He's your key to resolving this."

"No," Ellington said, his gaze drifting off into space. He slowly shook his head, then turned his eyes back on her. "Caswell was supposed to be the fall guy. He did all the dirty work, but he was sloppy. All the evidence points back to him for a reason. Now he's a liability because he knows too much."

Angela pondered his comment, seeming to follow his train of thought. "You think Harmon will try to kill him?"

"If it's him, he's done a good job of tying up all the other loose ends thus far. It's not unreasonable to think that Caswell might be in danger once he's no longer of any use."

"So, what do you want to do now?" Angela asked.

Ellington began to text on his cell phone, his thumbs typing swiftly. When he was done, his final message sent, he turned to answer her question. "We wait. I just texted Mingus. Let's see what he comes back with. Until then, I need to speak with my mother."

"How can I help?"

"How much time do you have?"

"That all depends on…" Her smile was teasing as her voice faded to a seductive whisper.

Ellington took a step forward, his arms sliding back around her torso. He leaned to kiss her cheek, hugging her warmly. "I'd love to just sit and talk."

Her smile was canyon-wide as she responded. "I'd like that. I'd like that a lot."

Ellington was starting to question his own sanity as he and Angela sat and talked about their families. Mostly his, although she, too, had a few questionable relatives. He imagined a family reunion would be a wealth of entertainment if they were ever to bring their kin together. He liked that they were able to laugh, despite the seriousness of his current situation.

"I'm sure you're exaggerating," Angela was saying as he told her about Simone outing his brother's girlfriend.

His baby sister had been less than enthusiastic about having a journalist in the family, and despite Davis's fondness for Neema Kamau, the truth of her career choice and her dishonesty about it had been a source of consternation for them all. Ellington shook his head. "No exaggeration here! Simone was vicious. She was like a hurricane the way she stormed in, stirred up trouble and then tiptoed out like she hadn't made our baby brother cry as she devastated his life. It was not pretty! They recovered and things are good with them now, but it was touch and go there for a while."

"I think your sister has me beat. I was ten years old the last time I made my brother cry. He broke the head off my favorite doll. I nailed him in the nuts!"

Ellington winced. "Ouch! That wasn't very nice."

Angela shrugged. "I only threw one punch."

He laughed. "Remind me to never make you mad!"

Before she could respond, his cell phone vibrated against the table. He sat forward in his seat and practically snatched the device from where it rested. He read the text message that beeped for his attention.

"My mother is on her way here. She's turning the corner now." Ellington sighed, a low gust of air blowing out of his mouth.

"On that note," Angela said, rising from her seat, "I'm going to head out so you two can have some privacy."

"Don't hurry off. I'm sure my mother would love to meet you."

"Your mother is looking for answers about one of her children. She has no interest in the woman you just had in your bed. Mothers are funny about things like that."

Ellington chuckled. "At least stay long enough for me to introduce you."

"As I do an evening version of that walk of shame?

I don't think that's the first impression I'm looking to make with your mother."

"Shame?"

"You know what I mean."

"I'm going to tell my mother anyway. I tell her everything."

"Everything?"

His smile could have warmed the earth it was so bold and bright. He laughed. "Okay. Almost everything."

Angela shook her head, giggling with him. "I would love to meet your mother, but I don't think now would be a good time."

"Then come for family dinner on Sunday. Mom makes a killer mac and cheese!"

"Family dinner?"

"You scared?"

This time it was Angela's smile lighting up the room. "Family dinner. That sounds serious."

He took a step forward and pulled her against him, wrapping his arms tightly around her torso. Their lips met in a gentle kiss, just a hint of tongue teasing the prospect of more. Ellington pulled his face from hers and stared deep into her dark eyes.

"It is serious. I'm falling hard for you, Angela Stanfield, and I want the whole world to know it. Starting with my family would mean the world to me."

She bit down against her bottom lip, the words like the sweetest caress against her ear. Because she had fallen for him, too. She was so lost in the depths of possibility that existed between them that she couldn't fathom what life would look like if he weren't a part of her world. She nodded her head and smiled.

"Then I guess I'll be coming for family dinner on Sunday," she responded, her lips moving back against his.

The kiss was warm and intoxicating, the heat between them rising so swiftly that it surprised them both. The moment was suddenly interrupted when Ellington's phone rang for his attention. He cursed softly and she laughed.

"That's the second time I've been trying to get me some and this phone has rung," he muttered. He tapped her backside as he answered the call. "Hello!"

"Yes, ma'am…yes…okay…on our way…" Disconnecting the call, he eyed Angela with a raised brow. "That was my mother. She said she needs help with some bags in her car and that I should, and I quote, bring whoever it is I'm cuddled up with down to the parking garage to give her a hand, unquote."

"I'm going to like your mother," Angela laughed. "So much for me sneaking out without being seen!"

His phone rang a second time. "It's my office. I need to take this," he said. "My secretary always calls to give me an update before she leaves for the night."

"I'll go down to help your mom. It'll give me a chance to talk about you."

He gave her a quick peck on the lips. "You're so funny!"

Angela laughed as she moved to the door. She paused for a minute to stare at him. Ellington had turned his attention back to his phone call. His expression was serious, his focus on the matter at hand. She hadn't said it aloud, but she'd fallen for him, too. She'd fallen hard, landing headfirst in a vat of emotion that had her excited and scared in the same breath. Despite her best efforts to ignore and deny it, Angela had fallen head over heels in love.

Ellington gave her one last smile and a wink of his eye as she stepped across the threshold and closed the door behind her.

* * *

There was no missing the elegant woman who stood behind the luxury vehicle. Judith Harmon Black's resemblance to her children was undeniable. Ellington had his mother's eyes and the same intense stare. She was looking off into the distance, her brow furrowed. A hint of panic painted her expression. The look was disconcerting, and Angela found herself suddenly on edge.

"Judge Black? Is something wrong?"

The matriarch's head snapped toward Angela's voice. Her eyes were wide, and she looked like she'd been snatched out of a nightmare. She eyed Angela with reservation, seeming unnerved by her presence.

"I didn't mean to frighten you," Angela said softly. "My name's Angela. Angela Stanfield. I'm Ellington's friend."

Judith tossed a lingering look over her shoulder before turning back to Angela. Angela continued talking, hoping to ease the woman's anxiety.

"Ellington had to take a call and asked me to come give you a hand with your bags."

Judith took a deep inhale of air, then forced a smile to her face. She extended her hand in greeting. "Angela, it's very nice to meet you," she said softly.

Angela smiled back. "Are you okay?"

Judith tossed a second look over her shoulder. "I heard something and then I thought I saw someone. At first, I thought it was Ellington, but...well..." She suddenly hesitated, falling into thought.

Angela bristled. The words *I thought it was Ellington* played over again in her head. Was it possible Fabian Scott was mere steps away from them? Her eyes skated around the garage's interior, nothing seeming out of the ordinary. There were a fair number of cars parked for the time of day but she fathomed that was normal. Her mind began to race as she contemplated her options were they to come face-to-face with the man hell-bent on terrorizing his biological family. She was suddenly unnerved.

"Judge Black, why don't we grab those bags and head upstairs. I'm sure it was nothing for you to worry about," she said, the little white lie rolling off her tongue. Because Angela was worried, and Ellington's mother had every reason to be even if she didn't yet know it. Had there been someone there? Someone who looked like the four sons she did claim? Was the child she'd given up for adoption close by, following and watching them? There was a lot to consider but first she wanted to ensure the matriarch's safety.

"I'm not usually so flighty, despite what my children may have told you," Judith said with a soft chuckle. She seemed to shake the unease from herself, filling her lungs with oxygen as she regained her composure. She smiled again and her eyes brightened. "So, where is that son of mine?"

"He had a call. From his office," Angela repeated.

"You did say that." Judith nodded. "Well, I'm glad you were able to get him to take a break and relax for a moment. Ellington never relaxes, always trying to fix something that's broken." Judith moved around to the back of her SUV. The rear was loaded with an assortment of bags from a local grocery store. "He also never has anything in his refrigerator or his cupboards. I just thought I'd drop a few things off and check up on him at the same time. I also wanted to meet you. I've heard a lot about you and the work you've been doing to help Parker. I wanted to personally say thank you."

"That's very kind of you," Angela responded, "but I

really haven't done very much. I actually wish I could do more."

Judith passed Angela a handful of bags, then turned back into the vehicle to gather the rest. "Well, everyone had only good things to say about you and that goes far in this family."

Judith was focused on the remaining shopping bags, sorting and resorting the items inside. Her actions were anxiety-laden, seeming to fulfill an unspoken need to regain a semblance of control. Something had clearly frightened her, and she didn't have the words to voice her fear to Angela because Angela was a stranger and not one she was confident she could trust. Angela understood and debated whether she should say something about what she knew. Concerned the matriarch might not take kindly to her personal business having been a point of discussion.

So focused on Judith, Angela didn't notice the white-paneled van that pulled out of the parking spot behind them. As it came to an abrupt stop beside the two women, the doors sliding open swiftly, it was already too late. Seconds later, those coveted groceries lay sprawled across the concrete floor and Angela and Judith were gone.

Chapter 13

Angela's head hurt, the back of her skull feeling like she'd been hit with a sledgehammer. Which was partly true. The man who'd grabbed her had been mammoth in size, hulking over her small frame. She hadn't gone down without a fight, though, and it was the fight that had landed her unconscious on her ass. She vaguely remembered the van that had suddenly rolled up on them, the rumble of tires and screech of brakes jarring. A team of men had jumped swiftly from the vehicle, the precision they executed telling. They were professionals, not a ragtag team of misfits. Judge Black had screamed and then a large hand had pressed a towel laced with chloroform over her mouth. As Angela tussled with the man whose arm was strangling her around the neck, she'd caught glimpses of Ellington's mother being lifted and tossed into the van.

She'd connected her elbow with her wrangler's face,

shattering the bones in his nose. And as blood spewed from his nostrils, she'd landed a swift kick to his knee cap. He'd gone down like a load of bricks and her next kick had easily fractured his cheekbones. She had lunged for the van, hoping against all odds that she could grab hold of Judith and keep their attackers from completing their mission. That's when someone had hit her hard against the back of her head. Just like that, everything around her had gone black.

Now, slowly opening her eyes, she mentally assessed the damage to her body. Nothing felt broken but she was bruised black-and-blue and feeling it. Her shoulder felt like it might have been dislocated, but it had shifted back in place and was achy. Her head hurt more than anything, and she would have given up a lung, or her firstborn, for two aspirin and a shot of Jack Daniels. She took a slow deep breath and then a second.

Her eyes shifted slowly around the dimly lit room. The space was cavernous, some type of warehouse that hadn't been used in ages. Dust particles were thick, swirling in heavy waves below the high industrial fans that tossed hot air from one wall to the other. She was tied to a wooden chair, her legs and hands bound with plastic zip ties. As her vision adjusted to the darkness, she realized Judge Black was tied to a similar chair across from her, and the matriarch was eyeing her with concern.

"You're awake!" Judith whispered excitedly, relief flooding her pale face.

Angela tried to smile, nodding her head slowly. "Are you hurt?" she questioned.

The older woman shook her head. "No. I'm good. I was worried about you."

"I'll be fine. Do you know where we are?"

"No," she answered with a shrug. "When I came to there was no one here but us."

"How long ago was that?"

"Maybe an hour. Maybe longer. I'm not quite sure."

Angela took another deep breath as she struggled against the ties around her wrists. She blew the air out in a heavy sigh.

"This is all my fault," Judith said, tears beginning to stream down her face.

Angela shook her head. "No, ma'am. This is not your fault."

"You don't understand. This wouldn't have happened if…"

Angela cut her off. "Please don't do that to yourself. You have no control over what your adult children do. Not even the ones you raised and definitely not the one you didn't raise."

There was an awkward pause as the matriarch stared at her. Then she nodded her head. "Ellington told you about the son I gave up for adoption."

"When he and Mingus suspected he might be behind all of this," Angela said softly.

Judith's eyes widened and then her tears kicked into second gear. Angela regretted not being able to give the woman a hug, not that one would have made her feel better or less responsible for what was happening to them.

The lights in the room brightened, a spotlight seeming to beam down upon them. Both women blinked, the sudden glow making it difficult to see. They heard him before they saw him, the voice a deep, rich timbre that could have played smoothly on the radio.

"Well, isn't this something!" Fabian Scott said as he moved toward them. "Hello, Mother!"

He came to a standstill at Angela's side, his gaze focused on the woman who'd given birth to him. Staring up at him, Angela was in awe of how much he and Ellington looked like each other. He was the spitting image of his brothers, the family resemblance running deep in his veins. He was clearly his mother's son, with the same chiseled features and pale eyes. His complexion was ruddier, seeming to hint at an Irish ancestry, and his auburn hair was the warmest shade of ginger red. He reminded Angela of the actor Damian Lewis and she suspected those features came from his father's side of his biological tree.

"Did you miss me?" he asked with a manic chuckle.

"Why are you doing this, Fabian?" Judith questioned, her tone calm.

"So, you do know who I am! I'm surprised you even know my name."

"Why would you be surprised? I gave you that name," she answered. "You were named after my great-uncle, Fabian Harmon. It was the one thing I asked your adoptive parents to promise to give you and they agreed."

"You knew my parents?" Fabian gripped the back of the chair Angela sat in, the information seeming to throw him off guard.

"Because your adoption was private, I selected your parents. I needed to know that you would be with a family that would love and care for you the way I couldn't. That you would have the life I wasn't able to give you."

"That you didn't *want* to give me. But you managed to give it to your other children!"

"It wasn't like that," Judith said with a soft sigh.

"What? You were pragmatic about throwing me away and that's supposed to make me feel better about being abandoned?"

There was something in his tone that gave Angela

pause. His pain was palpable, and steely, feeling like a sharp-edged knife cutting through butter. There was something inside him that was hollow and filled with anger and hatred. It felt dark and combustible, as if he'd lost himself in it with no hope of ever finding his way back. His mother felt it, too, her tears straining against the inside of her eyelids as she struggled not to sob openly.

"Clearly," Angela interjected, "things aren't what you thought they were. Why don't you let us go so that you two can talk and clear up the confusion?"

The comment seemed to jostle Fabian's memory, reminding him that she was there. He took a step from her, turning an about-face to stare. He laughed again, finding her comment amusing.

"Investigator Stanfield!" He smirked. "May I call you Angela? I mean, you and my brother have become close, so that practically makes us family. Although you'll find the Black family aren't welcoming of too many strangers. They keep their inner circle small, and close. I thought getting past my mother's husband would be the biggest challenge, but it seems you don't get in without my mother's approval. But if you don't believe me, just ask the wives. I hear the sons of Judith Black are all mama's boys! All of them except me, of course!" He laughed awkwardly.

Fabian tossed Judith a look. "People do like to gossip about you, Mother. I hear you can be quite the *bitch* when you want to be." He spat the words, putting as much emphasis on the insult as he could muster.

Judith sighed, pushing a heavy breath out of her lungs. "Watch your mouth. You can be as angry as you want but I will not tolerate your disrespect. Even though I wasn't there, I know you were raised better than that."

Fabian bristled. He bit back a retort and then he suddenly laughed, amused by his mother chastising him. He shook his head, his words coming with a hint of venom in his tone. "I was raised well. The Scotts were a nice couple. They insisted on family dinner together every night, church on Sundays and discipline that bordered on abuse. But my adoptive mother was a nasty drunk and my father didn't have much of a backbone when it came to standing up to her. You wouldn't have known that, though. Things changed after the old man lost his good government job and began to beat on her. We kept that information to ourselves, though. Heaven forbid if the neighbors discovered we weren't the picture-perfect family everyone thought we were! But you know about the necessity of appearances, don't you, Mother?"

Judith's eyes widened and she blinked rapidly to keep her tears from spilling past her lashes. "I didn't know," she said, her voice a loud whisper.

He shrugged his shoulders, then turned his attention back toward Angela. "I expected more from you, Angela. I practically spoon-fed you the clues to solve this case."

She paused for a split second before responding. Then said, "The clues you left were intended to put the blame on the wrong people."

He shrugged. "Maybe so. Then again, maybe not. It all depends on how you want to look at it."

"Why did you kill the district attorney?"

"I didn't. His ex-wife did. But you already know that. She was not happy about my brother destroying her marriage."

Judith snapped. "Parker had nothing to do with the demise of their relationship. They were divorced years before he and Jonathan met. You will not put that on him."

"Maybe not, but you have to admit, Mother, their relationship destroyed any chance of reconciliation and Vivian Wyler really wanted to reconcile with her hubby.

She hated that Parker was in the way of that. It was just by happenstance that I became acquainted with dear, dear Vivian. She was visiting the husband one day when I was shadowing your *second* son. It was a nasty little scene and I immediately sensed she could use a friend. When I reached out to her, she cried on my shoulder a time or two and I was delighted to give her some advice. No man should have treated her so badly and she needed to know she could do something about that."

"So, you told her how to kill Jonathan knowing Parker would be blamed."

Fabian shrugged his broad shoulder, but he didn't answer.

Angela continued. "Why did you kill Vivian?"

"I had nothing to do with that, either!" he exclaimed as he drew his hand to his chest, feigning shock and awe. "You'll be challenged to connect me to anyone's murder, Investigator! I've never killed anyone," he said emphatically. "I'm sure if you keep digging, you'll discover Detective Caswell murdered Vivian and his two men. I'm sure he feared they might tattle on him and his many bad deeds. Dirty cops always worry about someone turning on them. It's such a shame!"

Angela nodded. "So, you sent me the note and that tape."

His head snapped. "What note and tape?"

She eyed him warily, her gaze studying him intently. Fabian didn't know about the note or the tape that implicated him. Which meant he probably didn't know that Officer Danube was actually a federal agent.

She smiled. "I guess if you're asking then I might be a better investigator than you thought."

His eyes narrowed into thin slits. "What tape?" he snapped harshly.

Angela leaned forward in her seat. "The tape that Caswell made in case things went south and he needed to protect himself."

"You're lying," Fabian laughed. "Caswell's not that smart. Try again, Angela."

This time she shrugged, giving him a side-eye and no verbal response.

He stared and she realized he wasn't as confident as he wanted her to believe. He visibly shook his concerns away, turning back to his mother. He looked as if there was something more he wanted to say to her but he couldn't find the words he needed to express himself. Instead, he moved to her side and dropped to his knees, still eyeing her intently.

"This didn't have to happen, Mother. This is all your fault. All you had to do was love me."

"Because I loved you is why I did what I did."

Fabian laid his head in his mother's lap, wrapping his arms around her waist. "No," he sighed. "You really didn't, so don't lie."

Time seemed to stand still as he rested himself against the woman. Judith's tears had finally fallen past her lashes, raining down the curve of her cheeks. Moments later Fabian rose from where he knelt and Angela realized he, too, had been crying.

When he finally spoke, he'd composed himself, and his singsong tone felt awkward and sorely out of place. "Well, ladies, this has been fun, but I need to run. A few final errands I need to tend to," he said. He gave them both a smile and with one last check of his mother's ties and a kiss to her cheek, he turned and exited the space.

Ellington was still on the phone, taking notes and issuing orders when his doorbell rang. The ring was followed by a harsh rap that sounded like calloused knuckles against the wood. He instinctively knew it wasn't his mother or Angela knocking. He looked at his watch, realizing how much time had passed since the two women were supposed to meet up in the garage. His anxiety level suddenly soared, and he broke out into a sweat.

"Let me call you back," he said, disconnecting his call abruptly. He hurried to the front door, snatching it open. Mingus stood on the other side.

"What's wrong?" his brother questioned, their two gazes colliding like two billiard balls atop a baize-covered pool table.

"Did you see Angela or Mom in the parking garage?"

"I didn't go into the garage. I'm parked on the street. Why?"

"Angela went down to help Mom with her bags. They should have been back up here by now."

Mingus spun back toward the elevator, not needing Ellington to say anything else. Ellington opened the front closet and took a Glock 19 from the weapons case on the top shelf. He grabbed the keys to his front door and followed after his brother, the door slamming harshly behind them. The ride to the lower level was quiet, neither having anything to say. The elevator hummed softly, and soft jazz played out of the speakers. A million thoughts were spinning through Ellington's head, and he was finding it difficult to focus. Worry washed over him like a tidal wave. Although he hoped they would find the two women in deep conversation, gossiping about him and his antics, something just didn't feel right.

As they descended to the amenities level of the highrise apartment building, Mingus pulled his own revolver from the waistband of his jeans. Ellington checked the chamber on his weapon. When the elevator doors opened, the two stepped out in perfect sync, weapons raised as one looked left and the other right. They exited through the heavy steel doors to the parking garage and moved swiftly toward visitor parking.

Their mother's Jaguar F-Pace was still parked where she'd left it. The cargo hood was open, with bags of groceries spilled out of the back compartment. Cans of vegetables and fruit had rolled across the concrete floor and a loaf of bread that had been squashed beneath someone's foot rested near the rear tire. Blood splatters had begun to darken against the floor and the sight of it felt like a punch to Ellington's gut.

He reached down to pick up his mother's Coach bag from the ground. Her wallet and ID were still inside, allowing him to rule out robbery as a motive for their disappearance. He and Mingus exchanged a look. "Call Dad and wait for the forensics team," he snapped. "Then meet me in the security office. We need to take a look at the security tape."

Mingus nodded. "You going to be okay?" he questioned, noting the expression on his brother's face.

Ellington looked like he might explode, his cheeks a deep shade of red. He was visibly shaking, and it was taking every ounce of fortitude he possessed to maintain his cool.

"No," Ellington quipped. "I won't be okay until I know Angela and Mom are both safe."

Mingus pressed a large hand against his brother's shoulder. "We'll find them," he said, determination resonating in his tone.

"We better," Ellington responded. "I love those two women more than anything else in this world. Nothing can happen to them on my watch. Nothing."

Mingus nodded, understanding washing over him. He pulled his cell phone to his ear and waited for their father to answer on the other end. Ellington watched until the line connected and then he turned toward the entrance, moving toward the security office and the uniformed security guard he knew was napping soundly until it was time to make his rounds. Time wasn't on their side and they would have to act quickly if there was any hope of finding the two women safe and sound.

He stole a quick glance over his shoulder, eyeing his brother. Mingus had gone into investigative mode, assessing the scene with a keen eye. He held his cell phone, snapping pictures of the SUV and the food that lay on the ground. Ellington knew he would see things others might miss. Things that might lead them to their mother and Angela.

He paused to take a deep breath to still his nerves. He had said aloud to Mingus that he loved Angela, the words spilling past his lips before he could catch them. Truth had a way of taking on a life of its own and there was much truth in what he was feeling for Angela Stanfield. Suddenly, the thought of losing her had him in a slight panic.

He loved her. He loved her with every fiber of his being, and he had never felt that for any woman before her. She had managed to take up occupancy in his heart, laying claim to space his mother and sisters had occupied completely until he'd needed to make room for what he was feeling for Angela. Angela and his mother meant the world to him, and his world had suddenly imploded in a way he could never have anticipated.

When Mingus finally joined him in the security office, Ellington had the security guard jacked up against the wall by his collar. He was raging, threatening to bruise the young man if he didn't get the information he was demanding.

Mingus leaned back against the wooden counter and shook his head. "You are so out of your element," he said wryly.

Ellington snarled as he let the guy go. "We don't have time to wait for a warrant and he's giving me a hard time." Frustration painted his expression like bad weather on a spring day. "Now I need to see that security tape. The lives of two women may depend on it."

The security guard pulled himself upright, straightening his collar. He was a small man, standing no more than five feet tall. He looked like he might break if you shook him too hard. Ellington's ire didn't have him rattled, seeming instead to have solidified his defiance. "And I can't just give that to you without a warrant," he repeated for the umpteenth time. He glared in the attorney's direction.

Ellington was about to grab him a second time when Mingus stepped between the two. He shook his head at his brother, gesturing with a quick nod for him to take a step back. Ellington heaved a heavy sigh. He turned an about-face and moved across the room, folding his arms tightly around his torso.

Mingus turned to the security guard. "What's your name?"

The young man cleared his throat before he spoke. "Ben... I mean Benjamin...Crawford."

Mingus gave him a slight smile. "Well, Benjamin Crawford, there is a team of police officers in the garage at this very minute investigating the suspected kidnapping of a federal court judge and a special state investigator. And I have no doubts the press is already converging outside for information. How you handle what happens next will either make you a hero or put you in jail for impeding an investigation."

"I haven't done anything. I've been following the rules. At least I was trying to until he assaulted me." He pointed his index finger at Ellington, who responded with an eye roll.

"And following the rules is necessary and commendable," Mingus said with a nod. "But did he actually assault you or was it him just being overly anxious since one of the women missing is our mother and the other woman is his girlfriend? I'm sure you understand how something like that could make a man act out of character. Right? Imagine if it was your mother."

The man named Ben shrugged his narrow shoulders. "I guess so."

Mingus continued. "Besides, I like how you stood your ground. It shows you're a man of integrity. I'm sure your employers will be equally impressed when my brother and I give you a stellar review for how you're handling this situation."

"I should probably go up to talk to the police. We have rules."

Mingus reached into his jacket pocket. He pulled out a roll of cash the size of a large fist. "I know you can't legally give us the security tape, but the police chief will be down here in a few minutes, and he'll have a warrant."

"Then I have to wait for the police chief."

Mingus peeled off two $100 bills, toying with them between his fingers. "I'm sure with the right incentive you wouldn't have a problem leaving the two of us here to wait while you go up to the garage to talk with the officers. Just a little something for your inconvenience."

Ben looked from Mingus to Ellington and back.

Mingus pulled another bill from the roll in his hands. He eyed the uniformed man with a raised brow. Ellington still stood with his arms crossed tightly around his torso.

He tapped one foot against the tiled floor, still wanting to smash something beneath his fist.

Mingus peeled off one last bill. "This offer is about to disappear, Ben. And you need to get up to the garage before you get into trouble. So, what are you going to do?"

Ben stole a quick glance toward Ellington, his sense of morality suddenly floundering. He snatched the money from Mingus's hand as he headed toward the door. "I'll be back with the police chief. You two can wait here, but don't you touch nothing!" he said as he pocketed the cash.

When the door closed behind him, Ellington shook his head. "So much for his integrity," he quipped.

Mingus laughed. "Every man has his price. And since when do you go around manhandling potential witnesses? Did you hit your head on the way down here?"

Ellington had moved around the counter to the camera equipment, studying the buttons momentarily. "Why is it okay when you do it but not okay when I do it?"

"I don't have a law license to lose, that's why. Besides, brute force should always be a last resort. Like Mom taught us, you get more with honey than you can with vinegar."

"Well, that was some pricey honey. Your boy Ben took you for three hundred dollars."

"Four, but who's counting."

"And you are too damn calm about all of this," Ellington said, his eyes wide. "Isn't this driving you crazy? Why aren't you climbing the walls, too?"

Mingus shrugged. "One of us has to stay focused."

"It's hard for me to focus when I'm worried. And I'll be honest," Ellington said, his voice dropping slightly. "I'm scared. What if something…"

His brother stalled his comment, cutting him off before he could get his thought out. "I can stay calm because I trust we will find them. And when we do, they will both be safe."

"But what if…"

"But nothing," Mingus snapped. "Thinking what-if won't help them and it doesn't do us any good, either. I can stay calm because after we find them, I plan to make whoever did this pay for all the worry, fear and frustration we are feeling."

Shaking his head, Ellington gestured toward the security feed as he rewound the tape and then pushed Play. "Here, look," he said pointing.

His brother moved behind him to stare over his shoulder. Both men watched as their mother pulled her car into the empty parking space. There was a moment of pause before she exited the vehicle and Ellington knew that he'd been on the phone with her, amused that she'd caught him with his hands in Angela's cookie jar. When she finally exited the car, she'd gone right to the rear, reaching for the bags inside. Suddenly she spun to her right, something or someone startling her.

"Do we have that camera?" Mingus questioned.

"Hold on," Ellington said as he pushed buttons, changing the image on one of the other screens. He rewound the feed, adjusting the time to when their mother had jumped with fright. "There," he said, pointing.

They watched as a tall figure stood watching her, and for the first time Ellington got a clear visual of their older brother. He could only begin to imagine what his mother had to be feeling when she, too, had seen him, realization flooding through her. She jumped again, but this time it was Angela walking up on her that pulled her attention away. When she looked back, her firstborn child was gone.

"Son of a..." Ellington muttered, stalling the expletive on the tip of his tongue.

They continued watching as the two women chatted. Something their mother said caused Angela's body language to shift. He could almost feel her tense, her stance suddenly defensive. He felt as if she were trying to move his mother along as she took half the grocery bags in her hands, gesturing with her head toward the bank of elevators across the way. She was focused on Judith when a white-paneled van pulled alongside them.

Two minutes later he pushed Pause on the video. "It's not either's blood," Ellington said, a wave of relief washing over him.

"Your girl can scrap," Mingus said, his grin a mile wide. "She's got a mean left hook!"

Ellington nodded, equally impressed with the fight she'd given the man who'd accosted them. "When we find him, I plan to put my fist in his face, though. Just so you know."

"What face? He's going to need some reconstructive surgery after what she did to him."

Ellington shrugged, his own grin as wide as his brother's.

"We need to go," Mingus said as he texted a message on his cell phone. "I'll get Dad to send us whatever he finds on the license plate for that truck. I'll also let him know where we're headed."

"Where are we going?"

"To check the hospitals. We need to find a man with a broken face."

"Let's hope he's there," Ellington concluded. "Because when I break the rest of him, he won't have far to go for help."

"You want him to get help?" Mingus laughed.

"Not really, but I'm trying to remember the Christian values our mother instilled in us."

"You're a good man, Ellington Black. I tend to follow the kill-or-be-killed philosophy of our father. Or shoot first and ask questions later."

"Look in that cabinet over there and see if there are any blank discs. I want to make a copy of the tape. We'll take it with us just to make sure nothing happens to it."

"What about that warrant?" Mingus questioned.

"That'll secure the original copy that we'll be able to use in court. No one needs to know our copy even exists."

"And if they find out?"

Ellington shrugged, cutting an eye at his brother. "We'll be forthcoming about how we got our hands on it."

Mingus gasped, feigning surprise and shock. "You mean you won't lie? What kind of attorney are you?"

"The best, and no, I won't lie. But I might have to re-imagine the truth and wrap it in a lot of legalese."

"You do know that's why people hate lawyers, right?"

"It's a hazard of the profession. Now, let's go find our mother and my girl, please."

A few minutes later Ellington and Mingus headed toward the door. As they reached the exit, Ben suddenly rushed after them.

"Hey, where are you going? The police chief says he needs to have a word with you two about that security tape."

"What tape?" Ellington questioned.

"You know! That tape you said you needed to see! The security tape of the kidnapping."

Ellington and his brother exchanged a quick look, amusement dipped in arrogance dancing out of their eyes.

"Should we?" Mingus questioned.

Ellington shook his head. "No, but we're going to do it anyway."

His brother smirked. "Our mother would not be proud of us right now."

Ellington nodded. "Well, I won't tell if you don't."

Neither said another word, both chuckling under their breath as they gave Ben a wave. Then just like that, they disappeared out the door.

Chapter 14

"I'm proud of all my children," Judith was saying as Angela struggled against the restraints that held her hostage to that chair. "Don't get me wrong, I know better than most that not one is a perfect angel, but they've done well. They've become productive members of society, they're happy and healthy, and they strive to do good in this world. A mother couldn't ask for more."

Angela gave her a faint smile. "You should be proud. I've met all your children and they're an impressive lot."

"I heard that you and Simone hit it off famously. I have no doubts you and Vaughan will become fast friends as well. She's not as spirited as her sister, but definitely not as conservative as Parker, or even Ellington."

"I never took Ellington for being conservative."

"With some things he's very much so. He's a traditionalist at heart. But I imagine as you two continue to discover the best and the worst of each other, you'll see what I mean."

Angela smiled again. "I really like your son, Judge Black. He's a very special man."

"Yes, he is. And I'd venture to say that you might be falling in love with him. Your eyes shimmer and your cheeks get flushed when you talk about him."

The smile on Angela's face widened. "Love has always been a four-letter word in my vocabulary. A *dirty* four-letter word."

Judith chuckled. "Mine, too! Until it grabs hold of you and doesn't let go." She blew a soft sigh. "Now, how the hell are we getting out of here? Because I would really like to go home to the people that I love."

Angela pondered her comment. She'd been assessing their situation since Judith's wayward son had left them. Once or twice one of his minions had looked in on them, the large brute waving a firearm in their direction. His efforts to intimidate them were less than successful: neither woman was impressed with his curses and threats. But Fabian hadn't returned, and it didn't appear that he was expected anytime soon. Meanwhile, their babysitter was more interested in the television show he was watching in the other room than he was in guarding them.

"Don't take this the wrong way, Judge, but I'd like to go home to the people you love, too!" Angela finally responded.

"So, again, any suggestions on how to get us out of this predicament?"

"I've always been partial to a good fight. I say we go kicking and screaming since our friend out there doesn't seem amenable to our politer requests for him to let us go."

Judith laughed. "I see why my son is so infatuated

with you. You're fiercely independent, you have tons of spirit and you don't take yourself too seriously. He's always been drawn to women who challenge him, and I imagine you keep Ellington on his toes."

She chuckled again before continuing. Her expression was more stoic, her temperament turning serious. "If you say fight, then we fight." She leaned forward ever so slightly, her voice dropping to the slightest whisper. "Now, what's the plan?"

Angela leaned forward in her own chair, scooting the chair legs closer. "We need a diversion. One that will take his attention off me for a moment."

The matriarch grinned. "And I thought you would need me to do something hard!"

The confidence in her tone and the gleam in her bright eyes warmed Angela's spirit. In spite of their current situation, she, too, laughed heartily.

Ellington connected the Bluetooth in his car to his cell phone as he answered the incoming call. His father's voice bellowed out of the speakers.

"What the hell are you and your brother up to?" Jerome screamed.

There was a hint of worry that rang on the back end of his words, concern he hoped to shadow behind a cloud of hot air and anger. His frustration was palpable, flooding the airwaves between their two phones and billowing through the vehicle like rising mist.

"We're on a mission to find your woman," Mingus answered as the two brothers exchanged gazes. "And Ellington's woman, too."

"Why is this security guard annoying me? He says you two harangued him for some damn tape and then took off."

"We found what we needed. Now we're following up on another lead," Ellington answered.

"What do you need from me?" their father questioned.

"Space," Mingus answered. "We may break a law or two and we can't afford your guys getting in our way."

"Do what you need to do," Jerome answered. "And call me when you know something."

"Yes, sir," Ellington said, his voice dropping ever so slightly.

"And don't come home until you find your mother," the patriarch added, his voice breaking for the first time. "And I mean that. Bring my wife home!"

Ellington didn't bother to respond, instead disconnecting the call as he pushed the car forward even faster.

Minutes later the two brothers entered the University of Chicago Medical Center, moving swiftly through the emergency room doors. Hospital staff eyed them both warily until a physician's assistant wearing pale yellow scrubs, a floral-printed hijab and a bright smile between dimpled cheeks recognized Ellington. She greeted him warmly, that smile like a sliver of sunshine on a dark day.

"Attorney Black, it's good to see you!" A wealth of color tinged her face a warm red, and there was a hint of excitement in her tone.

"The pleasure is all mine, Arnita!" Ellington answered. "How is your husband doing?"

"He's doing exceptionally well. The settlement money we received has been a blessing. We can finally afford the physical therapy he needed. I can't begin to tell you how much I appreciate everything you did to help us with that."

"I only did what was necessary," Ellington answered. "I'm glad I was able to be of service."

Her smile widened. "So, what brings you here?"

He gestured toward Mingus. "My brother and I are trying to find someone. A man. He's a big guy and he would have come in a few hours ago for an injury to his face. We think he may have been admitted here."

The woman gave Mingus a quick once-over, then smiled again before she turned her attention back to Ellington. "That would probably be Mr. Harris. John Harris. He said he accidentally rode his moped into a tree. One of the nurses teased him about being too old to be on a moped but he didn't find that funny." She chuckled.

"Where can we find this Mr. Harris?" Mingus questioned. "We'd like to pay him a visit and see how he's doing."

The young woman eyed him again, her second stare a little more wary. She kept her gaze locked on the man, but her comment was meant for Ellington. "You're not ambulance chasing, are you, Attorney Black?"

Ellington shook his head. "No, not at all. It's just important that we have a chat with Mr. Harris. A woman's life depends on it."

Arnita stared at him for a quiet moment, his comment spinning through her head. Her smiled turned, a frown pulling at her lips.

"They moved him upstairs to a room," she finally answered. She eased behind the counter at the nurses' station and began typing into a computer. She nodded. "Room 335. Just check in with the charge nurse at the desk. He was scheduled for surgery so you might not be able to see him. My system isn't showing me what his visitor status is, but typically visitation is restricted to immediate family."

"Oh, we will see him," Mingus mumbled, a hint of attitude in his tone.

Arnita's eyes narrowed, and she cut her gaze back toward Ellington.

"I'm sure it won't be a problem," he said. "We appreciate all of your assistance."

She smiled brightly, the tension in her face easing. "Thank you again, Attorney Black."

"It was good to see you, Arnita. Please give your husband my regards."

Ellington could feel the woman's eyes boring into his back as he and his brother headed toward the hospital elevator. He wanted to look back, curious to see if she suspected their intentions were less than honorable. If maybe she were passing judgment on them both. Not that he cared what she or anyone else thought, because in that moment his only concern was getting the answers they needed to find Angela and his mother.

"Try not to get me disbarred," he said to his brother as the elevator moved slowly to the third floor.

Mingus shrugged. "Try not to get yourself disbarred. You're the one assaulting innocent bystanders. I can only imagine what you plan to do to Mr. Harris!"

"I did not assault that security guard."

"Could have fooled him. He looked scared hanging a foot off the floor with your hands around his neck."

"I'm going to hell," Ellington said as he pulled both palms across his head.

Mingus laughed but before he could respond, the elevator doors opened and Ellington was out of the conveyor, turning right down the length of hallway. His brother followed after him, tossing a quick glance behind them to see who might be there.

The door to room 335 was open and a nurse stood at the bedside checking on the patient. His head was bandaged, the bruises to his face hidden behind layers of white gauze. What could be seen of his eyes was nominal, the flesh red and swollen around two black marbles. She startled as the two men entered the room, moving to the other side of the bed.

"I'm sorry, but he just came up from surgery. Are you family?"

Ellington nodded. "Cousins. We heard about the accident and came as quickly as we could."

She gave them both a slight smile. "Well, I'll need you to limit your visit to five minutes at most. He needs to rest."

"Thank you," Ellington responded.

The two stood quietly as she finished checking his blood pressure and oxygen levels. She typed notes into a tablet, then exited the room. "Five minutes," she called out over her shoulder, "and I'll be back to check on him." She gave them one last stare before she shut the door behind herself.

With a wave of his hand Ellington watched her leave. When she was out of sight, he turned his attention to the man lying in the bed. "This won't take long," he muttered under his breath. "This won't take long at all."

Judith screamed at the top of her lungs, shouting for someone's attention. After a few minutes, Fabian's underling showed himself, annoyance painted across his face.

"What?" the young man snapped, his mouth filled with the last bite of a peanut butter and jelly sandwich he had been trying to finish.

"I have to use the restroom, please," Judith said politely, her voice even and controlled.

"Can't," the man quipped. "You gotta hold it." He turned as if to walk away.

Judith screamed again. It was bloodcurdling, sounding like the soundtrack to a Guillermo del Toro horror movie. It echoed around the large, empty space and even Angela jumped in her seat. When he turned back around, she gave him a polite smile. "This is an emergency, dear. I would not expect you to understand, but if you do not allow me the use of the restroom, it will not bode well for you later on."

The look he gave her was comical and Angela bit down on her bottom lip to keep from laughing out loud. His brow was furrowed, and confusion glossed over his expression. His eyes darted from side to side as if he were trying to consider the ramifications of his actions or decipher the meaning of what it meant to not bode well.

"Boss man said under no circumstances was I to let either of you loose."

Judith shook her head. "I'm sorry, dear, but what is your name?"

"They call me Bullet." His chest swelled with pride, as if the significance of his nickname was renowned.

Judith blinked, her stoic expression much like that of a stern science teacher Angela once had. The matriarch asked again, her tone a little firmer. "What did your mother name you, baby?"

The kid they called Bullet hesitated before responding. When he answered, you could hear the reluctance in his voice, a spirited debate waging war in his head. Should he tell her or shouldn't he. "Brandon," he finally answered reluctantly.

"Brandon, the *boss man* is my son, and I will deal with him later. Would you let someone make your mother suffer so unmercifully?"

He shook his head, dreadlocks waving from side to side. "Nah! But I ain't gone tie up my mother, either."

"Well, that's admirable. Clearly you are treating your

mother far better than my son is currently treating me. Now untie me and show me the way to the restroom. You can stand outside the door if you must. It's not like you need to worry about her going anyplace." Judith tossed Angela a dismissive gesture.

Brandon's hesitation was palpable. He was clearly challenged with what he should do versus what he'd been ordered to do. Realizing he was in a no-win situation, he pulled a pocketknife from the back pocket of his denim jeans and cut the plastic ties that held her bound to the chair. Judith stood, wringing her hands together as she shook the blood back into her wrists and fingers.

"Thank you, Brandon. Now, where's that bathroom?" she questioned as she headed toward the door he'd entered from. She tossed Angela a quick look and a wink of her eye.

Brandon followed after her like an obedient puppy, still flustered by the turn of events as Judith began to interrogate him, firing questions at him faster than he could comprehend.

"Where'd you go to school, Brandon? Are you an only child or do you have siblings? Have you thought about your long-term goals, young man?"

As the two disappeared from the room, Brandon muttering his answers under his breath, Angela swung into action.

The assortment of survival courses she'd taken over the years had taught her a thing or two. Basics had included how to light a fire without a match. How to set a fracture in the wild. And her personal favorite, how to avoid encountering bears. There was also a long list of things she'd been taught *not* to do, with not panicking being at the top of that list. She was acutely aware of the repercussions were she to do a maneuver the wrong way.

They had also put her in proximity to persons she would probably never have befriended. There was Magnus and Wyatt, the two brothers who lived off the grid and were more than prepared for the apocalypse. And Jenny-Lynn, the former madam who had made it her life's mission to give working girls the skills to keep themselves safe from their male customers.

As she strained against the plastic zip ties that bound her hands behind her back, a sliver of doubt pitched through Angela's stomach. What if she couldn't free herself in time? What would happen to them if they couldn't get away? Would Ellington be able to forgive her if she failed and something happened to his mother?

She took a deep breath, drawing on all her training to cast that doubt away. Because if nothing else, each course had given her confidence in her own self-sufficiency. Angela knew there was no challenge she couldn't face head-on and master, including the situation she currently found herself in.

She twisted and pulled at her right hand, the ties rubbing harshly against her wrists. She'd been working at them since shaking off the stupor from the head slam. She had finally loosened enough flexibility in the plastic to free her thumb and then wriggle her whole hand through the loop that confined her. She ignored the pain from the wooden chair cutting into her upper arms. She took a swift moment to assess the ties around her ankles. She was firmly secured to the piece of furniture, unable to move without dragging the chair with her. There with nothing for her to cut herself free, and not enough time to try and work them loose. So, with a big inhale of air, she suddenly jumped and slammed her body and the wooden chair against the concrete floor. The move was awkward but impactful, as the chair broke into pieces, the chair legs disconnecting from the seat. The two fingers she broke on her left hand were a casualty she would worry about later, she mused as she pulled her hand to her chest, clutching them tightly to keep herself from screaming out in pain.

She took another deep breath of air and then a third, blinking away the tears that pressed against the length of her lashes. She would feel the bruises later, she thought as she pulled the chair leg from the zip tie around her right ankle and what was left of the other from her left ankle. Finally able to move unimpeded, she shook the blood back into her appendages, grateful to get the circulation moving. She grabbed the chair leg that hadn't splintered into pieces and rushed toward the door, knowing the noise might bring someone to check on her before she was ready to greet them. Standing behind the door and wielding that piece of wood like a club, she waited, prepared to fight for her life.

The two brothers rushed out of the hospital back to Ellington's car. As he started the engine and pulled into traffic, Mingus was on the phone with his office shouting out orders. The man in the hospital had given them enough information to send them on another chase. This time they needed to find the warehouse where he claimed the two women were being held. Scared of the pain they had threatened upon him, he'd pointed them in their direction but hadn't been able to give them a definitive address before the nurse returned and shooed them out. Ellington listened in on his brother's conversation, his own mind racing with thoughts.

Frustration was like a dark mask across Mingus's face. His voice was raised, and he was trying not to shout at the person on the other end. But the answers he needed weren't coming fast enough, his demands feeling impossible to accomplish with such short notice.

He yelled. "I need to know who owns all the property within a five-block radius. Text the information to me and I don't want to hear it's going to take a minute. Call our contacts down at the city and tell them I said I needed the answer yesterday. My mother's life depends on it!" Ellington felt his brother's frustration, the wealth of it mixing with his own like lighter fluid and a match. He sensed that had there been one available and Mingus had been able, he would have slammed the cell phone against a brick wall.

"Think about this for a minute," Ellington interjected. "I think Fabian has them somewhere *near* Peace Row. Harris said it was like an old, empty warehouse, right? But that whole neighborhood feels like an abandoned warehouse district."

Mingus gave him a slight shrug. "Make it make sense."

Ellington nodded. "It's the most reasonable explanation I can come up with. All of this has been about hurting us, and subsequently hurting Mom. Taking those things near and dear to her loved ones seems to be how he operates. We own all the property on that block and the next. If he's anywhere, he'd be there."

"But where exactly? And how would he be getting in and out without someone noticing? When Armstrong began his renovations, he hired a security firm to monitor all the property."

"He did, because he had an entire team of homeless men squatting on the premises next door," Ellington reminded him.

"When was the last time you inspected the property?" Mingus questioned.

"The day we closed. I've had no reason to hang out

there since. I don't plan to renovate my building for at least another year. Maybe even two."

"But heaven forbid something happened to your girl-friend there, you'd never step foot in the place again," Mingus mused.

Ellington tossed his brother a look, then gunned the engine. Mingus dialed Armstrong and connected the call to the car's Bluetooth. Stalled at a red light, they waited for him to answer.

Armstrong's voice came through. "What's up? You find Mom?"

"What do you know about the security firm watching the property at Peace Row?" Mingus questioned.

"They came highly recommended. Everyone shows up when they're supposed to, and I get weekly reports. You all get them, too, but obviously no one reads their emails," he said snidely before he continued. "We haven't had any trespassers since we hired them. Why are you asking?"

"Anyone else coming in and out lately?" Ellington asked.

"Just the contractors."

"Same team who renovated the night club?"

"Yes and no. They're under new ownership. The same team for the most part. One or two new guys."

"I need names and a number for the owner," Mingus snapped.

"That's in my office. What's going on?"

"We're outside," Ellington quipped as he pulled his car into a parking space by the nightclub's front door. "We think Mom and Angela might be hostage in one of the empty buildings."

"I'm on my way out," Armstrong snapped.

"Send those names over to my secretary first," Mingus said. "I'm texting her now to get background checks on all of them."

The phone line went dead, and the two brothers hesitated for a split second. Mingus had resorted to texting orders instead of shouting them and Ellington used the time to catch his breath and get his thoughts together. He didn't say it aloud, but he was scared. Even with what they did know, there was just as much they didn't. Thinking the two women might be here, on Black family property, was a reach and not one he had a lot of confidence in, but they didn't have any other leads that made more sense. It was a lot of property to search, the brick buildings stretching the length of a whole block. Most of them had been condemned by the city and deemed unsafe. For the briefest second, he didn't know where they should begin. But mostly, he was worried that they might be wrong.

Angela still held that wooden leg above her head, two hands wrapped tightly around one end of it. She closed her eyes, took a deep breath and listened, her head cocked slightly to the side. Noises were far and few, but the faintest whispers seemed magnified as she stood listening. Somewhere in the distance she could hear Judith still chattering away. At one point Brandon laughed, the lilt of it seeming out of place. There was something in their exchange that had her questioning how he'd gotten himself tangled up with Judith's son and why he was so willing to do the man's bidding. He seemed like a nice kid, but clearly, he had lost his way. Angela took another deep breath. From what she could hear, Judith was intent on putting him back on the right path.

Angela suddenly bristled, her eyes widening. She heard him well before she saw him, his voice raised as he shouted at someone. When she didn't hear anyone reply she reasoned he must be talking over a cell phone. His footsteps were heavy as he slowly ascended up a flight of stairs toward them. He suddenly stopped, things quiet except for the small television playing in the outer room. Then the footsteps stomped back down in the direction they'd come from. They had lost their advantage, Angela thought. Taking down Brandon was one thing. Taking down two men, one willing to kill without regret, might prove to be more problematic. She slowly lowered the chair leg as she reassessed her options.

There was a closet to the left of the door. She pulled it open and stared inside. It had been a storage room and was still filled with dust-covered boxes, cobwebs and she imagined a rodent or two. Moving back to the door she peeked out just as Judith scurried quickly into the other room. Behind her Brandon blocked the exit, his attention focused on the stairwell. He, too, listened as Fabian yelled into his cell phone from someplace below. The two women locked eyes and Angela could see the fear that rose like a morning mist in the matriarch's stare.

She reached out and grabbed Judith's arm. Pulling her back into the room, she guided her to that storage closet, gesturing for her to hide herself behind a stack of boxes in the rear of the space. Then she secured the door. She wasn't going to make it easy for either man to get to them, and she wasn't going to allow either of them to be taken without a fight. Angela braced herself for the worst, prayed for grace and readied herself to swing that wooden chair leg like she was up to bat at the World Series with the bases loaded, two outs, two strikes on her and the title on the line. She felt the pressure of the world on her shoulders, but she was ready to swing that bat with every ounce of her might.

Seconds later there was a clamor of noise in the room on the other side of the door. Fabian's voice was rushed, his words choppy as he chastised Brandon. The faintest shouts rose from someplace in the distance and Fabian cursed, espousing profanity like a newly found language. There was more shouting and more voices and then a loud series of booms that sounded like fireworks erupting. And then, just as quickly, a quiet stillness descended around them. It felt surreal and unnatural, and her own fear began to swallow Angela whole. She jumped when Judith suddenly stepped in behind her, dropping her hand against Angela's shoulder. Suddenly, they both smelled smoke, and panic began to trickle between them like a faint stream of water from a faucet.

Theirs was a quiet exchange, no words necessary as Angela reached for the doorknob to pull the door open. It wouldn't give on the first pull, so she tugged harder, Judith's hands clasped atop hers as she pulled with her. When the door finally opened, flames were just beginning to spread, a fire erupting with a vengeance in the outer room. It crackled as it kissed paper strewn across the floor. The heat was rising as the flames grabbed hold of rotted beams and held on, embers beginning to smolder. The two women glanced at each other. Angela shook her head and cursed. Judith began to cry.

"Stay low!" Angela cautioned as she looked for items to block the gap at the bottom of the closet door. The smoke had become too thick in the outer room, the air incredibly thin. It was becoming difficult to breathe. Despite her best efforts to keep the flames at bay, the fire was spreading rapidly. She had tried her hardest to find a way out, but every route had come up short, blocked by flames and heat. The closet was their last hope, and it was a slim one at best. That someone would find them before the fire engulfed what was left of the building was what they hoped for, and for just the briefest moment neither woman believed in wishes coming true.

"He'll come for you," Judith suddenly whispered, her strength beginning to wane. "Ellington will come for you. Just like my Jerome will come for me."

Angela nodded. "I want to believe that," she said softly, a hacking cough catching in her chest.

"He will. Just trust it," the matriarch said as she rubbed her hand across Angela's back and shoulders.

Angela gasped and choked on the dry air again. The temperature was continuing to rise and she knew time wasn't on their side. Her eyes were becoming heavy and her chest hurt. Judith was beginning to feel it as well, her breathing labored. She slid into the far corner, her head hanging low, her cheeks wet with tears. Angela wanted to believe that Ellington's mother was right but nothing about their situation felt like their story was going to end with a happily-ever-after.

She suddenly began to bang an oversize ratchet wrench against the concrete floor. The wrench had fallen out of a box she'd knocked off the shelf as they'd hidden from their captors and looked for tools to protect themselves. Angela had abandoned that wooden chair leg for the steel instrument, knowing it would do far more damage if she needed it. Now, the only purpose it served was to make enough noise that someone might hear and come rescue them. That Ellington and his family would save them.

Angela continued to bang the heavy steel against the concrete. Each loud bang felt like a battle cry as she threw every ounce of energy into swinging the wrench up and down. She banged and banged and kept banging until she had little else to give. And then she heard him, the faintest voice cutting through the rising haze.

"Fire department! Call out! Anyone here? Fire department! Call out!"

From the corner of the room, Judith laughed, excitement building in her tone. She coughed, choking on the thick smoke. "It's the cavalry, Angela! Come to save us!"

Ellington felt like it had taken the fire department hours to get there and not the 6.4 minutes that had passed from the time the first call was placed. They were not prepared for the explosions that had gone off through the building, nor the flames that had barricaded the route up the stairs, preventing them access. They still had no idea who was inside or if Angela and his mother were safe. What they were certain of was Fabian Scott's role in all of it, their wayward half brother proving to be quite the nemesis. Racing after Fabian had been futile. He'd successfully evaded them, disappearing right before their eyes. He'd been there and then he was gone, a wall of fire standing in his place. They weren't even sure if he had made it out of the building. Ellington kept questioning if the move had been a suicide mission, frightened that Fabian had taken the two women Ellington loved most with him.

He felt Mingus staring, an admonishment crossing his face. Ellington didn't dare voice the negative thoughts racing through his head. He knew that if he did, it would send his brother, with his glass-half-full disposition, into rage mode and the two would go toe-to-toe. But his faith was wavering, and his anxiety was rising as the fire continued to rage out of control.

Minutes later their father moved toward them, his stoic expression causing Ellington's heart to race. He took two steps in the man's direction, his own expression questioning. "What?" he asked, his voice cracking ever so slightly.

"They're bringing out a body. I don't know anything else yet."

Ellington felt his throat tighten and the air being sucked from his chest. His legs began to shake, and he took a step back to lean against the hood of his car.

His father eyed him intently but didn't say anything. Neither was accustomed to feeling so vulnerable in front of the other. Ellington could only begin to imagine what his father was feeling because he felt completely out of control. They both turned as two firefighters suddenly stepped out of the building, dragging a man between them. EMS personnel met them at the entrance with a stretcher. They passed him off and just as quickly ran back inside. The man on the stretcher wasn't moving as the paramedics began to work on him. Breathing a sigh of relief, Ellington suddenly felt guilty. Whoever he was, he was someone's son, or husband, or father. Someone loved him and would be worried, no matter what his connection was to everything going on. Once he was identified, there'd be answers and Ellington had questions. A host of questions that had his nerves in a tight knot. Who was this man? What did he know? How was he involved? Could he tell them about his mother or Angela?

Ellington's heart suddenly dropped into the pit of his stomach. He watched as the paramedics pulled the white sheet up and over the man's head. One of them slowly shook his head at the fire chief who had arrived on scene and was standing alongside the police superintendent. Neither man showed an ounce of emotion. Ellington was broken and he knew it was painted all over his face.

Another fire engine from another fire precinct arrived on-site to join those already there. There didn't seem to be enough help as the center of the building suddenly collapsed. There was a wealth of activity with fire personnel racing back and forth for more tools and water hoses, and Ellington felt completely helpless, unable to offer an ounce of assistance.

They all heard the call over the radio, the fire chief depressing the talk button on his receiver to ask the firefighter on the other end to repeat what he'd just said.

"We've found two women. Both are alive. We're bringing them out and clearing the building now, Commander! I don't know how much longer this floor is going to hold!"

"Roger that!"

"They're okay," Armstrong muttered as he slapped Mingus on the back. "They're okay."

Jerome tossed his sons the faintest smile. Despite Armstrong's pronouncement they knew not to get their hopes up. Even Jerome would wait until he held Judith in his arms to celebrate. But by the grace of God, things didn't feel quite so bleak, and Ellington suddenly had a sliver of hope to hold on to.

Chapter 15

The squall of sirens rushing toward the hospital pierced the night air. Angela lay with her eyes closed. Someone had placed an oxygen mask over her face and cool air was blowing into her lungs. Blowing away the smoke and dust that had slowly tried to suffocate her. She thought she heard Ellington's voice through the layers of fog that clouded her head. It was warm and soothing, and he had called her "baby." Then there was nothing she could discern, as noises and voices she couldn't identify bled into each other.

When she next opened her eyes she was tucked comfortably in a hospital bed and hooked to monitors that were recording her heart rate and blood pressure. Her right arm and hand were in a cast and as she examined it, she smiled. Ellington had signed his name and had drawn a circle of hearts for emphasis.

She took a deep breath, grateful that her lungs no

longer burned with each inhale of oxygen. Grateful for the firemen that had found them, one lifting her into his arms to carry her out of the building. She'd gone in one ambulance and Judith had been transported in another. She was grateful that they both had survived and lived to tell the story.

A nurse entered the room, moving around the bed to check on her. When she realized Angela was awake, she smiled down at her. "Good morning. How are you feeling?"

Angela nodded. "Like I've been hit by a truck."

"No such luck. A few broken bones, residual smoke inhalation and no doubt a major headache. Other than that, you're good. The doctor will be in soon to check on you, but I guess if your oxygen levels are good, they'll release you later this afternoon. But don't quote me on that. Your doctor will have the final say."

Angela chuckled. "You've been doing this awhile."

"Over thirty years. Which is why I'll tell you when you do get home, drink plenty of water. It'll help move any mucus out of your chest. You might have a residual cough because your lungs are still fragile. And just rest. Let your body heal."

Angela nodded. "Yes, ma'am."

The nurse winked an eye in Angela's direction. "I'll be back to check on you. Try to get some sleep."

"I will."

"Oh, and your husband says he'll be right back. He wanted to go check on his mother."

"My husband?" Angela questioned, lifting her upper body slightly. The monitor beeped, her heart rate suddenly increasing.

"He slept in that chair most of the night," her nurse said, gesturing toward the seat in the corner. "I don't know anything about him, but he definitely seems like a keeper." She moved to the door and made her exit.

Angela grinned and settled back against the pillows.

Ellington couldn't begin to imagine what his mother saw in his expression, but when he entered her hospital room and she laid eyes on him, she began to chuckle. Her giggles swelled to gut-deep laughter and he found himself laughing with her. His father sat on the side of his wife's bed, shaking his head at the two of them as he also giggled. The laughter felt freeing, allowing them to finally relax after all the drama they'd just gone through.

"What?" he questioned. "What's so funny?"

"You look like you're twelve again, when your brothers would pick on you and you were plotting something against them that you knew was going to get you in trouble. It's funny because you're not twelve and that look just brings me such joy!" She extended her arms in his direction, gesturing with her hands. "It's so good to see you, son!"

"How are you feeling?" Ellington asked as he caught his breath. He leaned to kiss his mother's cheek as she pulled him close and hugged him tightly.

"I feel fine. I'm ready to get home."

Jerome gave her a look. "You'll be ready to leave when the doctor says you're ready to leave. You need to rest, not rush back to business as usual. Besides, we haven't found Scott yet. Until we do, you'll have round-the-clock protection, and I won't be leaving your side."

Judith rolled her eyes. "Your father is being overprotective."

"You had him worried. Hell, you had all of us worried!"

Judith smiled warmly. "How's Angela? Have you seen her?"

Her son nodded. "They let me sleep in her room last night. She was still out when I left to come visit you, but the doctor said she's doing exceptionally well considering what you two went through."

"That's a pretty special woman you have there. Please, don't mess it up. I really like her. It's going to make it very hard for anyone else if things don't work out with you two."

Ellington shook his head, the slightest smirk pulling at his thin lips. "I guess it's a good thing I really like her, then."

"Is that how you feel, son? You just *like* her?" His father's gaze was questioning.

"No, sir. It's definitely more than that, but I'd like to tell Angela I'm in love with her before I tell everyone else."

Jerome grinned, he and Judith exchanging smug looks. "That's fair," his father said.

"I need to get back to Angela. I don't want her to wake up and think I'm not here for her. I'll check back later or if things change, come find me, please."

His father nodded.

"I love you, Ellington!"

"I love you, too, Mom!"

Ellington tiptoed back into Angela's room. Her eyes were closed, and she appeared to be sleeping peacefully. After pressing a damp kiss to her forehead, he moved to the uncomfortable chair that still held the imprint of his butt cheeks and took a seat. He was beginning to get anxious, concerned that she hadn't wakened. He needed her to open her eyes and call his name. He was desperate to know that she was well. That things between them were good. All he wanted was to hold her in his arms and tell her he loved her and maybe have her say the words back to him.

He'd harangued her doctor for answers, lying that he was family. Her husband. He would probably go to hell for that tall tale, too, he thought. But he needed to be close to her and he would have been devastated had they cast him out to a waiting room or, worse, the parking lot. He'd broken rules but Angela was worth breaking them all for. Now he was missing her. Missing her laugh and the way her cheeks dimpled when she smiled. He swiped a tear from his eye and took a deep inhale of air as he whispered a silent prayer for her healing and recovery.

"Did you get him?"

Startled from his thoughts as he dozed on and off, Ellington looked up to find Angela eyeing him with a raised brow. Her voice cracked slightly, the tone husky as she questioned him a second time. "Did you catch your brother?"

He rose from the seat, moving swiftly to her side. "No. He's still out there."

"Make sure there's a protective detail on your mom. She's not safe."

He nodded. "My father's not leaving her side. Fabian won't be able to get to her, or to you." He took a seat on the side of the bed, needing to be close to her as he studied her face.

Angela extended her good arm and pressed her fingers to his chest. "I was worried about you," she said softly.

Ellington looked confused. "Worried about *me*? Why would you have worried about me?"

"I didn't think you were going to find us in time, which meant I would have had to haunt you for the rest of your life. That would not have been pretty. I'm sure me carrying a grudge into the afterlife would be sheer hell for someone."

He laughed, slowly shaking his head from side to side. "I'm glad I won't be dealing with your ghostly form anytime soon."

"Me, too," she whispered softly. Angela reached up to press her mouth to his, kissing him gently.

He kissed her back, trembling slightly. He wrapped his arms around her torso. "I was scared," he said, the vulnerability in his voice jolting. "I'm not going to lie. I kept imagining the worst and it scared me to death. I don't know what I would have done if anything had happened to you. To either of you."

"That sounds serious. Like you might actually care about me."

He shook his head, then cupped his hand beneath her chin to lift her gaze to his own. "No! It's more than just caring about you. I've fallen in love with you, Angela Stanfield. I love you and I have no interest in going back to my life without you." He kissed her a second time, his lips lingering longer than the first time.

When he finally pulled himself from her, Angela tapped her fingers gently against his chest, her good hand sliding around his neck until she could brush the short length of curls along the nape of his neck with her fingers. "I love you, too," she said, tears misting her gaze.

A familiar voice echoing from the door suddenly interrupted the moment. "Looks like you two didn't waste any time! I love you! Do you love me?" Mingus said, mimicking the two of them. His voice rose to a high pitch. "I do! I love you!"

Ellington and Angela stared at each other, amusement washing over them. He kissed her one last time before turning to give his brother an evil eye. "How old are you?"

"Old enough to know you two look good together. I'm happy for you."

"Well, thank you," Angela responded. She leaned her head against Ellington's shoulder.

Mingus continued. "I hate to interrupt this tête-à-tête you two have going on, but I needed to deliver a message. Our mother has arranged for Angela to recuperate at the Black family home to ensure her safety. Angela, I've taken the liberty of moving your belongings from your hotel room to the guest bedroom. I'm also told that once the doctor gives you an all clear, arrangements have been made for you to also have a private nurse until you're back on your feet and feeling better."

Ellington nodded. "Mom didn't need to do that. I was planning to take her to my place to stay with me. I was going to take care of her."

"Mom said you'd say that, so she wanted you to know she's putting clean sheets on your old bed and Dad's arranged twenty-four-hour security for the family when you all are not at the house."

"You all? What about you?" Ellington questioned.

"I am security. I'll keep an eye on me," Mingus said smugly.

"Judith is very kind," Angela interjected. "And I appreciate your family's generosity, but that's too much. I'll be okay."

"She said you'd say that, too, and I was to inform you that she wasn't giving you an option. She said you could argue the point with her once you both get to the house."

Angela laughed. "Well, I guess there's not much else for me to say. I know not to tangle with your mother!"

"Have you spoken to the doctor?" Ellington asked.

"He was here while you were visiting your mother. He said as long as I maintain my oxygen levels, he'll release me later this afternoon."

"That works," Mingus interjected. "He told Mom the same thing, so we'll only have to make one trip."

"Thanks, bro!" Ellington said.

"No thanks necessary. Besides, I can't wait to tell Angela the trouble you caused trying to rescue her. Assault, theft, damage to property..."

Angela's eyes widened. "Assault?"

"I didn't," Ellington said, shaking his head. "It was just a misunderstanding."

"Is that how you plan to answer the lawsuit against you? It was a misunderstanding?"

"Lawsuit? I can't wait to hear this," Angela laughed.

"Go away, Mingus," Ellington quipped.

"Going. Oh, and before I forget, your sister's cooking dinner tonight."

"Who, Vaughan?"

"Nope! Simone! So, try to swipe some stomach meds before you leave. We might need them if she actually cooks."

Ellington winced. "I would be scared, but knowing Simone, we'll be eating Thai food from some restaurant she couldn't resist."

"We should be so lucky," Mingus responded. "By the way," he said as he turned to exit the room, "I really am happy for you. Not as happy as your mother, but happy."

"Thanks," Ellington said, turning his full attention back to Angela. "Everything about this woman makes my heart sing!"

"Before you two lock lips again, I need your ear for a minute. I'll send him right back, Angela. I promise," Mingus said, his expression shifting to serious.

The couple eyed each other for a swift moment before Ellington rose from the bedside to follow after his brother. He tossed a look over his shoulder as Angela settled back down against the pillows and closed her eyes. He took a deep breath, shutting the door after him.

Mingus turned toward him as the two found a quiet corner in the hallway. "This isn't over," he said. "You need to be careful. Fabian's still out there somewhere. And from what Mom told us about their time together, he's not happy."

"How in hell did he get out of that building?"

"We may never know with all the damage, but there's no sign of his body in the ashes."

Ellington sighed, his hands clutching his hips. "What do you need from me?"

"You just take care of your girl. She should be safe at the house with our old people. Dad has the entire department on the lookout for him and I've put my whole team on the case. We've also got some help from Danube and his people."

"Danube? What's his angle?"

Mingus blew hot air past his full lips. "Fabian is a person of interest in the murder of Mike Caswell. Detective Caswell's body was found in his home last night. It looks like a suicide, but with everything we know so far, it may very well be something else."

Ellington's eyes widened. "Caswell is dead?"

His brother shrugged. "Caswell is the last person who could connect Fabian to everything that's happened. Him and Danube. But since we don't think he knows Danube works for the agency or what Danube may know, we believe Caswell was the last loose string he thinks he needed to take care of."

"Except for Mom and Angela. They might be in even more danger."

"We're not going to let anything happen to either one of them. Just stay close. We'll find him."

"Keep me posted," Ellington said, his mind beginning to race as he contemplated where Fabian might be hanging out.

His brother tossed up a dismissive hand. As he disappeared down the hallway toward the elevator, Ellington was past ready for it to all be over. He needed a beach, with a drink in his hand, Angela by his side and the ocean waves lulling them both into the sweetest nirvana. His mother's son was making that dream near impossible and he wasn't happy about it. Until Fabian was found, he'd follow in his father's footsteps and keep the woman he loved close to his side. He hurried back in the direction of Angela's room.

Chapter 16

Despite the laughter that rang through the hired limousine, Angela sensed that their suspect still being on the loose was keeping Ellington from taking a relaxing breath. The Black family were all on edge and the tension in the car spiraled through the air like the vapor above boiling water. Their effort to keep the conversation casual required effort none of them were interested in giving and so they settled into awkward silences and nervous laughter to distract themselves.

Ellington seemed to read her mind, reaching for her hand. He clasped her fingers between his own and gave her the slightest squeeze. His mother sat across the way and she smiled at the two of them as she leaned into her husband's side.

"You two bring hope to the table. There's a lot of promise in what the future may hold for you. It makes me feel better about things," she said softly, the comment like a warm blanket around their shoulders.

The couple smiled, exchanging a quick look with each other.

"I truly appreciate everything you've done, Judge Black. We made a great team," Angela said.

"We put the capital *T* in team, you and I," Judith responded. "I firmly believe we wouldn't be here right now if it hadn't been for you. Because you didn't have to fight your way into that van to try and save me. You put yourself in harm's way to help me and I won't ever forget that. I owe you my life. If there is ever any way I can repay you, just ask and it's yours."

"I only did what I knew was right to do. You don't owe me anything for that."

"Young lady, I'd collect on that if I were you," Jerome interjected. "My wife doesn't often pledge her allegiance to anyone. Not even these bigheaded kids of ours!"

"No lies detected there," Ellington muttered.

Angela laughed. "You should be ashamed of yourself. There is no one who would believe that about your mother!"

"Thank you, Angela," Judith said. She eyed both men with a hint of scorn in her gaze. "They know there's nothing I wouldn't do for my children. I just don't coddle their bad behavior, put up with their whining or entertain any nonsense from them. I don't need to pledge my allegiance to them. I'm their mother. They were all born with my allegiance."

Another awkward silence descended on the space. Thoughts of Fabian seemed to cross all their minds at the same time. Judith's gaze dropped to the floor and tears misted her oceanic eyes. Jerome turned to stare out the limo's window. Angela met the look Ellington gave her and the two shared a moment of empathy for his mother's situation.

Angela wished she had the words to make things better for the matriarch. She knew just how much Judith loved her wayward son. How her sacrifice had shaped her world and his and defined the future they found themselves in. She didn't know if Ellington's mother would ever share all the details of what had happened with her eldest son and Angela knew it wasn't her story to tell. Whether it was ever spoken aloud, Angela knew enough to confirm that love had motivated Judith's decisions and her allegiance to her baby boy was why she'd inevitably let him go. Sadly, he had misconstrued her love for abandonment, and it had haunted him into a hellish nightmare where he was intent on pulling everyone into the dark abyss with him.

"We'll find him," Jerome said, gently tapping his wife's thigh. His voice was a loud whisper as he repeated the comment. "We'll find him, and everything will go back to normal."

Judith shook her head. "I don't think I know what normal is anymore."

"Wait until Simone starts whining about absolutely nothing. It won't take you long to remember," Ellington said with a warm chuckle. He shook his head.

"Simone whining will be music to my ears for about two minutes," Judith said.

"I'd bet a dollar to a dime you wouldn't last two minutes," Ellington said.

Jerome laughed heartily. "That baby will buy your sister those two minutes. But I wouldn't recommend the rest of you trying your mother."

Judith tossed up her hands and laughed with them. She changed the subject. "Did you call everyone?" she questioned, her eyes shifting in Ellington's direction.

He nodded. "Simone is already at the house waiting

for the food to be delivered. Vaughan has a meeting and will be late, but she promises to show up well before dessert. Armstrong and Mingus have to pick up their women but promise to be on time and Davis's woman said she'll get him there in time to bless the table. Parker is going to join us via video chat."

"We need to bring him home," Judith said, directing the comment at her husband. "We know the truth, so he should come home. You have to make that happen. He has to be with his family now."

Jerome nodded but said nothing.

"Please," Judith concluded. "Bring him home as soon as you have Fabian behind bars."

Jerome draped his arm around her shoulder and kissed her cheek. He still hadn't said anything, but he didn't need to. Angela stared at the two of them. They were a beautiful couple. She had picture-perfect features: high cheekbones, black eyes like dark ice and a buttermilk complexion. She wore no makeup and her lush, silver gray hair had been pulled back into a loose ponytail. Her expression was pained, but she'd forced a smile to her face, impressions still being important to her. The family had an image to maintain, and she would not disappoint or embarrass her family. She was a beautiful complement to her husband. He was tall, dark and handsome. Like his sons, he exuded a formidable presence. He wore an expensive silk suit and a polished cotton dress shirt, and had no concern for his image. He was comfortable in his skin and unbothered by what others thought of him. Ellington had inherited the best of both.

Minutes later the limo pulled into the driveway of Jerome and Judith Black's home. The property was located in the heart of Chicago's historic Gold Coast neighborhood. It was situated on a large corner lot, its stone-and-brick architecture timeless. The police superintendent opened the door before the driver put the car into Park and held out his hand to take his wife's. Ellington exited next and turned to help Angela. Stepping out of the vehicle, she took a deep breath of fresh air and then a second, gratitude washing over her.

"You two head on in and check on Simone," Jerome said. "I need to speak with Ellington. We'll be right behind you." He leaned to kiss his wife's cheek.

Judith stared at the two men, then nodded. She understood her husband's request was more command than request, so she gestured for Angela to follow her. She pushed the door expecting it to open. When it didn't, that seemed to surprise her.

Angela paused, a wave of heat rippling across her spine. Judith seemed to read her mind.

"There was a time when we rarely ever had to lock our door. Most times none of us ever think about it during daylight hours. Nighttime is different. But with everything going on I guess we'll have to do better," the matriarch mused.

Pulling a key from her pocket, she inserted it into the lock and pushed a second time.

Silence greeted them as she called out, "Simone! Hello! Anybody here?"

Angela followed on the older woman's heels as she led them through the front foyer and past the formal living room. There was no missing the home's beauty. The solid wood-and-glass front door with its ornate iron details was stunning, promising an outsider that there was more to come. Stepping through the entrance was like stepping into a whole other world, a busy Chicago lifestyle easily left behind for the comfort and quiet of the family retreat. Angela was duly impressed as she took in the polished wood, lush fabrics and warm decor.

Ellington's mother moved down a short length of hallway. She came to an abrupt stop at the entrance to the family room. Her body tensed and she began to visibly shake. She tossed a quick look over her shoulder, her eyes wide with fear. Moving swiftly to her side, Angela turned to stare where she stared, her own gaze burning as she suddenly felt like the air had been sucked out of the room.

Fabian Scott stood room center. He waved a large gun toward the two of them, gesturing for them to enter and take a seat. Beside him Simone sat in a wingback chair, her hands clasped protectively across her pregnant belly. Tears streamed down her face. Fabian pushed the muzzle of his gun against her stomach, the gesture made to emphasize his control. He looked from Judith to Angela and back. He smiled, a treacly bend to his lips that felt disingenuous at best and psychotic at worst. His left hand wrapped in white gauze and his clothes were stained with black soot. There was a nervous tick in his face and it twitched anxiously, jumping for attention. At first glance he looked frightening, like he'd just stepped out of a John Carpenter horror movie. He was evil personified, and had invaded the calming sanctity of the family home.

"Welcome, Mother!" Fabian said sardonically. "I missed you."

Angela pressed her hand against Judith's lower back. The gesture was strengthening, and the matriarch took a deep inhale of air to stall her rising nerves.

Judith's expression was scolding, her voice commanding. "Fabian, if you need to point a gun at someone you point that thing at me. Not your sister. She and her baby have nothing to do with this."

The man shrugged. "No, they don't. But I want to make sure you know exactly what I'm willing to do."

"What's your endgame, Fabian?" Angela asked. She took a small step toward him. "What are you hoping to have accomplished when this is all over?"

He flinched, clearly annoyed by Angela's presence. "Why are you here, Investigator Stanfield? Are you family now?"

"Answer my question first and then I'll answer yours. How do you want this to end, Fabian?"

He paused. "I want my mother to hurt like she has never hurt before. I want to take everything she loves from her. I want…"

"You want her to know how you feel," Angela interjected.

"Yes!"

"And destroying people who have nothing to do with the two of you? Why do that to them?"

"You're right," he snapped. He suddenly pointed the gun at Judith.

Angela took another step, easing in front of the matriarch. "You know I can't let that happen, either, right?"

"I can shoot you first. Then her. Or—" he pointed the weapon back at Simone "—I can just end the next generation of Judith Black's legacy."

"Or you can put the gun down and we can talk about this. This can be fixed before anyone else gets hurt. You just need to let us help you." Angela's tone was calming, meant to ease the tension wafting between them.

Fabian shook his head vehemently. "No!" he screamed. "No talking! I'm tired of talking. Talking to people who don't care. Talking to therapists. Talking to you. No!"

Angela suddenly felt a large hand on her shoulder. Ellington had entered the room and he moved in front of her and his mother, standing protectively.

"Then talk to me," he said. "Brother to brother. Because I care. Let me help you."

"I don't need your damn help!" Fabian snarled. He suddenly tapped his free hand against his forehead, his ire rising as he found himself suddenly cornered. He pushed the gun's muzzle harder against Simone's stomach and she cried out with fear. When she did, he lifted it back toward Ellington, pointing it at his brother instead.

No one expected the loud bang that came next. The sound of gunfire surprised them all. The moment was surreal, playing out in slow motion. Bang! Bang! Bang! The first bullet hit Fabian in the shoulder, blowing out the muscles that controlled his hand. The gun fell, hitting the tiled floor harshly. Shock and awe washed over his face as his body recoiled from the second and third shots that hit him square in the chest. He grabbed at air, his eyes locked on the family who'd been eyeing him warily, and then he fell backward to the floor, gasping for each breath he could manage.

Everyone turned at the same time, in the direction from where the shots were fired. Jerome still held his weapon high, his right hand propped against his left to steady his aim. Angela rushed forward, helping Simone to her feet. Blood was spattered against her face, her tears raining in shades of red over her cheeks. She was shaking as Angela guided her from the family room toward the formal dining room. The two women passed Armstrong and Mingus as the two brothers rushed in to see what was going on after hearing the gunshots.

Ellington and his father locked gazes. Tears misted the old man's eyes. "Don't touch anything in this room.

And do not give a statement until I give you permission to do so. Is that understood?" Ellington said, his tone a loud whisper.

Jerome nodded.

After quickly assessing the scene, Armstrong was on his police radio. "This is Detective Black. Badge number 14297. We have an officer-involved shooting at the police superintendent's private residence. I need you to rush an ambulance to that address."

A random voice responded. "10-4, Detective."

Armstrong turned his attention to his father. "Dad, I need to relieve you of your gun. We need to do this by the book."

The patriarch nodded, finally allowing his hands to drop down to his sides. He deposited the gun onto the glass-topped end table in the corner. Behind them a mournful wail suddenly filled the room. They turned to see Judith on the floor beside Fabian. His head rested in her lap as she gently trailed her fingers along his profile. Her torso rocked slowly back and forth as she began to sob. Mingus stood above her, a hand resting gently against her shoulder. He looked up and shook his head at his brothers.

Armstrong depressed his radio button. "Cancel that ambulance. We need the medical examiner and a homicide team ASAP."

"10-4, Detective Black."

Ellington moved to his mother's side and knelt down beside her. He choked back his own tears, hating to see the pain washing over her so abundantly. "Mom, please let go. You need to go in the other room and sit with Simone. Please."

Judith looked up, her eyes shifting from one son to the other. First Ellington, then Mingus and Armstrong. When her gaze landed on Jerome, her expression hardened, her tears freezing from the glacial stare she gave him. She took a deep inhale of air, then lashed out with a level of venom that shook every one of them to their core. "Damn you! Damn you! You killed my son, Jerome Black! Damn you to hell!"

Angela had moved back into the room, feeling every ounce of the frustration and emotion sweeping between them. She took a breath and held it deep in her lungs before speaking. "We still need that ambulance," she said, interrupting the moment. "Simone's water just broke. She's in labor." She turned toward Judith, extending her hand. "Judge Black, she's crying for you. She wants her mother."

With a quick nod of her head Judith pressed a tender kiss to Fabian's forehead. She gently eased his head back to the floor. With help from Mingus and Ellington she stood, pulling herself upright. She swiped the tears from her face, straightened her clothes, then swept past them to the dining room, where her youngest daughter waited.

The quiet in the room was deafening. They all knew it would only last for the briefest moment before the space would be overwhelmed with the presence of Chicago's finest. The noise level would rise until none of them would be able to hear themselves think.

Jerome turned, easing toward the front door. The weight of his actions bore down on him, and he looked weary. Mingus followed after his father. Armstrong was already giving direction to the first officers on-site, turning the investigation over to a senior detective as he recused himself from the case. He followed his family to the front of the home.

Ellington moved against Angela, wrapping his arms tightly around her. He kissed the top of her head. He held her, oblivious to the wave of activity around them.

He held her until EMS carried Simone from the house, Judith holding tightly to her daughter's hand. He held her, refusing to let her go, and Angela clung to him with equal urgency.

It had taken mere seconds for things to change. Ellington couldn't begin to fathom how his family would come back from all that had happened. He worried for his parents, who'd always been able to overcome the worst. He feared they would never again find balance with each other. He had always thought the two of them invincible, nothing and no one being able to knock them from the pedestals where they reigned. For some time now he'd seen them fragile, and seconds ago, with his mother raging at his father, he'd seen them broken, splintered beyond reasonable repair. In that moment, Angela felt like the surest thing in his life. He loved her and she loved him, and he had no intentions of ever letting her go. And so he held on to her until a uniformed officer tapped them both on the shoulder for questioning.

Epilogue

After forty-two hours of labor, Nino Jerome Reilly was born to Paul Reilly and Simone Black-Reilly. The newest addition to their family tree weighed in at six pounds, thirteen ounces. The entire Black family, siblings and spouses, had gathered in the hospital waiting room for the miraculous moment. Angela was honored to share in their joy, most especially since the Black family had closed ranks on all outsiders pending the resolution of their mounting legal issues.

Ellington had been fielding one phone call after another, doing double duty as big brother and attorney du jour. Because of their father's position in the community the FBI had stepped in to oversee the investigation and interviews. The process was exhausting, and despite his best efforts to not let it show, Angela could see Ellington was tired, physically and emotionally. If they could both go to bed, pull the covers over their heads and disappear, they would. But right then, the luxury of disappearing from their lives didn't seem possible.

Ellington was suddenly standing beside her, leaning to kiss her cheek. "I've got good news finally," he said, addressing everyone in the room.

They all fell quiet, the circles of casual banter shutting down as his family turned to stare. "Parker has been totally exonerated. With the evidence submitted, especially the cassette tape, Agent Danube's statement and the results of Angela's investigation, the state had dropped all charges against him."

"Thank God!" Vaughan exclaimed.

"What's going to happen with Dad?" Davis said, asking the question they were all thinking.

"It's not official yet, but they will probably declare the shooting justified. It was all captured on the home's security cameras and the video aligns with everyone's statements. Simone is the only person they haven't been able to speak with yet."

"This is such a mess," Vaughan intoned. "If they weren't on the verge of divorce before, they are now."

"Don't talk like that," Armstrong snapped. "Mom and Dad always manage to work things out. They'll get through this."

"He killed her firstborn child. That one might be hard to forgive," Vaughan said.

"Her firstborn child was trying to kill all of us. I think he had good reason to do what he did. Especially when Simone and the baby were being threatened," Mingus quipped. "Fabian pointing that damn gun at you and Mom just solidified what Dad needed to do."

Ellington sighed. "No matter what happens, we need to support them both. This is not the time for any of us to take sides. I can't begin to imagine what they're going through. The next few months will be hard for them both. Let's not make it worse, please."

They all fell silent. The moment was interrupted by Simone's husband, Paul. He came rushing into the room, a wide smile on his face.

"Simone will be moved to a private room shortly, then you all can go see her. Our son is doing exceptionally well. I can't wait for you all to see him."

"Congratulations," Ellington gushed. "We're all very excited for you two."

Paul nodded. His voice dropped an octave. "Your mother is still with Simone and she's called for your father. She wants to speak with the two of them first."

Ellington's eyes widened. "That might not be such a good idea."

"That's what I thought, but she's insisting. Keep your fingers crossed," Paul responded. "And maybe say a prayer, or two."

"Or three or four," Vaughan piped in.

Ellington shook his head. He dropped into the seat beside Angela.

"So, tell me about the baby's name," Angela said. "Is Nino a family name?"

"Sort of," Ellington answered.

"No, it's not," Vaughan chimed. "That's our sister naming that baby after herself."

Her brothers laughed.

Ellington continued. "Simone is named after Nina Simone. Had the baby been a girl she had planned to name her Nina. Since he's not a girl, she named him Nino, after herself."

"What I said!" Vaughan chuckled.

"I think it's a great name. Not too fussy but distinguished," Angela stated.

"So, when are you two tying the knot?" Vaughan asked, changing the subject.

Angela stammered, "We... It's... I..."

Ellington laughed. "Don't answer her. She's been marrying us off since we were kids."

"That's not true. I only ask when you guys meet people I like."

"You should be flattered," Ellington remarked. "My sister likes you."

"You've dated worse," Vaughan said. "If Angela only knew. Maybe I'll tell her."

Angela laughed. "I can't wait to hear those stories!"

"No," Ellington said with a shake of his head. "You really can. They're not that interesting."

Mingus laughed. "No lies detected there!"

Ellington tossed up his hands. "Can you all ever give a brother a break?"

"No!" his siblings chimed simultaneously.

Angela laughed heartily.

Mingus gestured for her attention. "Can I steal you for a moment?"

Ellington gave them both a look and shrugged. Before he could comment, his cell phone buzzed. He winked an eye in her direction, then shifted his attention to the caller on the line. Angela rose from her seat and followed Mingus out of the waiting room into the hallway.

"What's up?" she asked when they'd found a quiet corner to talk.

"I'd like to offer you a job."

Angela's eyes widened with surprise. "A job? Working for your agency?"

He nodded. "I think you'd be a good fit and I need someone with management and investigative skills who can handle themselves in the field and in the office. Someone who can take charge when I can't."

"I don't often play by the rules to get a job done."

"Which is why I like you. It's what makes my business successful. We think out of the box and we're not afraid to ruffle feathers when we need to. We don't follow rules, we make them."

"It's definitely something to consider. I honestly hadn't thought about what I would do next."

"Give it some thought. We can talk again in a few days. I can detail the salary and the few perks that come with being my second-in-command, and hopefully make it worth your while."

"Thank you. I appreciate that," she said.

Mingus gave her a nod. "And if no one's said it already, I hope you know how much my family and I appreciate all you did to help Parker. We also like you and Ellington together, so forgive them if my sisters and their enthusiasm get a bit overbearing. It's not personal. They do everyone like that. Just ask my wife."

Angela laughed. "Well, thank you again."

With a quick glance at his wristwatch, Mingus moved back to the waiting room. Standing there, Angela wasn't sure what to think. The prospect of employment with the Black Detective Agency was actually intriguing to her. It was something she would definitely give serious consideration.

Movement at the end of the hallway drew her attention. Jerome and Judith had exited a room and stood toe to toe in what appeared to be a heated discussion. Then just like that it wasn't, and they seemed calm. Jerome reached out and pulled his wife to him, both wrapping their arms tightly around each other. Her body heaved up and down and Angela realized Judith was crying. She watched as he wiped her tears away with his fingers and then he kissed her, a gentle touch from his lips to hers. The intimate moment pierced Angela's heart, tying her heartstrings in a million knots. Whatever had been said, whatever they shared, there was no denying the magnitude of their love for each other. She could feel it like a warm breeze billowing through the air. It bounced from wall to wall, and it was as pure as anything she could even begin to imagine.

What they shared was what Angela wanted for herself. She wanted companionship that could survive the hard times. That didn't hide when life wasn't easy. A partner who listened and heard her through the noise that could cloud one's judgment or turn a heart cold. She needed a man who was first and foremost her friend, before he was her lover. Someone she trusted with her heart and her soul, who didn't hesitate to trust her with their own. And in that moment if she was certain about any one thing, she was certain about Ellington Black. She wanted what his parents had, and she wanted that with him.

Ellington tiptoed around the bed searching for his wristwatch. Angela was still sleeping soundly, and he didn't want to disturb her rest. He knelt down beside the bed, reaching his hand along the carpeted floor but found nothing. When he rose, Angela's eyes were open, and she was staring at him. Her lips lifted in the sweetest smile.

"Good morning," she said, stretching her limbs against the mattress.

"Good afternoon," he answered. "I didn't mean to wake you."

"What time is it?"

"Just after one o'clock."

"Why didn't you wake me?"

"You needed your rest."

"I never sleep this late," Angela said, stretching up and out again.

"It's also Thursday."

Her voice cracked, shock washing over her face. "Thursday? That's not possible."

He nodded. "It is. You've been asleep for three whole days. But don't feel bad. I slept for two."

"Wow!" she said, her eyes darting back and forth as she considered the time that had passed. "What did I miss?" she asked.

Ellington climbed onto the bed beside her. He wrapped his arm around her as she laid her head on his chest. He gently trailed his fingers against her bare skin.

"Well, my father was cleared of any wrongdoing. He's already back in the office and still fighting with the mayor."

"That's good to hear. How did the mayor feel about everything that happened?"

"All he cared about was there not being any kind of blemish on the city under his watch. He's just happy for it to all go away as he starts his reelection campaign."

Angela sighed, her head shaking slowly from side to side.

"Simone and the baby are out of the hospital and home. She's driving everyone crazy trying to hire the perfect nanny."

Angela laughed. "I didn't see that coming. I thought she'd want to be a stay-at-home mom."

"We are talking about Simone. You've met her? Haven't you?"

"I know who we're talking about." She laughed.

"I was just checking. You sounded confused there for a moment."

Angela shook her head. "How's your mom doing?"

Ellington paused before responding. "She's in Morocco."

Angela pushed herself upright. "Morocco? When did she...?"

"She decided to take a sabbatical. She needed some time to herself, and Simone's husband has a home there. Once Simone was settled at home with the baby, she took off."

"I'm so sorry."

Ellington shrugged. "She's missed, but we understand Dad plans to join her in a few weeks, so it's not all bad."

"How are you doing?" Angela asked. She snuggled her body closer to his.

"Better," Ellington answered.

She reached to kiss his lips, allowing her mouth to linger sweetly against his. Her hand slid the length of his torso, down past his belly button. Her fingers crept past the waistband of his boxers and tangled in the first strands of pubic hair that she touched. She pulled at them gently, twirling the strands around her fingers. Ellington inhaled swiftly.

"Much better," he muttered. The muscles below his waist had hardened and his body began to feel like he was on fire.

Angela suddenly withdrew her hand. She rolled from him and pulled herself from the bed.

Ellington reached for her. "Where are you going?"

"I need a shower."

"And I need you. Desperately!"

She laughed. "I won't be long."

He threw his legs off the side of the bed. "I could wash your back."

"You could."

He stood up and pushed his shorts to the floor. His

body exposed his desire. His erection stood at full mast, begging for her attention.

"Looks like you have a personal problem there," she said teasingly.

"It's not personal at all. It's all your fault."

She laughed. "My fault? Please!"

Ellington shrugged his shoulders, then slightly rotated his hips, his male member waving from side to side. "I didn't do this."

She changed the subject abruptly. "How would you feel about me taking a job with your brother?"

"My brother?"

"Mingus offered me a job with his agency."

Ellington paused, reflecting on the comment. He nodded. "If it means you'll be staying, I'm fine with it."

Angela laughed. "It definitely means I'll be staying. And if I accept, I'll need to start looking for an apartment."

"Why? You can move in here with me."

"That's not going to happen," Angela responded. "Not yet."

"Why not?"

"Because we're still getting to know each other. We both need our own space until we're ready to take our relationship to the next level."

"That makes no sense. I love you and you love me, so why..."

"Because we do love each other," she interrupted. "And I don't think we need to rush into anything. This is new for both of us, and I don't want to mess it up. If we hope to have what your parents have, then we're going to have to build our relationship on a solid foundation of trust and friendship and communication. If I just move in with you, sex will just muddy that up."

"I don't agree," he said. "I think we can have it all and have sex, too!"

Amusement danced out of her eyes, and she laughed again. "I didn't say we wouldn't be having sex at all," she said. "I'm just saying we need to slow things down and date."

"I like dating."

Angela grinned. "And I like sex, and dating." She turned toward the bathroom and the shower, stopping to pause in the doorway. "You coming?" she asked as she disappeared in the other room.

Ellington grinned, falling headfirst into his feelings. Something like joy swept through his spirit. "Hell yeah!" he muttered excitedly. "Angela Stanfield, I will follow you to the ends of eternity."

* * * * *

Don't miss the previous volumes in the
To Serve and Seduce miniseries:

Seduced by the Badge
Tempted by the Badge
Reunited by the Badge
Stalked by Secrets